HARDPRESSED

Meredith Wild

WATERHOUSE
PRESS

PRINTED IN THE UNITED STATES OF AMERICA

ISBN: 978-0-9897684-4-3

For Jonathan

CHAPTER ONE

"I can't believe I'm doing this again," I said.

Blake slid his arm around my shoulders. He pulled me close and I relaxed into his familiar warmth. We stepped out of his office building and headed a few blocks down the street. He leaned down and gave me a reassuring kiss on the cheek.

"No funny business this time, I promise."

I laughed and rolled my eyes. "Very reassuring."

I almost believed him. The past few weeks had been intense, but something had changed between us. I could joke, but he had my trust now. After all my fervent protests and desperate attempts to fight the way I felt about him, I'd finally let him in. At least more than I'd ever let anyone else in, and nothing had ever felt more right.

He flashed me a mischievous smile. "Don't worry. There was no way I could get Fiona to pull a stunt like that again."

Dressed in white capris and a navy chiffon shell, Blake's sister, Fiona, waited ahead of us near the entryway of a quaint café. We stopped directly in front of the entrance. The engraved sign above read *Mocha*. A young patron swung the door open and the deep aroma of freshly ground coffee and chocolate wafted out, setting off happy signals all over my body. I'd nearly forgotten about our original mission when Fiona motioned us toward an unmarked door next to the café.

"We're upstairs." She ushered us up a narrow staircase to the second floor.

"Who owns the building, Fiona?" I tried to make it sound like small talk, but who was I kidding? The fact that we were a few short strides from a steady caffeine source was already a major selling point, but Fiona knew my position on renting from Blake or any of his subsidiaries. I trusted Blake, but that didn't mean he wasn't still committed to becoming intricately involved in my business dealings at every possible opportunity.

Blake had plenty of his own contradictions. He could be sweet and heart-wrenchingly tender one moment and be driving me into a fiery rage with his compulsive controlling tendencies the next. He could micro-manage the hell out of my growing business during the day and fuck me straight out of my mind the second we walked through the door every night. Granted, sometimes I needed both, but I still wasn't sure how I felt about all this dominance in my life. Letting him in scared me, but I was learning to be more open to it, to trust him as much as I could.

Today, a part of me, the part of me that needed separation and independence from Blake, wanted to make absolutely sure he wasn't pulling a fast one on me again.

"I can assure you that Blake has no ownership stake in the property," Fiona reassured me.

That was all well and good, but not so long ago she'd sold me on a beautifully updated apartment within the same Comm Ave brownstone that Blake not only owned, but also lived in. The tenuous line between our personal lives and businesses was already too blurred. I was holding firm on this one.

"I'm glad to hear it."

Fiona dug into her purse. Despite my misgivings, my anticipation grew. She unlocked the door and we filed into the space. The long room was small, at least compared to Blake's. Though musty and in dire need of a cleaning crew, the space held promise. Behind me Blake sighed.

"Fiona, seriously. This is the best you could do?"

She shot him an annoyed look.

"We—Erica and I—discussed her budget, and for the location and size, this is a fair option. Obviously the space could use some TLC, but you have to admit it has potential."

I took a long look around, envisioning the many possibilities. I had been so busy keeping things running out of my apartment, all while hiring, that I hadn't had a chance to get excited about this move. But this would be fun.

"I love the wood floors."

"They're filthy." Blake scuffed the sole of his shoe on the floor, drawing a faint line through the dust.

"Have a little vision, Blake. We just need to clean it up, and with a few enhancements, this could definitely have a cool design studio feel."

"Exactly. Exposed brick never goes out," Fiona added.

"Pretty old." Blake wrinkled his nose.

I laughed and slapped him on the shoulder. "Show me a building in Boston that isn't old."

The space was a far cry from the Landon Group's renovated modern offices, but I had modest and realistic expectations. The current state of the space left much to be desired, but with some elbow grease and a few additions, we could make this work.

We stopped in front of the large windows facing the

street. A flutter of excitement coursed through me. Giving the business its own address would be a major milestone and make everything we'd accomplished so far seem much more real.

I turned to gauge Fiona's reaction. "I think I like it. What do you think?"

Fiona pursed her lips and looked around. "The price is fair and the lease term gives you options for growth. All things considered, I would say this is a safe bet. Can you see yourself here?"

"I can." I smiled, having renewed faith in Fiona's brokering skills. At the end of the day, we needed a comfortable, affordable working space for the new team members of Clozpin, the fashion social network I'd spent the past year growing.

"Let me make some calls and see if I can get the price down for you. Because Blake's right, this place is kind of dirty. Plus, if you plan on fixing it up, that gives us a bargaining chip." Fiona pulled out her phone and exited toward the hallway, leaving us alone again.

"You didn't ask me what I think." Blake gave me a crooked grin.

"That's because I already know what you think."

"I could give you twice the square footage and you wouldn't even need to leave the building to come visit me. Plus you'd get the girlfriend rate, which I think you'll find is unmatched in this part of town."

Blake's uninvited assistance in all matters was a lost cause. Sure, he was controlling, compulsive, and persistent as all hell, but he was ultimately a fixer. When the people he cared about ran into problems or wanted for anything, he came to the rescue, sparing no expense in the process.

"I appreciate the offer. I really do. But you can't put a price on independence, Blake." We'd had this conversation before, and I was standing my ground. He needed to trust me to make things work on my own. This trust thing went both ways.

"You can be independent. We'll put it all in writing."

"In my experience, putting it in writing only commits me to being dependent on your ample resources for a minimum length of time." Blake already had me bound to a year-long lease with my apartment, though he'd yet to cash any of my rent checks.

"Call it rent control. You could lock in the girlfriend rate for, say, a twenty-year lease, and then we could negotiate from there." He encircled me in his arms, pressing me firmly against his chest, his lips inches from mine.

My heart pounded. This went beyond our usual banter of trying to outwit each other. We had only been together a matter of weeks and he was already thinking about the long-term? My lips parted slightly as I struggled to take a full breath. Blake's words and his proximity made my world spin, time and again. No one had ever affected me like this, and I was gradually learning to enjoy the roller coaster.

"Nice try," I whispered.

He growled and closed his mouth over mine. He claimed me with gentle urgency, teasing me with tiny licks of his tongue.

"You drive me crazy, Erica."

"Oh?" I breathed, trying not to moan as the air left me.

"Yes, in every conceivable way. Let's get out of here. Fiona can wrap up the paperwork if you're intent on renting this dump."

He grabbed my hips and sandwiched me between his rock hard body and the wall behind me. I didn't know what it was about him pinning me to hard surfaces, but I fucking loved it. I slid my hands through his hair and kissed him back helplessly, so easily forgetting myself in his embrace. What time was it? Where did I need to be later? I mentally ran through every possible obstacle between me and being naked with Blake. His thigh found the space between my legs, exerting the perfect amount of pressure so the crease of my jeans rubbed me through my panties.

"Oh, God."

"I swear, if there was a clean surface in this place, I'd fuck you on it right now."

I giggled. "You're bad."

His eyes went dark. "You have no idea."

"Ahem."

Fiona leaned into the doorway, wide-eyed.

Blake stepped back abruptly, leaving me dizzy and momentarily confused. For the first time ever, I witnessed him flush as he ran his fingers through his hair, seemingly embarrassed at having been caught making out in front of his little sister.

"If you two are finished, I got the price down another couple hundred. Can we make a decision on this, or do you want to see some more places in different parts of town?"

I straightened and stepped away from Blake to join her, knowing the farther away I was, the more clearly I could think.

"Decision's made. Let's do this."

★ ★ ★

"You new to the neighborhood?"

The busty redhead serving up two steaming *creme brulee* lattes interrupted my train of thought as I checked through my email with obsessive care.

"Sort of. I'm renting commercial space upstairs."

"Rock and roll. I've been here a few years. I opened the café with my parents but they retired, so it's just me and the crew now."

"Wow, congrats. I didn't realize you were the owner." I'd seen her several times since scouting out the neighborhood and practicing my route to work. Okay, so I was mainly over-eager to move into the office, and the compelling smells coming from Mocha lured me in regularly.

"Most people don't. They're pretty surprised when they ask for a supervisor and they're still looking at me."

We laughed, and I held out my hand to hers. "I'm Erica."

"Simone. These are on the house."

"Awesome, thank you."

"No worries." She sauntered back to the coffee bar with curves that even I envied. Simone had a presence in the place and she made a mean latte, so she wasn't easy to forget. The patrons around me followed her with their gazes until she was safely hidden behind the counter.

Liz pushed through the door and found me at my table.

"Wow, you're wicked tan," I said, admiring Liz's ability to look like a catalogue model with presumably very little effort. Somehow her perfect blond bob looked even lighter than the last time we'd met over coffee. My own hair was pulled up into a messy bun, and I was dressed in a pair of well-loved, thoroughly ripped blue jeans and a tie-dyed tank top, ready to clean up the office space before our furniture arrived.

"Thanks! Barcelona was amazing. You have to go sometime. My parents rented a villa and I basically hung out on the beach the whole time. Absolute bliss."

"Sounds amazing."

"So what have you been up to?" She took a sip of her latte.

"I got my funding for the business, so I found office space and now I'm renovating and hiring."

"Holy crap, congratulations!"

"Thanks."

"What are you hiring for?"

"We have a couple new programmers, but I'm sort of agonizing over finding a marketing director. No one has wowed me yet, but I need someone soon. I can't wear that hat with all the other things I have going on."

"Oh my God, I know the perfect person." She clapped her hands together and then started rummaging through her purse.

"Yeah?"

"My friend Risa. She's been working for a marketing company for the past few summers. She graduated with us and is on the job hunt now. She's crazy into fashion. You would love her."

I raised my eyebrows. Not like I especially *loved* fashion. Sure I ran a fashion social network, but that was business. Obsessing over fashion was Alli's gig, but since Alli was the one I was replacing, maybe this girl would be worth talking to.

"I'm trying to replace my business partner who moved to New York for work, so she'd have to be willing to take on a lot of responsibility for meager start-up pay. Not really everyone's dream job."

Liz shook her head, seeming undeterred. "Sounds perfect, actually. You should talk to her. I could be wrong about what she's looking for, but connecting with her couldn't hurt. You never know."

I shrugged. "All right, but I can't make any promises, okay?"

"Absolutely. She's a friend but we're not super close so if it doesn't work out, no hard feelings."

"Okay, cool."

I waited for her to send me the info on her phone, and I let my mind wander to everything I had to do before we set up shop upstairs.

"I'm really glad we reconnected, Erica." Liz smiled sweetly, bringing me back to the moment.

"Me too."

"I thought a lot about what you said when I was away." Her expression changed, her features softening. "I should have been more understanding of the whole situation. I had nothing to compare it to, so I probably didn't react the way I should have. I'm sorry I couldn't be the one to help you through it, but I want to try to be a better friend to you now, if it's not too late." Her voice lowered when she spoke to me, even though the coffee shop was humming with other customers wrapped up in their own conversations.

"Of course not. Don't worry about it."

I waved away her apology and all the emotions it

threatened to conjure. One of the reasons we'd grown distant to begin with was the constant reminder of the difficult time in my life that we had shared. I did want to give our friendship another chance, but I seriously hoped that didn't mean reliving the past every time we met up.

"We're talking ancient history, Liz. I've moved on and I'm not interested in dwelling on it. I have a million other things to think about right now."

"Right." She nodded. "I don't know how you do it. I couldn't imagine running a business. I wouldn't even know where to start."

"There's definitely a learning curve, but you could say that about anything, I guess. How's your job going?" She must have already started her position at one of the large investment firms in the city.

"Great, actually, except I'm in spreadsheet hell right now. But I'm learning a lot and trying to figure it all out. I think I like it. Plus, there are tons of hot guys who work at the firm. Major bonus."

I laughed, remembering how boy crazy she had been when we'd shared a dorm room our freshmen year. In fact, her love of boys and parties might have been what had landed us off campus at a frat house one night. I shook my head, pushing thoughts of that terrible night with Mark out of my mind.

Now that I knew the identity of the man who'd raped me, I was even more determined not to let the experience rule me. I was stronger than the pain he had left me with, and I had come too far to lament the innocence he'd stolen.

"I'd love to come see the new office sometime," she said.

"Sure, as soon as we get everything set up you should come by. On that note, I really better run. The furniture is being delivered tomorrow, and I've got a long night of cleaning ahead of me."

"No worries. It was great seeing you."

"You too." I smiled and offered her a quick hug.

I hurried up to the second floor. I hadn't seen the place since I'd made the decision to rent it. I was giddy to start making it our own, even if that meant getting a little dirty.

I stopped in front of the door. It was completely unrecognizable from the old door a few days ago. The wood had been painted a satin gray and the window was frosted, leaving a transparent silhouette of our company logo in the center. I turned the key in the shiny chrome handle and opened the door.

The original floors were now shiny and renewed from being refinished and lacquered. Ornate white trim lined the windows and the walls where they met the ceiling. A new ceiling fan and track lighting brought the space into the twenty-first century.

I grabbed my phone and called Fiona.

"Hey, Erica."

"Do you have something you want to tell me?"

"What? Oh."

"I thought we were past this." I tried to keep my tone even, but when was she going to learn to keep Blake out of my business?

"Erica, he's my big brother. What do you want me to do? He wanted to do something to help. You know how he is."

Yes, I knew how he was and how impossible he

made it to say no, especially when he had his sights set on something. I walked around the room admiring how the space had completely transformed since I'd last seen it. I couldn't imagine anything better. All I could think to do was mentally map out furniture placement. Blake had done the rest. Damn it all.

"Well it looks amazing. It's perfect."

"I know. I sneaked a peek before giving you the keys. He did a great job. Just what I envisioned." Her wariness at my reaction had clearly waned, her excitement shining through.

I sighed and tapped my foot. Damn it, I was excited too.

"All right, I'm still mad at you though," I said, thoroughly unconvincing.

"I'll buy you a drink sometime and you'll forget all about it."

"I usually need a few drinks to forget."

She laughed. "Not going to argue with that. Well, enjoy the space. Congrats."

"Thanks, I'll talk to you later."

I dropped my bag—heavy with cleaning supplies that were now unnecessary—to the floor. I sat cross-legged in the middle of the room, taking it all in. Every baby step we'd taken with the business these past few weeks had seemed overwhelming, and Blake never failed to take everything up a notch.

Just then the door opened, and Blake's frame filled the doorway. His hands were full with a bottle of champagne, a blanket, and a brown paper bag. A knowing grin curved his lips.

"How's my favorite boss?"

"Can't complain," I said flatly, looking up at his impressive frame towering over me.

He unfolded the blanket, sat down, and patted the spot next to him for me to join him there.

"What's all this?"

"I was thinking we could have an office picnic to celebrate the new digs."

He smirked and twisted the cork off the champagne, then poured the bubbly into two glasses he retrieved from the bag.

Our gazes locked. He was gauging my mood.

"You mad?"

"Maybe," I lied. Luckily he'd done such an amazing job that I'd already forgiven him and his accomplice.

His eyebrows shot up as if he were waiting for me to react. I got a little lost in his eyes. His beautiful hazel irises under thick, long lashes were the centerpiece on a face that took my breath away with alarming regularity. The sharp lines of his jaw. His lightly tanned skin and full delicious lips that reminded me of the terrible, wonderful things they could do to me. I could stare at him for hours and never tire of the way he made me feel. Possessed and obsessed. I'd never felt so wanted or so enraptured by another human being. Blake was the whole gorgeous, maddening package, and I loved every inch of him.

I sighed, hoping I didn't look as hopelessly in love as I felt. "I'm accepting your insanity."

"Good girl." He visibly relaxed and flashed me a smile.

Eager to be closer, I accepted his earlier invitation and shifted to join him on the blanket. I took the glass of champagne he handed to me and took a sip.

"Do you like it?"

"I love it." Despite his misgivings about the location, he seemed to have had some vision for the place after all.

"I hoped you would."

"Why the change of heart?"

He frowned. "What do you mean?"

"You made no bones about hating this place when we looked at it."

"Obviously I was going to want you closer. But this is what you wanted. You're accepting my 'insanity' as you call it, and I'm accepting your obstinacy."

I stared at him a moment. I couldn't quite argue with his description of me. "Some might call that progress."

He smiled in a way that made me believe no one had come this far with him before. We hadn't talked about it, but Blake didn't strike me as someone who made compromises often. Frankly, neither of us did, but somehow we were figuring it out. Remodeling the office was way over the top, but accepting my decision was a step in the right direction.

I sipped the chilled bubbly. Silence settled over the room. "You need to let me struggle a little bit, you know."

He raised his eyebrows. "Do you hear yourself?"

"Yes, I do. And I know I won't grow if I always have you butting in before I can face a challenge or make a mistake. I want those opportunities, otherwise I'll just bumble along in this fantasy world where you make all my problems go away and I'll never know what it's really like to run a business."

He exhaled loudly. "All right, then. How involved do you want me to be?"

"How about you let me ask for your help when I need it?"

He shook his head. "You'll never do that."

I rolled my eyes, but he was partially right. I was stubborn as hell and rarely reached out for help.

"Hey." He caught my chin, turning me toward him. "I'm proud of you."

"For what? Roping you in for four million dollars?"

He laughed. "If that was all part of your master plan, then yes, I'm extremely proud, because I never saw that coming."

I smirked despite myself. I would have done just about anything to avoid taking his money, and he knew it.

"Seriously though, this is a big step. I want you to remember to enjoy the moment."

And I did just that. Being with Blake made every moment just a little sweeter. A lot sweeter. He gave everything a kind of wonder that made me question how I'd ever survived the tedious existence I called life before he walked in and turned everything upside down.

"I am, thanks to you." I leaned in closer and met his lips.

He cradled my face in his palm and traced his tongue along my lips, coaxing them open, dipping into my mouth with soft lashes of his tongue.

"Aren't you going to ask me what's in the bag?"

I pulled back a fraction, breathless and a little dazed on his taste and scent. Clean, rough, and masculine, uniquely Blake. He turned away and unpacked the contents of the brown bag. He set out a container of strawberries, whipped cream, and a small glass jar of gourmet chocolate sauce.

"What kind of picnic did you have in mind?"

He held up the glass jar. "They drizzle this amazing

chocolate sauce on the lattes and confections downstairs. I guess it's not for sale, but when I politely explained to them that I'd be licking it off your naked body to christen the new office, they finally obliged."

I giggled and tried to imagine that unlikely conversation between him and Simone. He twisted the lid off and offered it to me. I dipped my finger in the chocolate and then into my mouth. The chocolate coated my tongue, the taste decadent and divine, the experience only heightened by the surety that Blake would be making good on his plans shortly.

"I thought you were opposed to office nooky," I said.

"This is *your* office. Different rules."

"Which I see you're already making." I dipped my finger through the chocolate sauce again, but before I could make it to my mouth, Blake pulled it swiftly into his and tongued my fingertip suggestively.

"Take your shirt off and lie down."

I grinned and rose slowly to my knees, pulling my tank top off. "You're bossy today."

He pulled a black silk mask out of the bag and slipped it over my eyes. "It's not a mood, baby. It's who I am. You'd do well to remember that."

His breath was warm against my collarbone. I held my breath in anticipation of his mouth on me but was surprised instead to feel his hand slide up my back. His fingers deftly unhooked my bra and I heard the garment land a few feet away. Bare-chested and chilled by the cool room, I was acutely aware of my present vulnerability.

"Lie down and don't make me repeat myself again."

I released the breath I'd been holding, suddenly

weakened by the command and the edge in his voice. Arguing with his simple but forceful request was a distant thought, quickly overwhelmed by the desire to have him take control of my body for as long as he saw fit.

I obeyed and lay down on my back, resting my palms on the textured fabric of the blanket, cool against the heat that prickled beneath my flesh. He unbuttoned my jeans and tugged them down my hips, stopping just short of my pubic bone.

He trailed hot open-mouthed kisses along my belly that had me breathless for more. I arched into his touch as he caressed the juts of my hipbones with his thumbs.

"I love this part of you," he murmured. "One of many. Your body… Erica, you're so fucking sexy."

"Touch me."

"I plan to, but I'm getting ahead of myself. Stop squirming."

"You're torturing me," I whimpered.

He laughed quietly. "Not nearly."

With that he left me, creating an unwelcome distance between us. The room chilled again. Where was he and what was he doing? I shivered at the first drop of liquid sliding into my navel. He drizzled a trail up my chest, circling my nipples, each beading under the sensation.

"Do you like strawberries?"

I smiled at the hint. "Yes."

"Good. I'm going to feed you one."

The fresh aroma of strawberries mingled with the chocolate as he rested a piece of fruit on my lower lip. I opened my mouth, but Blake kept it just out of reach. I arched to grasp it until he finally let me sink my teeth into it. I chewed and swallowed, savoring the flavor and the new experience of combining my obsession with Blake with my love of food. Strange, but I couldn't argue with having too much of a good thing, or many good things, in this case.

He pressed an unexpected kiss to my throat, nibbling my flesh. He traveled down my collarbone and passed between my breasts. His tongue slowed and circled one peak after the next. He sucked and licked slow velvety strokes all over my torso, spreading his attentions to any remote expanse of skin. I gasped at the sensation of his tongue taunting and taking its sweet time to lick my flesh clean. Once he had, he slid a hand into my jeans and cupped my sex over my now soaked panties.

"I'm going to fuck you now, Erica. Do you want that?"

His breath over the wet flesh of my nipple gave me gooseflesh, my skin electric from all the ways he'd tantalized it.

I moaned a loud affirmative, my hands nearly numb from gripping the blanket with restraint. Ready to burst, I released them and found his hair, fisting the silky strands that slid between my fingers as I held his mouth tight to my breast. He nipped me gently and I yelped.

He took me by the wrists and replaced them above my head. "Stay still."

The bag crinkled again, and then he bound my wrists with some kind of silky fabric and tightened the knot, leaving no question about my ability to wriggle free from it.

He stripped me from the waist down and I heard his clothes drop to the floor at my feet before his body covered mine.

I twisted my wrists, a pointless effort since I had no

way of breaking free on my own. As I did, my heartbeat ratcheted to a rapid rate, panic seeping in. He'd done this before, left me helpless, unable to touch him or move. Those bonds had been a little easier to negotiate, but these didn't budge. I couldn't see him now. I was helpless and in the dark. A cold fear crept in, replacing Blake with a nightmare, the darkest memory.

"Blake." My voice was uneven, tainted with the uneasiness that grew. I wasn't sure if I could do this.

His hand rested over my heart, my chest rising rapidly with the breathing I could no longer control.

"Shh, baby. I've got you," he murmured.

He covered my body with the warmth of his own, claiming my mouth with his, tender and full of love, silencing my fears. He kissed my jaw and moved to the sensitive skin of my neck, just below my ear.

"Do you feel me? It's me, baby. It'll always be me."

With those words, my body went lax beneath him. I released the fists I'd been clenching and focused on his touch, unlike any other. No one had ever touched me the way he did, like he knew my body better than I did.

Slowly the panic subsided, melting away as he reintroduced himself to my body, his voice bringing me back to the moment, our moment.

"I've been hard all day thinking about you like this. Do you have any idea how impossible it is to work that way? Thinking about your tight little body quivering under me, ready for me?"

Inch by inch my skin came alive, quickening as his hands and his mouth claimed me. Urgent touches and hot, wet kisses. His voice talking me through every motion, every plan. My hips circled into the motion of his fingers massaging me, sliding through my wet folds and inside of me, a promise of what was to come.

My focus pinpointed on the contact. I was panting, aimlessly wondering how much longer I could hold out like this. God, the man loved torturing me.

"You okay?" He circled my wrists gently and feathered down the sensitive skin on the underside of my arms.

I roused myself from my longing to consider his question. Panic was so far in my rearview. I could think of nothing but the sweet inevitable of having him inside me.

"More than okay. Don't stop."

He spread my legs around him. He notched at my opening and pushed in, slow enough to drive me a little crazy. I held my breath until he was rooted, stretching me fully. He took my mouth in a deep kiss, and I took my next breath from him as he ground his hips gently, reminding me how deeply he could possess me in every way. I moaned, and fire spread through my veins, heating me from limb to limb as I clung to his body the only way I could. I hooked my ankles behind his thighs, urging him into me, the need to have him moving inside me almost more than I could bear.

He slipped his arm around my waist and splayed his hand at my tailbone, protecting me from the hard floor as he thrust into me harder. I gasped, relief and ecstasy flooding me.

He rocked into me, finding a steady rhythm. Between kisses, he murmured in my ear. "Love you, baby. Being inside you…like this. Controlling your pleasure. I need this."

He whispered the things he wanted to do to me, how

every minute inside me made him feel, staying with me so I'd never forget who was loving me.

"Blake, oh God…" There was nothing but the sound of his voice and his cock plunging into me. No distractions, only the fierce claim of his body over mine. My lip trembled as the tension mounted.

"That's it. Now you're going to come loud and hard and introduce me to the neighbors."

He took my hands in one of his, holding them tight above me while the other found my hip. Then, lifting me a few inches off the floor, he drove in hard so his cock hit the spot inside me that made everything go white behind the black.

His name left my lips in a hoarse cry. Colors exploded behind my eyes as my body seized around his, the tremble rocketing through my core.

"Christ, Erica… Fuck, just like that."

My toes curled as he rolled into the last few strokes that took us both over the edge. He gripped my hips roughly and buried himself in me one last time with a loud moan.

He collapsed over me, his body slick and fevered. I twisted my hands again, wanting to touch him and soothe him through the aftershocks. He untied the fabric deftly, freeing me. I squinted against the light pouring into the room when he slipped off the mask.

Blake's face was relaxed but his eyes were dark and serious. He stroked my face reverently, pushing tiny strands of hair away as we caught our breath.

"I missed your eyes. Next time I want to see them every minute I make love to you, all the way to the end. I want you to see what you do to me."

CHAPTER TWO

"I *love* fashion."

I didn't doubt it. Dressed in a sleek black designer wrap dress matched with heels that I would absolutely fall over in, Risa Corvi was very well maintained. Almost too put together. She didn't have the effortless beauty that Alli carried, but nothing was out of place, from her shoulder-length jet-black hair to her fresh French manicure.

She came across as high-maintenance. I bet she got her eyebrows waxed like clockwork too. Sadly, I could probably take a few notes from her. I scanned her resume. For an entry-level candidate, she boasted some impressive work, but I was still skeptical about hiring a friend of a friend.

"I can see that. Tell me about some of the campaigns you've worked on."

Risa pulled out a large portfolio case with sections of printed material organized by campaign. Every page was aligned perfectly and the content was equally clean-cut and professional. Lots of stock photo models sporting fake and perfect smiles, because their retirement accounts were making them *that* happy. The technique was overused and a far cry from who we were as a company.

"This is great, Risa. But to be honest, these are very mainstream. We want to be mainstream, but we also want an edge to our brand that makes it feel young, exclusive, and hip."

"I completely understand. These are very safe. Obviously I was limited by what the client wanted here, but I could explore many more directions with Clozpin. We can do edgy high fashion and make it clean and elegant, you know? Simple but sexy."

She talked a good game, but could she deliver? I flipped through the rest of the portfolio and studied her a moment.

"How do you feel about networking and sales? Landing new accounts is possibly the most critical component to this position. You can love fashion all day long, but you need to be able to sell it."

"Agreed, but it's really difficult to sell something you don't love. I can sell this service, and if I have to do after-hours events for the networking effort, I'm totally fine with that."

I sat back in my chair and weighed her words. She was hungry. No one could deny that. In the past couple weeks of interviews, I hadn't come across anyone who exuded as much passion as she had in the past five minutes.

We had no real office culture, so I had no idea how she would gel with Sid and his new troupe of techies. More importantly, how would she gel with me? The clock was ticking on getting our newly funded plans in place, and I needed to make a decision. Hiring her on the spot seemed rash, but she was basically perfect.

She took a deep breath. "Listen, I understand this is your baby, Erica. You seem like someone who would be great to work with and learn from. The decision is yours of course, but I'd really love to be a part of this team."

She bore into me with her dark blue eyes, waiting to pounce on the next interview question, no doubt.

"You're fine with the pay?"

"Absolutely." She waved her hand definitively.

I clicked my pen, stalling even though I'd already made the decision. "Fine."

"Fine?"

"Let's do this."

A huge smile spread across her face. "Really? Oh my God, you won't regret it."

I stood, and when we shook hands, hers trembled slightly in my own. Wow, was she that nervous?

"You can start on Monday. We'll sort out the paperwork when you get in."

"Awesome, thank you so much." The smile plastered all over her face wasn't going anywhere, I could tell.

★ ★ ★

Alli stretched out on the blanket beside me while I tossed crumbs to the ducks in the pond. The public gardens were just a few blocks from my apartment, and on a beautiful warm day like today, the park was alive with families, tourists, and people like us. I'd cut out of work early to pick her up, and we decided some sunshine was the first item on the agenda for her long weekend visit with me.

"I forgot how much I love summer here." Her eyes were hazy and wistful, like her thoughts were here but also someplace else.

"You miss Boston yet?"

Alli propped up on her elbow. "I think I do. New York kind of sucks you into its vortex. Sometimes I have a hard time imagining my life outside the city, but I have to say, I am enjoying the change of scenery. I needed a break."

The past several weeks had been an adjustment for both of us. After three years of sharing a dorm to being two hundred miles away, our friendship had been strained. But deep down, I knew distance alone couldn't shake what we had.

"No doubt. Any news from Heath?"

"He's doing well."

"I thought maybe you'd go see him, you know, instead of me." I was glad she hadn't, of course. After bringing her up to speed on everything that had happened between Blake and me and then having Mark show up seemingly out of nowhere, we'd both agreed that we needed face time.

"Friends first, biatch." She smiled and gave me a little poke.

I retaliated by aiming a few breadcrumbs at her perfectly tousled soft brown locks falling down her back.

"Do you think you'll visit him in L.A.?"

"No. He needs his time there, and frankly, I need time too. I finally got my own place, and the move has been strangely liberating. Every day I felt like I was waiting for him there. Now I'm finally starting my life in the city, without every moment revolving around him and us."

I nodded, knowing full well how important independence could be in a new relationship. Keeping Blake at arm's length was a constant struggle when I wanted nothing more than to be enveloped in the safety and security of his hyper-controlled world. Blake's world was safe, but it wasn't always reality.

"That makes sense. When does he get back from rehab?"

"Another month or so. Not sure yet."

"What then? Are you going to pick up the pieces and try again?"

"I think so. We haven't made any commitments, but—" She lay back and stared up at the trees above us.

"What is it?"

"I just… I miss him. That's all."

I paused, not wanting to push her either way. She was struggling with their separation, but I still wasn't convinced Heath was good for her. Even if he was Blake's little brother.

"Sometimes all I can hear is people judging us."

I cringed a little, praying she hadn't read my expression or my mind.

"Like, what the fuck am I doing wasting my time with someone like him? My friends, even you, think he's trouble, and I admit it, he's got problems. But I can't give up on us. He deserves another chance." She wiped away a tear before it had a chance to fall.

I lay down next to her on the blanket and waited for her to collect herself. Finding out Heath had a drug problem had been a shock, but I couldn't ignore the fact that they were hopelessly in love. I'd never seen Alli so blissed out, and Heath had taken her there. I hoped she could do the same for him, enough to lure him away from an addiction that could ruin their chance for happiness together.

"Alli, I care about you, and I want you to be happy. If I come across as judgy, it's because I'm worried about your well being, not because I question Heath's value as a person. Trust me, I know full well that no one and no relationship is perfect. He's got issues, but all hope is not lost, I'm sure."

She turned her head and gave me a weak smile. "Thanks."

"If he can get his shit together, you can still make this work. Just be smart about it. That's all I want."

She laughed. "I'm trying. I'm not very smart when it comes to being in love, I guess."

"Maybe this break is good. Obviously he needs to work through some of his own issues, but also you both can have time to really think about your relationship without being so wrapped up in the intensity of it."

"You're right. I'm already getting into a better mind-set, you know, the more time we spend apart." She took a deep breath. "Anyway, enough about me and my problems. What about you and Blake? Is he still driving you crazy?"

"You know it."

"In a good way or a bad way?"

"Both, but we're figuring it out."

She gave me a grin. "I think Blake has met his match with you, Erica."

"Oh?"

"Yeah, I'm sure you don't take any of his shit. Mr. Software Billionaire probably has no idea how to deal with you putting him in his place."

I laughed at the picture she drew of us. She might have been right. I couldn't imagine many people challenging Blake the way I did. I did it for self-preservation though, not sport. Still, the tug of war drove us both crazy. Mostly good crazy.

"He keeps me on my toes, and he could probably say the same about me. Never a dull moment, that's for sure." I smiled to myself and my heart did a little flip at the thought of him. Blake was full of challenges. I never knew what the hell to expect from him, but that was just another part of our relationship that I couldn't get enough of. The rush, the negotiating, and when the occasion called for it, the sweet surrender.

"Okay, the look on your face is making me nauseous."

I laughed. "Sorry."

"Don't be. I'm just bitter and lonely. Anyway, stand your ground. I know you will, but those Landon men can be pretty damn persuasive."

She looked serious for a minute, then a smile curved her lips and we burst into a fit of laughter.

★ ★ ★

Walking into the office still took me aback sometimes. The space looked great with the subtle lighting and sleek workstations. Sid sat next to two of the newest team members. I leaned on the desk they huddled around. They paused and looked up.

"What's new, guys?"

Chris was about a decade older than we were. This wasn't his first job at a start-up, so he brought some experience that most of us lacked. A heavyset guy, he had bright red hair that was overgrown and curled up at his shoulders. Based on the past week's attire, he seemed to have an affinity for Hawaiian shirts.

On the other end of the spectrum, we had hired James as our dedicated designer and front-end developer. He was a different brand. With a mop of nearly black wavy hair, tanned skin, and bright blue eyes, he was by far the most naturally outgoing of the entire crew. Well-built with a touch of bad boy about him thanks to some ink that peeked out from his button-downs, he wasn't hard to look at either.

"Morning, Erica." He flashed a smile that caught me off guard.

I smiled back, surprised at being greeted with such enthusiasm so early in the morning. *Good hire*, I thought.

Sid blew out a breath, apparently not sharing James's mid-morning peppiness. "We're trying to figure out a plan for rolling out the upgrades we talked about, but it's a little hard with this band of misfits trying to take us down twenty-four hours a day."

"Uh-oh." I cringed a little, having no idea how to go about *technically* fixing this problem beyond harping on Blake to work his magic. He'd been frustratingly vague about his association with M89, but clearly, due to whatever he'd done to piss them off so royally, the hackers were not going to give up easily.

"Anyway, we're figuring it out. Don't worry about it." He scowled and focused on the monitor, stopping periodically to jot down some notes.

"Can I help?"

"Nope."

His answer was predictably curt. For the Sid I'd come to know, who was regularly grumpy due to his erratic sleep schedule, being met with challenges at ten in the morning was unacceptable. I rolled my eyes and caught James smirking.

"Keep me posted." I pushed off the desk and disappeared behind the Chinese curtain partitioning my office from the rest of the space. Due to the size of the room and the budget, I'd decided to forgo the privacy that a build out would afford, and in the end, I was grateful Blake had honored that wish with his secret remodel. I felt secluded enough to do my work in peace but still connected enough to tap into whatever Sid and his crew were up to. Plus, Risa would be joining us soon, and we'd likely have a lot more regular communicating to do. At least we spoke the same language.

When their informal meeting ended, I Skyped Sid to come talk to me. He came in, his tall frame towering over me at my desk. He settled into a chair across from me.

"What's with the attitude, Sid? We're on the same team here."

"I realize that, but I'm getting really sick of patching holes in a sinking boat."

"We're sinking?"

He sighed. "No. But constantly patching vulnerabilities and fixing shit they're breaking while trying to roll out new development is becoming pretty fucking tedious, Erica."

I sat back, stunned. Sid rarely swore, so his nerves were frayed. When my nerves were frayed, I cried in the privacy of my room or channeled my anger into being obsessively productive. When Sid's nerves were frayed, everyone suffered.

"What do we do? I want to help. I just have no idea how, Sid."

"Talk to your boyfriend. Doesn't he have all the answers?"

"Most of the time he does, yeah. But he doesn't have a magic pill for this. I'm at a loss."

Blake's strategy thus far had been to simply make the site completely impenetrable. Because I'd refused to let his team of programmers take over the site, the responsibility fell squarely on Sid. Now Chris and James shared the burden.

"On the ground-level, there are improvements I can make to the site. At some point, we'll need to redevelop it anyway to accommodate large-scale growth. The only thing I can think of is to work on that instead of doing these upgrades. Then at least we're working with a more solid foundation, since clearly we're going to be under attack for the foreseeable future."

"Sid, you're scaring me. Rebuild the site from the ground up? There has got to be another way. We're coming up on a critical marketing push."

"I'm not here to tell you what you want to hear. I suggest you talk to Blake. Whatever he did to bring this on, he should know how to fix it because this isn't what I signed on for."

Sid's response punched me in the gut.

"Okay, how about you get the guys squared away with their work for the day and you can take the day off. Come back refreshed, and hopefully I'll have some answers tomorrow."

I tried to keep my voice steady even though I wanted to tell him to grow the fuck up. Work was full of challenges. I had taken on the brunt of the ownership responsibilities, leaving him with the task of focusing on only what interested him—the development. Yet he marched around like the entire world was plotting against him. True, a small faction was in fact plotting against us, but he was being a little dramatic.

He huffed and left my pseudo-office. He mumbled some things to the guys and slumped back into his chair.

I smiled. Deep down, Sid was just as obstinate about giving up as I was. We had that in common.

CHAPTER THREE

Alli brushed on some bronzer while we got ready in my bathroom. She let me borrow a tight leopard-print skirt that fit like a glove. She took the liberty of pairing it with a black off-the-shoulder top. I had a feeling Blake might be stripping this outfit off me with his teeth in a few hours. God, I wanted him to.

After two days of dedicated girl time, Alli was venturing out to get dinner and drinks with some friends so Blake and I could catch up. My skin was crawling from missing him so much.

We'd survived brief periods of separation before, but usually those were colored by me being totally pissed at him, which helped stave off the unbearable attraction I had toward him. All I felt toward Blake right now was epic longing, especially after the mind-bending sex we'd had in the office a few days ago.

I loved spending time with Alli, and I was glad for the time away from our respective boys if it meant reviving the friendship that we'd spent the past three years building. Between the Landon brothers, we had plenty to work through. I'd brought her up to speed with everything that had happened, from Blake blowing up my business deal with Max, to the total mindfuck of having Mark show up out of nowhere.

Heath came up in our conversations with a frequency

that made me question how much she was really appreciating their time apart. Tonight she'd been quiet, though.

"Everything okay?"

She smiled too quickly. "Yeah, definitely."

I finished sprucing up, and when I walked out, Blake was lounging on the new living room set I'd purchased for the apartment. In a white collared shirt rolled up at the sleeves and dark blue jeans, he looked so fucking delectable that I thought seriously about straddling him right then and there.

When our gazes locked, his jaw dropped a fraction. The feeling was mutual.

"You ready?"

I smiled. Alli joined us and interrupted my laser focus on Blake's amazing body. He rose to greet her and brushed a quick kiss on her cheek.

"You look great, Alli. It's good to see you."

"Likewise." Her smile was tight, seemingly strained by some emotion that was bubbling under the surface.

I tried to read her body language. Was she nervous or embarrassed about seeing Blake after the Heath situation in New York?

"So I guess we're off," I said quietly, trying to break the awkwardness that hopefully only I was picking up on.

We said our goodbyes, and Blake ran his hand down my back and gave me a gentle push toward the door. The power and suggestion of his touch had my skin tingling, my nerves alert. I was suddenly cursing our dinner plans when I wanted nothing more than to drag him upstairs to his apartment and rock his world straight into the dawn.

★ ★ ★

We stepped out of the apartment and Blake led me upstairs, his fingers interlaced with mine.

"Did you forget something?"

Before he could answer, we walked through the doors of his apartment and the smells of a home-cooked meal filled the air. Blake had cooked without any help from me.

"Whoa." The kitchen was a mess, but by contrast the dining room table was neatly covered with several matching pottery serving dishes filled to the brim with pasta, salad, and bread. The room was dimly lit, the mood enhanced by flickering candles set throughout.

"I thought we could stay in," he murmured.

"But I got all dressed up." I leaned back into his embrace, letting his arms wrap around me.

"I'm glad you did. You look amazing. We'll be lucky to make it through dinner."

I bit my lip and my appetite wavered. Blake was by far the most mouth-watering item on any menu, but I needed fuel if I was going to ravage him all night like I'd planned.

"Everything looks great. I can't believe you did all this by yourself."

"I hope you like it."

We settled down at the table, and he poured us two glasses of wine as I helped myself to a plate of Blake's soon-to-be-famous spaghetti Bolognese, so he assured me. I took a bite and was pleasantly surprised. Spaghetti was hard to screw up, but with as little cooking experience as he had, I was prepared for the worst. A comfortable silence settled between us as we ate, but I was still thinking about Alli.

"How are things going with Alli?" Blake asked, as if reading my thoughts.

I bit into my garlic bread before answering. Alli was in a tough place right now, both lovesick and heartbroken by her turbulent relationship with Heath. I wasn't sure how much I should say.

"I think she's just going through a lot right now. With Heath and the move."

"The move?"

"She moved out of the condo."

"I hope she didn't do that on my account." His gaze rose to meet mine.

I shook my head, remembering Blake's once fervent insistence that I maintain some distance with Alli while she was involved with Heath. I had swiftly refused and ignored his wish, and thankfully that had been the end of the discussion. With everything I'd been going through at the time, the last thing I needed was to isolate myself from the few people I could go to for support.

"No. I think she needs some space to figure things out while Heath is gone. I don't think she's had a chance to be very independent since she moved to the city." I hesitated with the last thought. I wanted to tread lightly. Blake and Heath had their issues, but they were still brothers. I didn't want to cause problems between Heath and Alli if he didn't know about the move yet.

He nodded. "How's work?"

"Good and bad."

"Oh?"

I finished my last bite of the spaghetti before choosing my words.

"I hired a marketing director. She starts Monday and Alli is going to help me bring her up to speed with where she left off."

"And the bad?"

"I'm getting concerned with the security of the site. Sid is ready to pull his hair out. I don't know what to tell him." I risked a questioning look his way. I was approaching a subject he hated discussing.

He sat back and threw his napkin on the table. "You won't give me access to the code, Erica. What the hell do you want me to do?"

"It's not out of distrust, Blake. We need to be in control of the code for the long-term and you know that. Yet we all remain in the dark as to why we've been inexplicably and relentlessly attacked by this group."

He stared past me, avoiding my eyes and the pleading in them. An uneasy knot formed in my stomach. I hated his secrets. They ate at me like my own once used to, before I poured my heart and soul out to Blake. Revealing my past to him had lessened the burden, but I didn't know how to make him trust me the same way.

"You want my trust, Blake. This is why I have a hard time giving it so freely. You keep things from me."

"If I'm not forthcoming with information, it's for your own good."

"Can't I decide what's for my own good? Jesus, I'm not a child."

He muttered a curse under his breath, moved to the living room, and sank into the couch.

I chose a seat on the other couch, unsure how the rest of this conversation would go. A safer, less sexual distance might be better if we were going to accomplish anything constructive.

"You said you would fix this. You promised me. And if it's not that easy, fine, but I deserve to know what's really going on here. Maybe I can help."

He exhaled through his nose and let his head fall back on the couch. "You already know that I was a member of M89 when I was a teenager."

"Yes," I said quietly.

He leaned forward and rested his elbows on his knees, avoiding my eyes. "What you don't know is that I led the group with someone else."

"Who?" My voice was quiet and tentative. I didn't want to give him any reason not to tell me the things I so wanted—needed—to know.

"Cooper. His name was Brian Cooper."

I paused. "Was?"

His jaw ticked. He pushed back his dark brown hair that had grown longer since we'd met and fell unkempt across his forehead. I wanted to reach over and fix it but didn't want to interrupt the moment.

"He killed himself."

"Oh my God." I touched my hand to my mouth. No wonder he didn't want to talk about this. "When?"

"After the group was busted for hacking the bank accounts, they brought us all in. Except I'd been out of the operation for weeks. Cooper had been a friend, and when we came up with the original plan, I was on board for hacking the Wall Street guys, but then he'd wanted to start in on individual accounts. Regular people who invested their hopes of retirement with these jerks, but beyond that, had no connections to their Ponzi shit. I couldn't get behind it so I left the group. Our friendship was over, and obviously there was bad blood between us. When the Feds started questioning me…"

A heavy silence fell and my heart twisted. Blake was inextricably tied to the circumstances that had led to his young friend's suicide.

"Fuck, I don't know. I was young and pissed off and everything happened so fast." He rubbed his eyes with the heels of his hands, as if trying to erase whatever visions had conjured there.

"It's okay. Tell me." I moved from the adjacent couch to sit next to him, wanting to be close to him but worried about what he might say. But I wanted to know.

"I told them the truth. And because I cooperated, I basically got off and the investigators put the pressure on him. I wasn't trying to save myself, Erica. I just wanted to set the record straight. If I was going down with the ship, I wanted people to know what I stood for."

"Baby…" The words caught in my throat.

Pain shadowed his gaze. Years of regret had kept him from telling me this the first time the site went down.

"They didn't get far with him before he killed himself. That effectively ended the investigation. The funds were returned, and the rest of us got a slap on the wrist. Because we were all minors, they sealed the records. That's why most of what you read about me are just rumors. Only a handful of people really know what went down."

"How did the group stay active after all of this?"

"It didn't, but someone revived it a few years ago."

"An original member?"

"I doubt it, but I don't honestly know. I don't run in those circles anymore, but based on them being a persistent pain in my ass, whoever is behind this new generation of the group is holding a torch for Cooper. They probably worship him like he's some sort of goddamn martyr for the cause. What cause that might be is still a mystery to me."

"Have you tried to reach out to them?"

"No. I don't negotiate with terrorists."

The frustrated anger I'd come to recognize whenever we spoke about the hackers replaced the pained expression on his face. Blake was powerful and incredibly talented, but these people had somehow rattled him. That they did scared me, because he might be my last and only defense against them.

"Doesn't that seem like a hard line to take, considering how dedicated they are to ruining everything you touch?"

"We know their strategies. They're predictable, so my team has figured out efficient ways to keep them out of our business. They're vandals, but once you know their angle, you can outsmart them. I can't do the same for you until you let me."

"You're not looking at the source of the problem."

He sighed. "Whoever they are, they see him as a martyr. And I'm Benedict Arnold. Nothing about that will change as long as they exist."

"I think you're missing the point."

"I'll talk to Sid in the morning, all right? That's it."

The edge in his voice gave me pause. His vulnerability had disappeared, expertly masked behind his anger. But I knew better. He and Cooper had been friends once. Surely his death must have clung to him. Blake seemed to take personal responsibility for nearly everyone around him. I caught the reaction in his eyes when he spoke of him, but as quickly as he'd opened up, he'd closed himself off again.

I wanted to kiss him then, coax out the man I loved and soothe the pain that still lingered within him. I reached up tentatively and cupped his cheek in my palm. He turned into my gesture, placing his hand over mine and turning my palm up to kiss it gently before pulling it down onto the couch between us.

"Don't be mad at me," I muttered.

"I'm not. I don't like talking about this."

"You might feel better if you did."

He groaned and rolled his eyes. I could feel him slipping further away from me at the suggestion. I slid my hand under his shirt, appreciating every ridge of his abs under my fingertips. I was determined to lure him out of this mood he'd fallen into. Nothing took me away from the cacophony of my thoughts better than being naked with Blake. I suspected the same was true for him.

"I miss you."

His face relaxed and I smiled, relieved. He stroked my face reverently, tracing a path from my cheek to my chin. Before I could say anything more, he angled his lips over mine and took my mouth in a kiss. Soft and tender, the kiss quickly became heated. He pulled away abruptly.

"What?"

He looked past me. "I can't do this right now."

"What do you mean?"

I straddled him the way I'd wanted to, my skirt inching up indecently high. I pulled him into another kiss. I arched into his chest, leaving no space between us, rabid for his touch. No sooner had I fisted my hands in his hair, he pulled back, disengaging my fingers and holding them gently by my sides.

"Erica, stop. I need…to cool off."

Before I could question him, he patted my thigh gently, a signal to move off of him. Slowly I obliged. He retreated to the kitchen where he started to clean up. I joined him and started helping, but he stopped me.

"It's okay. I'll take care of this." He paused and faced me. Leaning against the counter with his hip, he looked deceptively casual considering the tension that rolled off him. "Listen, I've got some work to do for tomorrow, and it sounds like you do too. Do you mind if we call it an early night?"

I searched his eyes for answers, but he seemed as cold and closed off as ever. I stared, stunned and speechless, swallowing hard as the rejection settled over me. Had I pried too much? Didn't he understand my reasons for wanting to know?

Everything I thought to say back sounded feeble, desperate, in my mind. *Why don't you want to be with me? Why can't I stay?* The thought of him answering those questions honestly scared me. I wasn't sure if I wanted to know why he didn't want me tonight.

★ ★ ★

My apartment was empty and lifeless with no signs of Sid or Alli to console the loneliness and hurt that washed over me. Blake had never shot me down before. I was dressed to kill and the man had a marathon sex drive. Somehow we'd survived the past few days outside of each other's beds, but now he was pushing me away?

I dropped my purse on the counter and stood in the quiet darkness of the room, trying to figure out how Blake's confession about his past had driven such a wedge between us. I went to the bedroom and assessed myself in the mirror. I felt terrible. Blake hadn't just shot down a night in his bed. That he didn't want me cut me to the core, leaving me with a sick and hopeless feeling.

No. I couldn't let this go.

I headed back out, grabbing my keys on the way.

I let myself into Blake's apartment but he was nowhere to be found. I walked down to his bedroom where I heard the shower running. I hesitated at the doorway leading into the en suite bathroom. Through the glass, I could see Blake's hands pressed against the wall, water pouring down his massive unmoving frame. He was beautiful, despite the sadness that had crept over us and threatened our night. I took another step forward. He turned his head toward me.

I stood still, waiting for his reaction. He turned off the shower. My breath caught at the sight of him as he emerged. Under normal circumstances Blake was a sight to behold. Now, stark naked and dripping wet, he could not have been more impressive. A prime specimen of masculine beauty.

Goosebumps beaded his skin and his cock was as hard as stone, jutting out from his formidable frame.

What the fuck?

"Blake." My voice was barely a whisper.

"What do you want, Erica?"

His voice was flat, his face expressionless, as if I were a stranger. He toweled himself dry methodically.

"I—"

I had no words. My grand plan to sneak back into his apartment and seduce him, to not take no for an answer, had been shot to hell by the sudden realization that seduction might be a lost cause.

"Go home, Erica. I told you, I've got work to do."

"Bullshit. Do you want to explain to me why you've spent the past ten minutes taking a cold shower and now you've got the biggest cockstand I've ever seen, but you're cutting me off?"

"I don't want to fight with you. Can we just call it a night?"

He passed me and headed into the bedroom. I followed him, determined to get answers.

"We're talking about this. If you're going to shut me down, you can fucking tell me why." My voice shook. I was losing my cool and wild scenarios swept through my mind. "Are you seeing someone else?" I asked, incredulous. What had transpired since our last time together in the office? Had I done something wrong?

He scowled and fisted his hands. "Jesus Christ. No. Will you just leave me be?"

His words stung. I hated him in that moment. How could he make me feel so small and insignificant with his indifference when I was here damn near begging him for intimacy? "You're right. I don't need this shit."

He sighed. "Baby."

I turned and marched to the door. Before I could reach it, he outpaced me and slammed it shut in front of me. He caught my elbow and spun me to face him.

"What do you want from me, Erica?"

My breaths came fast. My heart raced with anger mingled with my steadily growing desire. I couldn't decide which emotion would win or which I was rooting for. But I wasn't here to fight with him.

"I want you to fuck me."

His jaw tensed and his grip on my arm tightened painfully.

"Why don't you want me?" My voice was small, almost unrecognizable. I weakened in his grasp, and my anger gave way to something else. A raw vulnerability that Blake had uncovered.

His next movements were so quick I could barely distinguish them. He pushed up my skirt and ripped off my panties in one violent motion, stinging my upper thighs as the fabric tore across my skin. A second later he hoisted me up around his waist and slammed me against the door. And then he was there. Plunging himself so deep that I screamed. I arched into the door, raw pain tearing through my core. I whimpered at the relief that followed. He was with me again, finally.

He thrust again and I cried out. Heat shot through me, my body melting around his.

I softened when I sensed Blake's stillness. His body was frozen against mine, eerily still. I opened my eyes to meet his intense and questioning gaze. God, he was beautiful. And he was mine, but somehow over the past couple hours I'd lost him. I had to keep him with me, to show him how desperately I needed him like this.

"Don't stop. Please," I begged.

I raked my fingers through his damp hair, fisting the strands gently. Tightening my legs around his waist, I churned my hips, urging his movement. I only needed the slightest friction to set off my orgasm. I was already slick around him. He barely moved when a quiet moan escaped my trembling lips. Warmth crept over my skin and I shuddered, my sex rippling over his length, my gaze never leaving his.

His lips parted slightly, his eyes misted with emotion. "You're going to be the death of me, I swear it."

I kissed him deeply. "Finish me. Don't make me beg," I breathed into his mouth.

"God help me, I've never wanted anything more. You... this." He pulled out and drove into me again.

I cursed, crying out with every punishing thrust that sent unimaginable sensations through my body. A blinding mix of pleasure, pain, anger, and love seized me, rocking me from one orgasm straight into the next. Unable to contain the frenzy that had taken over, I clung desperately to him, my mouth at his shoulder.

Every muscle tensed, taut and rigid, beneath my touch. My teeth pressed into his skin and I dug my nails in deep, scoring his flesh down to his elbow. My cunt tightened around him. He growled, quickening his pace.

"Look at me." His voice was tense with need. "I need to see you."

I harnessed all my strength to raise my gaze, meeting his. Taking in all his beauty weakened me in his arms, putty in his hands. Never mind what I did to him. This is what he did to me.

His eyes never left mine as he rammed me into the door with his final thrust.

I sucked in a sharp breath. "Blake!"

"Feel me. I want you to feel all of me, Erica," he rasped.

A strangled groan followed as he emptied himself into me and released the last orgasm my body could give.

We stood there only a moment before we collapsed to the floor. He rolled to his back onto the Oriental rug. I draped my body lazily over his, spent from what had just happened between us, but still needing the contact, to know that we were still connected, together.

We stayed like that, no words, no movements, until he slid my skirt up a fraction, thumbing the tender flesh where he'd removed the obstacle of my panties moments ago.

I glanced down, and his hands cupped my ass. "You're going to have bruises here too."

I looked back up to find his mouth set in a hard line. "Why would I care?"

"Maybe you should care."

I slid my hand up his chest. "I don't know what's going on in your head, but I wish you would talk to me. If you really don't want to, I can live with that too. But don't push me away. I can't take it."

"Is that what you call pushing you away? Using your body as a battering ram?"

I frowned at his description of what we'd just had. Sure, it was a little rough and I'd probably feel it tomorrow, but anytime we were together meant something.

I rose to my knees, straddled his thighs, and dropped my hands to either side of him. I tried to read his eyes but he avoided my penetrating gaze, worrying the reddened flesh at the crease of my thigh instead.

I pulled off my shirt and bra.

"What are you doing?"

"Getting your attention."

Heat passed over his eyes. "You have it."

"I like when you lose control like that, Blake. Don't turn it into something dirty and wrong."

His cock hardened beneath my thigh.

"What if it is? Giving you bruises…freaking you out."

"Is that why you've been cockblocking yourself all night?"

"What I feel…for you, Erica. With everything else that's going on, sometimes it's just too intense. I feel like I'm going to rip us both apart. I wanted tonight to be different. I really did." He closed his eyes for a moment. "You deserve to be worshipped. Loved."

I frowned, trying to figure out how my habitually domineering lover was slipping away from me. "I do feel loved. I like waking up to the memory of your hands on me, even if I'm a little sore. It's new for me, I'll admit it."

"I scared you before though." He held my gaze, daring me to say otherwise.

"Sometimes it does scare me, but I trust you." I paused. "I like the things we've done."

"Do you realize I haven't even begun to scratch the surface of the things I want to do to you?"

My breath caught, but I didn't waste time dwelling on the fear that rooted in my stomach. "Then let's dig deeper."

I doubted the words even as I said them, my heartbeat picking up speed again. Blake was already pushing me past boundaries I didn't even know I had. I was keeping up pretty well, but now, knowing his desires were that vast and beyond me, I couldn't help but feel a little in over my head.

"No." His voice was quiet but firm.

"Why?" I hoped I'd masked my doubts.

"Because this isn't right. I shouldn't want to…to *hurt* you or restrain you. It's fucked up, and it's the last thing you should have to think about with everything you've been through. I realized that last time. I took things too far. The second I tied you up, I regretted it."

"Then why didn't you stop?"

He was silent.

"Tell me."

He sighed. "Because I knew I could calm you down, show you how to enjoy it."

"And I did."

"That doesn't mean anything. I shouldn't have challenged you that way."

"I want to be challenged, Blake. If this is something you want, I want it too."

"No, it's not going to be like that. Erica, you can put that right out of your head. You're not going down this road for me. You were…raped, for Christ's sake. My compulsion for control when we're fucking is the last thing you need. You're not the right person for this."

A sickness punched me in the gut and my skin chilled. What if I couldn't be what he wanted? What he needed? I could posture all I wanted to in the boardroom, but my need for Blake's love had rooted itself well beyond any conscious control. "What do you mean?"

He sat up, bringing us chest to chest, warming me with his body. He stroked my back. "I mean I need to figure this out, for you, for us. Obviously I don't know the first thing about how to turn this off other than avoiding you sometimes. Tonight was…"

"Talking about Cooper set you off."

He closed his eyes, wincing at whatever memories played in his mind. He opened his eyes and kissed me sweetly.

"You're everything to me, baby. I don't want to move backwards and talk about the past. All that shit I have no control over."

"Having control over me makes you feel better though," I whispered.

He nodded. "I need to change that."

"What if I don't want you to?"

CHAPTER FOUR

My favorite redheaded barista set to work preparing our lattes-to-go as Alli tapped her nails on the counter.

"How was your night?" I asked.

"Good. Just a few drinks with the old crew. Yours?"

"Good." I glanced around the café, avoiding eye contact with her.

Blake had tried valiantly to avoid the topic by fucking me right out of my mind. Even though he was holding back, his strategy had worked famously. I didn't remember falling asleep, too tired and wasted to think about anything.

I wasn't sure how to navigate the gulf between us now. Blake had been a mystery to me in so many ways, but the more I uncovered about him, the more I fell hopelessly in love with the man. We had to figure our way through this somehow. Pulling away from me wasn't going to work.

I looked back to Alli. She lacked the usual glow of energy that added to her natural beauty. Today her eyes were swollen and tired. "Is everything okay?"

She brightened a bit. "Yeah, I'm fine."

"Were you out late?"

"No, actually I came back early."

I shook my head, confused, and waited for her to continue.

She slouched a little in defeat, letting the fatigue show in her features once more. "Heath didn't call yesterday. I'm worried."

"I'm sure everything is fine."

"We haven't gone a day without talking since he left. I was waiting up for his call, but nothing."

"I'm sure he'll call today. Don't worry."

She nodded and chewed her lip.

"Do you want to do the marketing meeting later so you can get some rest?" I placed my hand over hers, wishing my happy, exuberant friend would resurface. I barely recognized her this way.

"No, I'm fine. You're right. I'm sure it's nothing." She offered a weak smile.

Simone delivered our java and I paid, adding a generous tip. She waved as we headed back out.

We made the short walk upstairs. Risa was already there. I checked my watch. She was early. She greeted us with every ounce of vivacity that the two of us lacked. She wore black patterned crop pants and a black button up that came across as impeccably professional. In dark jeans and a Portofino blouse Alli had lent me, I'd taken advantage of the decidedly casual dress code that the guys had established.

"Alli, this is Risa Corvi, our new marketing director."

Risa held out her hand. "Alli, great to meet you. I'm so glad we could catch up today."

"Me too."

We settled at the small conference table at the far end of the office, and I brought Alli and Risa up to speed.

We had been at it for nearly an hour when Blake walked in, six-feet of delicious. My eyes fixed on him, as if his entrance had somehow sucked all the oxygen out of the room and I was waiting for permission from him to breathe again. I stopped staring long enough to catch Alli and Risa gawking too.

"Am I interrupting?" He flashed me a crooked grin and walked toward us with his hands in his pockets. He was in his usual work uniform, blue jeans and a snug fitting T-shirt advertising the conference we'd been to in Las Vegas. That had been a good trip.

Risa nearly tipped her chair over, jumping out of it to shake his hand, her eyes alight with obvious appreciation. "You must be Mr. Landon. I'm Risa Corvi."

"Call me Blake."

"We were running over some of the membership numbers, if you want to join us," I said quickly.

"Sure, let me talk to Sid first."

I nodded and watched him walk away, fully appreciating how fantastic his ass looked in jeans, and how they strained around his thighs. *Get a grip, Erica. You're at work.* Had I not gotten enough of him last night? Jesus, what was wrong with me?

I shook my head back into reality. Risa's gaze was riveted where mine had been. I cleared my throat to get her attention.

She turned back to me quickly. "Sorry. He's... Wow." She sighed and sifted through her notes.

Alli rolled her eyes. My body immediately tensed, going into irrational protective jealousy mode. I clicked my pen anxiously as I ran a few choice phrases for Risa through my mind. Unfortunately none of them were remotely appropriate to utter out loud. I bit my tongue, not wanting Risa's first meeting at work to be about her boss pulling a nutty staking claim over their investor who she also happened to be dating.

I took in a slow breath and tried to focus on my notes. Blake was gorgeous. He turned heads wherever he went, and this was no different.

"Where were we?" Alli interrupted me, apparently eager to wrap up.

Before I could get us back on track, my phone rang at my desk. "Excuse me a minute. You two carry on." I ducked behind the partition and searched for my phone in my purse. I froze when I saw the number. I snapped out of it quickly and picked up the call.

"Daniel, hi," I rushed, hoping I'd caught him before he hung up. I hadn't spoken to him since I'd left his house on the Cape a couple weeks ago, under circumstances that he was completely in the dark about. I wasn't sure if the lapse in time had been as awkward for him as it had been for me.

"Erica, how are you?"

I smiled at the sound of his deep and confident voice. "I'm doing well. How are you?"

"Oh, you know, busy with the campaign. But I wanted to ask about your plans for Friday. The firm is sponsoring the Spirit Gala this year and we have some extra tickets. A lot of important people will be there, maybe even a celebrity or two. Might be a good networking opportunity for you."

"That sounds wonderful. Are you sure?"

"Absolutely. I'd like to see you again."

"Thanks, same here. I meant to call, but..." In truth, I didn't really know how Daniel felt about staying in touch with me. Sure, he was my biological father, but we'd only recently discovered this. We barely knew each other. Outside of running into his stepson and my living nightmare, Mark, our visit had been pleasant and meaningful. I wanted a relationship with him, but between his run for governor and the corporate machine that was his life, I wasn't sure where I could possibly fit. We'd both agreed I should stay under the radar as his illegitimate daughter.

"No worries. I'll courier some tickets over. Invite Landon and anyone else who you'd like to mingle on your behalf."

"Sounds wonderful. Thanks so much."

"I'll look forward to seeing you then, Erica."

The affection I'd heard in his voice was abruptly cut off when the call ended. I stared at the phone a few moments longer until I heard Blake join me.

He wrapped his arms around me, his body curving behind mine.

"Everything okay?" he murmured, pressing a warm kiss to my neck.

I hugged my arms over his. I wanted to keep him close to me just in case he had any ideas about leaving abruptly. He sure as hell wouldn't be sending me off again anytime soon.

"What are you doing Friday night?" I asked.

"You."

My face heated and I turned in his arms until I faced him.

"That can be arranged, however Daniel invited us to some gala his firm is hosting and they have some extra tickets."

"Are you asking me out on a date?"

I smirked and considered a remark about last night's "date" that involved his home cooking and some very intense frustrated sex, but I thought better of it.

"Are you interested? I could probably find someone else in a pinch," I teased.

"Over my dead body." He tightened his embrace, pressing me deliciously close, melding my body to his.

"It's black tie. I'm assuming you can retire the witty T-shirts and clean up nice?"

"What do you think?"

My heart sped up at the mere vision of Blake in a tuxedo. What that might do to me in person was almost frightening. "I think I can't wait."

"I have to get back to work, but let's grab dinner with Alli since it's her last night in town."

"That would be nice."

"I'll text you when I get out."

He stepped back but I caught the hem of his shirt, as if I could hold him still with the tiny handful of fabric.

I didn't want him to go. Last night had been intense, and I needed to know he was still with me. As close as we'd been, emotionally stripped, the thought of him pushing me away again, ever, scared the hell out of me. I never wanted to feel that way again.

"What?"

"I want to keep you a little bit longer. Is that so wrong?"

"I won't argue with that." His eyes darkened and he came closer. Sliding his hands down my arms, he leaned down to kiss me.

All too aware of our serious lack of privacy, I froze, bracing myself for the onslaught of sensations he inspired. We were stealing a moment. His lips met mine, warm, controlled. I opened my lips to his but he broke away.

"Not this again," I muttered.

He answered my eye roll with a smirk and stroked the ridge of my lower lip with his thumb. "I think you have a fetish for office sex, sweetie," he whispered.

"You're my fetish, Blake. The setting doesn't much matter."

He laughed, the low rasp reverberating through me. I bit my lip too hard, replacing the tingle he'd left there with a twinge of pain.

"The feeling is mutual. That still doesn't fix our current predicament, however. I want to spread you out over this desk and fuck you 'til you scream, but as you once aptly noted, some of us have work to do."

"Shut up."

I caught a fistful of his shirt and pulled him back down to me, forcing his mouth onto mine, muffling a quiet growl that rumbled through him. He gave my ass a hard squeeze, pressing our bodies together and reminding me of last night's endeavors. His body, his presence, overwhelmed me so easily. A rush of desire intoxicated my senses, making me forget everything but the way he felt wrapped around me, his hands on me, his tongue inside me. I wanted more. I always did.

I vaguely heard the click of heels approaching. I tore myself away from his kiss and caught Risa gaping at us. A wave of pure female confidence surged through me. *Eat your heart out, honey.* Blake was mine, and I couldn't have made that more clear outside of the present moment. If she wanted to crush on him, she'd have to get in line.

Blake seemed to be waiting for my reaction. I smiled and gave him a quick kiss before pushing back slightly. "Bye, baby."

A twinkle of acknowledgement passed over his features. He was calculating to a fault, and he knew how jealous I could be. Sure, I was completely overreacting, but Risa got the picture.

He returned my knowing smile and stepped away slowly, giving her a polite nod on his way past.

"I'm so sorry. I didn't—" Risa was wide-eyed, her jaw agape.

I immediately regretted the choice. This was her first day, after all. "Don't be. I wanted to ask you something actually."

"Sure, what is it?"

"We've got tickets to the Spirit Gala on Friday night. Would you be interested in going and representing the company? You could bring a date, of course."

"I'd rather not."

I lifted my eyebrows.

"I mean, I'd love to go. I'd rather not bring a date. Networking is easier that way."

"Oh, right. That's fine. Let me know if you change your mind."

"Great, I can't wait." She smiled broadly and glanced down at the notebook she was holding. "Alli and I got through most of my questions, but she wanted me to run a few things by you that she wasn't sure about. Do you have a minute?"

"Sure. Have a seat here. I'll be back in a minute."

I left her there to find Alli, who was looking as restless as she had this morning, checking her phone at the conference table.

"You guys done?"

She nodded. "I think so. If you don't mind, I might head back to the apartment. I need to pack and catch up on some things for work."

"You're on vacation, you know."

"Not with this gig, unfortunately."

"All right, I'll see you tonight. We can grab dinner with Blake later if you're up for it."

"Sounds good." She rose to give me a quick hug, waved goodbye to Sid, and left.

★ ★ ★

Alli and I sat at a cocktail table in the open air bar, sipping pear martinis while we waited for Blake to join us. The weather was perfectly mild. The sun was setting and a warm breeze blew over us. Days like today made the long winter worth enduring. Everything felt possible. I only wished Alli felt the same way. She looked better, a little more rested, but something was still off.

"I can't believe you're leaving already. I feel like you just got here."

Alli had made the choice to work in New York while I chose to stay in Boston. Now our lives were taking root. I wanted to urge her to come back. With the business funded, she could. She knew that as well as I did, but I kept those thoughts to myself. She didn't need any more confusion, or worse, guilt, on top of everything else she was dealing with right now.

"I know. I don't feel ready to go back either."

"Maybe I can visit soon."

She brightened. "I would love that. I want you to see my new place."

"Me too. We'll see how things go, I guess. Work will probably be intense for a little while until everyone gets settled and we get into a routine."

"Right."

"What do you think of Risa?" We hadn't had a chance to catch up about her replacement at the company since the marketing powwow that morning.

She took another sip of her drink. "She's smart. She seems driven, like you. I think she'll do well."

Her matter-of-fact description made me wonder if she might be a little jealous. I had anticipated that she might be, but Alli was good-natured, and at the end of the day, she'd support any decision that was good for the business.

"I'm glad you think so. She's no Alli Malloy, but she seems passionate. I'm hoping after her crash course this afternoon she'll hit the ground running and take us to the next level."

"Hopefully. How do *you* like her?"

I caught her grin and knew immediately what she was aiming for. "I know what you're thinking, and no, I'm not going to freak out on her for ogling Blake. I'd be in for a lifetime of misery if I started doing that now. I swear, if I had a dollar for every time some woman stared a little too long, I wouldn't need angel funding."

"A lifetime, eh?"

I frowned. "Whatever. It's an expression, Alli."

She started laughing, then stopped abruptly. Her focus had shifted away from me. She paled.

"What's wrong?"

"Oh my God," she breathed.

I twisted in my seat, and my gaze quickly fixed on Blake walking side by side with none other than his brother.

Alli looked like she was seeing a ghost, except Heath was healthier than I'd ever seen him, with ruddy cheeks and bright eyes that never left hers. Something in the air shifted. I became as transfixed on the two of them as they were on each other.

Alli's color returned. She slid off the stool and pushed her hair back behind her ear with a shaky hand. She took a few cautious steps in his direction, and he took two long lunges in hers, scooping her up and into his arms. She squealed, and a broad smile crossed his face as he lifted her off the ground and into his embrace.

She wrapped her arms around his neck, nuzzling him there as he held her close. They stayed like that for what seemed like several minutes. When Alli pulled back, her eyes glistened with unshed tears. She pulled Heath close for a kiss, and he met her with equal fervor, as if he had been starved.

We shouldn't have been there—or they shouldn't have been there—but the fact that we all were didn't seem to matter to either of them. I nudged Blake and he nodded.

"Let's go see if the table's ready," he murmured.

We left them and checked in with the hostess who sat us promptly. I was still reeling.

"What just happened?" My adrenaline was still pumping. I was thrilled for Alli, but my head was spinning from how this had come about so quickly.

"He's back," Blake answered simply.

"For good?"

"As long as he stays out of trouble."

I looked across the restaurant to where the couple still stood. Alli was laughing and brushing tears away while Heath peppered her with kisses. They looked so incredibly happy. In a matter of moments, the cloud of doubt and misery hovering over my dearest friend had passed over. The joy I felt for her overwhelmed the concern that still lingered regarding their relationship.

"How was he able to leave so early?"

"I spoke to the judge and worked it all out. He got on the first plane back."

They joined us then, their energy palpable. Alli seemed like a new person. They both did.

"Erica, it's great to see you."

I stood and gave Heath a hug. He hugged me back, hard, then stepped back and gave me a half smile, as if he were trying to communicate something to me without words. Maybe he was sorry for shredding Alli emotionally for the past few weeks. I smiled back, suddenly unable to entertain any emotional reservation in the presence of their contagious joy.

"How have you been?" I cringed inwardly. Was that the wrong question to ask someone fresh out of rehab?

"Awesome. Never better."

The enthusiasm and confidence in his reply quelled my concern, and we all settled down at the table. He seemed so different. Not just healthy, but more real, more genuine somehow.

We ordered drinks and our meal. Heath stuck with water. I felt immediately guilty for wanting a second martini.

"Let's toast," Heath said as soon as the drinks arrived,

true to form.

"Absolutely," I agreed.

"What should we toast to?" Alli asked.

"To new beginnings…" His gaze shifted to Alli and she looked back at him, starry-eyed.

"To new beginnings," she murmured.

That was it. Any question there may have been about their relationship status post-rehab had just been answered. I only knew two other people so hopelessly in love, and I didn't even want to think about how destroyed I'd feel if I had to spend weeks away from Blake. I'd be a puddle of romantic goo just like these two.

"Well, this is timely," I said. "Alli heads back to New York tomorrow. Maybe you could travel together."

Heath coughed a little and rested his elbows on the table. He looked quickly to Blake and then to me.

"Actually, I'm going to be staying in Boston for a while."

Alli paled again and looked to him.

"What? Why?"

"The court situation. Blake got me back early, but I need to stay here for the rest of the time I would have been at the center in L.A. so I can finish the treatment here."

"But…" Alli cut herself off.

There were no "buts" about his options. He was lucky to be this close now.

"I didn't realize that." Alli faced forward, shifting her body away from him for the first time since they'd sat down together.

"We'll figure it out, okay?" His voice was quiet as he reached for her hand and cradled it in his own.

After a moment she swallowed and nodded. "Okay."

Her spark came back with a small smile.

The rest of the evening passed without incident. We made small talk, catching up and sharing stories. Heath asked me questions about the business that revealed how much Blake had already told him. That he'd spoken of me to Heath, despite the distance and circumstances, meant something to me. That he'd made this whole reunion happen meant even more.

Weeks ago, the four of us sitting here had seemed impossible. Blake hadn't wanted me associating with Alli, let alone Heath, with all the trouble he'd brought into her life. Now he'd gone out of his way to bring them back together. I couldn't make sense of it, but I was genuinely happy he'd done it.

Alli and Heath walked ahead of us on the way home. Alli giggled and leaned into him. I was half expecting them to break out into a sprint toward the nearest bedroom. Last time I was with the two of them, I could barely stomach it. This was different. I wasn't going through withdrawals from Blake like I had been in New York, and somehow their love just amplified ours. I leaned into Blake, and he circled my shoulders with his arm. I slid my hand around his waist and hooked my thumb on his belt loop, loving how we fit.

"Thank you," I said.

Things weren't perfect, but Alli was happy, I was happy, and Blake was the reason why.

★ ★ ★

I slipped far down into the tub. Another centimeter and my nose would have been submerged. I moaned into the warm water, letting waves of relaxation wash over me. Blake's fingers kneaded the soles of my feet with expert care. I wasn't sure what I'd done in a previous life to deserve this utterly perfect moment, but I was loving it.

When I'd been thoroughly massaged, I slipped out of his grasp. I repositioned myself on my knees, settling my legs snuggly on either side of his muscular thighs.

I followed the sharp line of his jaw with my fingers, appreciating every God-given feature that made me so impossibly attracted to him. "You're too good to me."

"No such thing," he murmured, planting a soft kiss on my lips.

"But you spoil me."

"You deserve to be spoiled."

I softened at his words. His face was relaxed, happy, a reflection of the moment. I almost felt undeserving of it, though I wasn't sure why.

Because of my mother's inheritance, I'd been given opportunities that most people had only dreamed of. But I couldn't remember the last time I'd felt spoiled, doted on by someone who held such affection for me outside of Marie. A little part of me couldn't completely accept it.

"How do you know if I deserve it?" I tried to read his beautiful hazel eyes. He flashed a megawatt smile, and my brain short-circuited.

"I know everything."

I cocked my head to the side and studied him with a grin. "How could I forget? Master of the universe."

He kissed my throat, taking advantage of the position. "Now you're catching on." His warm breath sent gooseflesh over my damp skin.

"Do you think they'll be okay?"

I twisted a strand of his hair around my fingertip.

He nodded. We shared concern about Alli and Heath's future, though they were probably disturbing the peace in Blake's spare bedroom as we spoke.

"What will he do now?"

"He'll stay with me for a little while to start, until we figure out his next move. In the meantime, I'll be getting him more involved at work. He needs to finally take the business seriously. He's been screwing around too long because I've let him. But responsibility is probably what he needs more than anything right now—something or someone to be accountable to other than his own superficial needs."

"I can't believe you did this for them. You didn't seem very optimistic about things before."

"I wasn't."

"What changed?"

He shifted beneath me and I sat back a little, sensing he needed space for what he wanted to say. He drenched the fine strands of his hair with the soapy bath water. I traced my hands over the hard curves of his pectorals. There was nothing sexier than wet Blake.

I tore myself away from the mental inventory of Blake's sexiest qualities to press him. "Talk."

He sighed. "I don't know. I guess I became more sympathetic to his position. Not the drug thing. Obviously I can't relate to that. But the desperation in his voice when he talked about Alli. Like he couldn't breathe without her, like anything he had left in him that was keeping him going, which probably wasn't much, was draining by the day not being near her."

He paused, dropped his hands into the water, and stroked my hips with his thumbs, tightening his hold possessively.

"He loves her." I finished his thought, as convinced as ever of what they shared.

"I know he does. The way he sounds when they aren't together, that's how I feel every time you run away from me. And I couldn't wish that on anyone else."

My heart shattered. All the times I'd pushed him away, out of fear, self-preservation, and pure, justifiable rage. But every time I did, my heart ached for him, a bone-deep pain that weakened me at the very core. A part of me wanted to keep that line drawn between us, keep him at a safe distance from my professional life. But fighting it so hard left me in pieces.

"I'm sorry." My voice was heavy with emotion.

He hushed me and pulled me closer so our bodies were flush. Wet, we slid against each other. His skin on mine, his arms wrapped around me, we were so close. Awareness simmered low in my belly, coiling slowly with every touch, but our motions were careful and deliberate as we caressed each other with infinite care. I was overwhelmed, racked by the potent emotions that had taken over in his presence.

Maybe Marie had been right. We'd passed the point of being the best we could be on our own. What we were together had become so much more powerful, a force that took my breath away and made everything secondary. As much as I hated to admit it, Blake Landon was fast becoming everything to me.

With every stroke of our tongues, roam of our hands, my heart swelled with love. With trust. As my touches became urgent, Blake's became more controlled, gentler when they should have possessed me with the fierce craving that we shared for each other. I pulled back, determined tonight would be different.

"I want you to take control tonight."

He leveled an even stare at me.

"Complete control. Whatever you need." I kept my voice steady even as I worried what I was getting myself into.

His body tensed beneath me. "Erica, we're not doing this, okay?"

"I love you and I want to do this for you. I trust you to take me as far as you think I can go. I… I can't promise anything because I don't know what you want exactly, but I want to try."

"Stop."

He shifted, giving me a little push to move back. A panic welled up in me.

"No, wait. Please." I sighed and pressed my temples, hating what I was about to admit. "A part of me…even when I'm fighting you every step of the way, there's a part of me that wants to give you control over everything. Real life submission." I cringed inwardly at the words as they left me. "The thought of letting go… I'd be lying if I said it wasn't a tempting and intoxicating notion. I've been taking care of myself for so long."

He brushed his knuckles over my cheek, and warmth washed over me. He was hearing me. I wanted to believe that he could somehow understand, sense the weight I carried with so few people to really rely on.

"You take care of people, and I know I could trust you with anything I gave you. I recognize that and I fight it, because it scares the hell out of me. I can't give you that much control in my life. I just can't. But I think with sex, I could give you the kind of control that you want."

"How are you supposed to do that? Flip a switch?"

"I think I can. I—"

"What about everything you've been through? How can you possibly think the things I want are healthy for you?"

"I don't know what you want. Show me and I'll tell you."

He sighed heavily. "Erica, you're a strong, independent woman. Unlike anyone I've ever met. You prove it to me every day, no matter how difficult I make it for you. And I don't want to try to take that away from you, to bend you to do things that you really don't want to."

"How do you know I don't want it?"

He shook his head and looked away. "What if I take things too far, and it's something we can't come back from?"

"I trust you."

I kissed him, reveling in the silken friction of our bodies beneath the water. He was hard. Maybe he already had plans. I'd show him I could be the right person for whatever he needed. Then a chilling thought crept into my mind.

Sophia.

I wasn't sure I'd even said her name out loud until Blake's expression turned cold. His lips tightened into a thin line.

"Don't, baby. We're not going there."

"No, wait. Was she on board for all this submissive stuff that turns you on so much?"

He hesitated.

"Just tell me," I snapped. I didn't want to dance around this with him.

He paused for a long moment. He nodded slowly, avoiding my eyes.

As quickly as he'd acknowledged the question, I wished he hadn't. *Fucking Sophia.* I hated her now more than I had before. The jealousy nearly paralyzed me. Being physically compared to Blake's model ex-girlfriend was hard enough. To know she'd been what he wanted sexually was almost more than I could take. I shrank back to my side of the tub. The water was becoming uncomfortably cool.

He eyed me. "It wasn't a matter of her 'getting on board' with things. She *wanted* to be submissive with me. It was her goddamn idea. Needless to say, taking a dominant role with her wasn't much of a challenge. But she always wanted to push things further. The things she wanted me to do bordered on dangerous at times. That's *not* what I want with you. But being in that kind of relationship for as long as we were…"

"It's what you crave now." I finished his thought, knowing it was true before he could confirm it.

"Sometimes, yes."

"The things we've done, were you testing me, to see what I could take?"

"In a way. I've pushed you. I think we both realize that."

"And the times when I've taken control…"

He leaned his head back against the tub. "It's been difficult for me. I've tried to be so careful with you, Erica. You have no idea."

"Tell me what you want, Blake."

"It really doesn't matter at this point."

"I deserve to know." I held my breath, waiting for him to speak.

"Total submission. Total control over your pleasure and pain." His voice was flat, matter-of-fact, as if he were negotiating a business deal and those were his terms.

My breath left me in a sharp exhale as the reality of his words hit me. Was that something I could give? A different kind of panic gripped me. I wrapped my arms around my knees, trying to stave off the chill that had now deepened. I couldn't lose Blake.

"Fine, I'll do it," I rushed before I could really think it through.

A deep groove marked his brow and his eyes widened slightly, as if my concession truly scared him. He sat up out of the water, leaning his arms on his knees. "Why would you do that?"

"Because you mean more to me than anyone ever has. I need to at least try."

"This isn't about pleasing me."

"You're right. This is about me loving you enough to take a chance. I think I'm finally getting used to that."

I stood up and toweled off on my way to the bedroom. I was trembling now, shivering. The water hadn't been that cool. I was terrified. Why? Blake had never really hurt me. *He'd never hurt me.* I stood at the edge of the bed, unsure what to do.

Blake came up behind me. I fisted my hands into the terry cloth of the towel that was bunched around between my breasts. I took a deep breath to quell the quiet tremors that staggered through me.

"This isn't what I want. What you're feeling now. We

haven't even done anything and you're scared to death."

I turned to face him. "Tell me what to do. I'm nervous. I'm afraid I'll do something wrong."

"No, you're afraid I'm going to hurt you."

I clenched my jaw and hated that he'd given voice to my fears—fears that were so deeply a part of me. They'd followed me around for years. I wanted to cry at the thought that I'd never be free from them. "I know you won't hurt me."

"If you're so sure, why are you scared?"

I swallowed hard. "You know why."

He lifted my chin, angling my face to his. His eyes brewed with emotion in the soft light of the room. He was deciding. I could see the calculations taking place. He was weighing the pull of his desire against the very real chance that I could freak out if he did something too far outside of my comfort zone.

I dropped my towel and pressed my body against his. His skin burned against mine. My body began to unwind at the warmth of the contact.

He palmed my breast and took my nipple between his fingertips, twisting the hardened tip gently. "What if I just want to toss you on the bed and fuck you senseless? Vanilla. Missionary. Hard."

I bit my lip. His words washed over me like a heat wave. That sounded very appealing, but he was dodging me. "I'm sure you can come up with something more creative than that."

He silenced me with a hard kiss. "Slow. We're going to go slow. I'm going to make love to you, baby."

His words sounded more like an affirmation than an

expression of what he really wanted, deep down. His hands were restless, carefully grasping and releasing me as if he were at war with his own body. His urgency lit the fire in me. A warm glow built in my core and shot through my limbs until my skin was as fevered as his.

I kissed him back, swallowing the affirmations that would sell us both short on what we wanted, craved. I gripped his shoulders, tangling my fingers in his hair. I couldn't get close enough. I wanted to coax out the animal that wanted to come at me with everything he had. I wasn't scared anymore. I needed him.

"Take me how you want me. Do anything you want. God, please. I need it, need you," I moaned, rubbing myself helplessly against him.

"No." He uttered the refusal through gritted teeth. His body was taut, frozen, as if a single movement would break his resolve.

I licked my lips, nearly wild with the sensation of his erection against my belly. I wanted him so badly I thought I would go mad. I couldn't wait anymore. In an instant, I lowered to my knees and caressed his length gently in my palms. I'd figure out how to be submissive with or without his help. I slid my mouth over the tip and sucked, swirling my tongue around the sensitive tip. I moaned, loving the taste of him, the subtle scent of his body.

He let out a sigh, as if he'd been holding his breath for far too long. I licked him, sucked him, and grazed my teeth ever so softly until he trembled slightly. Submissive or not, I held all the cards in this position. But maybe I didn't have to.

I slowed my motions and relaxed my mouth. I grabbed him from behind and pushed him deep until he hit the back of my throat. His breath whistled through his teeth. He slid out of me slowly, his cock resting on my lips. I dug my fingernails into his ass and he jolted forward into my mouth. I swallowed, undulating over the head of his cock.

"Fuck." He sifted his fingers through my hair, cradling my head. "What are you doing to me?"

"I want you to fuck my mouth. Control me with your hands. Show me what you want." The words came out like an order, but I couldn't help it. He needed to understand I was ready for this now.

"You don't listen to a damn word I say."

I smirked, gliding my tongue lazily over and around his length, in slow motion. I waited for him, pushing him deep again and again.

Letting out a low growl, he fisted his hand in my hair and his hips bucked slightly. I took him fully and eagerly with each careful thrust. Then he deepened them, hitting the back of my throat, giving me just as much as I could handle.

"You're so beautiful like this, baby...on your knees. All for me." He stroked my cheek and pulled back to let me catch my breath before doing exactly what I'd asked him to do. His grip on my hair tightened almost painfully as he maneuvered me, fucking my mouth with measured strokes. He sucked in a sharp breath, giving me more.

I moaned, loving the satin skin of his erection sliding against my tongue as I struggled to take all of him.

The sounds he made assured me that this was driving him nuts. A fine mist covered my skin as I gave myself over to the moment. I wanted to touch myself, to feel how wet he'd already made me, but I didn't. I kept my hands rested on the muscles of his thighs that had tensed into rock hard bunches.

I couldn't stop thinking about what he'd feel like inside me, pumping with the same fervor and passion. The sheer power of his body was evident in this position. My mouth couldn't sustain the fierce thrusts that he'd normally give me if we were fucking. He was carefully reined in for this more delicate position, but he was in complete control. I was so vulnerable, completely at his mercy. Trusting him, and letting him take his pleasure from me was intoxicating.

I lightly dug my nails into his thighs, my desire reaching a fever pitch.

"You okay?"

"Don't stop."

"I don't think I could if I wanted to. Feels too good. Fucking amazing actually."

I closed my mouth over him again and crept my fingers up and over his abs. They flexed and tightened with each careful thrust until he cried out, spurting hot semen down my throat. I swallowed and milked every last drop from him with my tongue.

He released me and pulled us onto the bed where he collapsed, laying me on his chest. He frowned with his eyes closed as he caught his breath. I pressed hot kisses along his chest, licking the dip of his collarbone. He grabbed my wrists, his eyes now open but still heavy with desire.

"You keep that up, you're going to get it."

"Would that be a punishment or a reward for blowing your mind?"

His face softened a little and he laughed. "I haven't decided yet. I can't think straight."

I hummed in anticipation. "I can't wait to find out."

I knew he couldn't go again so soon, yet I continued my sabotage of his torso with my mouth. I couldn't get enough of him. Pleasing him was addictive, and I needed another fix. I moved over his body eagerly. I licked the salt off his skin, still slick with sweat from his release. The clean, masculine scent of him drugged me with lust. Before I could go any lower, he flipped me onto my back. He pushed me up on the bed and spread my legs wide. I squirmed in anticipation. The only thing better than giving Blake head was getting it from him. He had a supremely talented mouth.

He posted himself in prime position and stared at me, his breath still coming hard. He touched me softly, up and down my thighs. I shifted anxiously, all too aware of the ache between my legs.

"Touch yourself."

"Why?"

"Just do it. Do everything you'd do if I weren't here about to fuck you right now."

Tentatively, I lowered my hand and started slow movements over my clit. Blake kissed me up and down my thighs, my calves, my ankles, everywhere but where I really wanted him the most.

"Do you think about me when you do this?" His warm breath sent chills over me. My body tightened in response.

"I haven't had to do this since we met. I much prefer your touch to my own. Why don't you touch me? Please."

"Don't stop. I want to watch you. Do you have a vibrator?"

I rolled my eyes, slightly insulted that he had to ask. "I'm a modern woman. Obviously I have a vibrator."

"Where is it?"

I hesitated, suddenly feeling as shy as I was modern. "In my underwear drawer. Why?"

He planted an open mouthed kiss on my inner thigh that made me gasp.

"Just wondering. Continue."

I obeyed, letting my fingers fall into a rhythm that my body knew well. The movements were easy and smooth because I was already wet. He could be inside me so easily now. No resistance.

"You're beautiful down here. So pretty and pink. I want to shave you sometime. Lick all the soft skin. Have you ever done that?"

I shook my head. I wasn't sure how I felt about this up close analysis of my lady parts. He was throwing me for a loop. I just wanted him to suck or fuck me already.

"I can't do this." For the first time in my life, pleasuring myself was starting to piss me off. I wanted his hands on me. I felt like I was settling for less, embarking on the solitary journey to orgasm as a means to an end. Nothing like the unexpected and deliriously pleasurable adventures that Blake took me on.

"Are you embarrassed?"

"No… A little, maybe. But I don't want to come this way."

"You won't. You're giving me what I want, and trust me, nothing and no one's going to make you come but me from now on. You're going to show me how you touch yourself, and then when you're just about to come, I'm going to put my cock in you. Can you handle that?"

"Can you use your mouth?" I pleaded.

He propped himself on his elbow and half rolled his eyes. "You know, Erica, you're not exactly being obedient. I've given you the game plan, which, lucky for you, doesn't involve any props because they're in my apartment. But if you keep talking, I'm going to just throw you over my knee and spank the hell out of you. Get it?"

I giggled, but my laughter faded. His gaze was dead serious. *Oh, he wasn't kidding.*

I took a deep breath and closed my eyes so I wouldn't be tempted to laugh. Challenging Blake was too fun, but I didn't want to be spanked like a petulant child right now.

I kept my eyes closed so I could concentrate, trying to forget that Blake was watching everything. I tensed and tightened, grabbing my breast, arching into my own touch. I was getting close, my motions becoming more urgent, less graceful. My mind spun. I imagined Blake was there instead. His name left my lips again and again. I needed him inside me. I was about to come when he caught my wrists, holding them tight to my sides.

"Have to taste you for a minute, baby." His tongue flattened and lashed across my clit. The slow and steady climb to my orgasm sharpened into a steep one. I cried out as the sensation of his mouth on me launched me perilously close to the precipice. I bucked my hips, desperate for him, for more delicious Blake contact. He tore away, but before I could protest, he'd buried his cock in me balls deep in one single thrust, quickly followed by another.

"Blake, oh God, I'm coming," I cried, my body shuddering with the searing pleasures overwhelming me.

"That's right, I want to feel you fist around my cock. You're so fucking tight already."

He kept up his punishing thrusts, thumbing my clit in careful circles until I came with a wild string of cries. I swore, in my mindless release, that nothing had ever felt that good. Ever.

Blake found his own pleasure somewhere in the blur of my orgasm and collapsed over me. We lay there in a wasted heap, our breathing shallow and uneven.

"Good girl," Blake whispered.

CHAPTER FIVE

I decided to go in late to work so I could see Alli off the next day. Heath and Blake were in the living room, talking quietly, catching up. For four people who cared about each other so much, we all had a lot of catching up to do.

I helped Alli pack since she'd lost time staying the night with Heath. I could tell from her frazzled and sleep deprived state that they'd had an intense night. Probably no less intense than the one that Blake and I had shared. She was right about these Landon men keeping us on our toes. Heaven help us both.

But her color was back and her mood was lively again. She struggled to zip up the luggage that always seemed to grow after a visit even though we hadn't done any shopping. She conquered it and stood back, hands on her hips. I checked the time. We only had a few more minutes before we sent her off to the airport.

"I guess this is it," I said. I tried not to think about how much time would go by before I saw Alli again.

Tears spilled over onto her cheeks. She pulled me into a tight hug and sniffled into my shoulder. We'd had a great visit, but I knew her tears weren't all for me.

"It's going to be okay, I promise."

"You promise?" She pulled back, holding my hands tightly in her own.

"I promise." *Come back and we can all be together,* I thought but swallowed the words. No point in going there. That was her choice to make. She knew she could always come back.

"Heath loves you and I love you."

"And you love Blake!" She giggled through her tears.

I hugged her again. We separated once Heath popped his head into the bedroom.

"Time to go, babe."

She gave me a little squeeze and waved goodbye, disappearing through the doorway with Heath.

Blake came up to me as a tear fell down my cheek. Damn it. I would miss that girl. He wiped it away and pulled me into a hug. I wrapped my arms around his waist, thankful that at least I'd never have to say goodbye to Blake any time soon. I couldn't and didn't want to imagine it, ever.

★ ★ ★

"Are you sure it's going to fit?"

I waited impatiently as Marie unzipped the garment bag and peeled away the enclosing plastic from the dry cleaners.

"I think so. I had the top taken out a bit."

I laughed a little as I held a modest arm around my breasts, which had always seemed a little too full for my petite frame. I stood in my bedroom in my underwear as Marie unveiled the dress. The floor-length gown was a rough black silk with a pattern of faded teal velvet embellishments.

I stepped into the dress and Marie zipped me up. The sweetheart top tightened around my chest comfortably. Grateful I wasn't busting out, I shuffled over to the mirror to see how the rest of the dress fit. The mermaid cut gown hugged my waist and hips perfectly, and the large swaths of the vintage fabric flowed out at my knees.

Marie stepped beside me, almost a head taller and looking as vibrant and gorgeous as ever. She'd been my mother's best friend, but over time she'd truly become one of mine as well. Sometimes she was the mother I needed, other times just a friend I could talk to about things I couldn't imagine talking to my mother about. Times like these though, she looked at me the way my mother would have. Her eyes clouded a bit as we admired the beautiful gown together.

"Sometimes I forget how much you look like her."

I smiled and swallowed back tears. Now that I knew my father, I could appreciate a little more how closely my features favored my late mother's. We shared the same blond locks and fair skin, but my father's eyes stared back at me.

I tensed suddenly at the thought of seeing him tonight. Nothing about that relationship was simple.

"Well, she had incredible taste."

Her eyebrows rose slightly. "Actually, Daniel bought this for her. She wore it to our senior ball."

"But she left it with you."

"She left a few things, out of convenience I suppose. Told me to donate them. But this was too beautiful not to keep. I'm so glad I did. Look at you." She slid her hands down my upper arms and gave them a little squeeze.

"It's perfect." I ran my hands over the fabric, loving the mix of soft and rough textures, from the velvet to the silk. The dress fit me so well. Somehow my mother had managed to give me a truly beautiful gift without even knowing it.

Before I could get emotional again, the door buzzed

in the kitchen. I shuffled out of the bedroom to answer it. A few seconds later I let in the courier. He was holding a pink box with a black sheer bow. His eyebrows rose as he examined my too-formal-for-midday outfit.

"Sorry, wardrobe change," I joked nervously.

"No apologies needed." He gave me an obvious once-over before fishing a piece of paper out of his pocket. "Um, I just need you to sign for this."

I scribbled my signature and took the box. I shut the door behind him and set the box on the table, eager to open it. I retrieved the tiny card tied to the bow and read it.

Erica,
Spoil me and wear this tonight.
Love, B

My heart sank a little. Shit, what if he'd bought me a dress? I couldn't part with this gown. The gala was still hours away but I already didn't want to take it off.

Reluctantly, I tugged the edge of the bow and pushed away the layers of pink tissue paper until I reached a pile of delicately folded black lace garments. I took out a strapless bra with matching panties and lace topped silk stockings. The man had expensive taste, and lingerie was no exception.

Marie came up behind me and let out a whistle.

"Okay, that's my cue. My work here is done."

Suddenly embarrassed, I dropped the garments back into the box.

"You're officially my formal attire savior. Thank you so much, Marie."

"Anytime, baby girl. I'm glad I could help. Please take

pictures! Oh—actually on that note. I forgot to tell you that Richard will be there with a photographer who's covering the event. Maybe he'll give you a plug in his piece."

"Awesome, I'll keep an eye out for him."

"He's tall, dark, and unwilling to commit. You can't miss him."

I laughed.

"Seriously though, he's seen photos of you all over my apartment, so I'm sure he'll introduce himself at some point."

"Got it. I'll be on the lookout."

She gave me a quick kiss and headed out, leaving me alone with nothing but the overwhelming anticipation of the night to come.

★ ★ ★

I'd slipped on the lingerie that Blake had given me and did a little spin in front of the mirror, assessing myself. My hair was pinned up, and loose curls framed my face. I wore diamond studs that had been my mother's and matched the diamond bangles that Blake had given to me.

What a lucky girl I am, I thought, giddy with anticipation. But trying to network with all this sexual anticipation was going to be interesting for sure.

Alli had taken off for New York already and Heath was now staying with Blake. Maybe that was a good thing. He'd mentioned props recently, and the thought of being subjected to his arsenal of dominating toys intimidated me a little. We could do enough with our bodies alone. Surely we didn't need help.

Just then, Blake's silhouette filled the doorway. My breath caught as I sized him up. The green in his eyes glowed against the stark black and white of his perfectly tailored tuxedo.

I watched his reflection as he walked slowly toward me, drinking me in from the back.

"You're early."

He stopped behind me, catching my gaze in the mirror. "I may have underestimated how tempting you would be in this little getup. Those panties do fantastic things for your ass."

"Serves you right," I teased, taking a step back so I could feel the heat of his body, perilously close.

He sucked in a sharp breath through his teeth. He rested a hand at my hip and pulled me back so our bodies met.

"I couldn't wait to see you in it."

"I missed you too." I smiled and leaned in, rolling my hand back, relieved to have him with me again. My body relaxed into his. Any time away from each other really dragged. *Could you sound more hopeless and dependent?* I ignored the little voice, and at least for now, gave in to being completed in his presence.

My smile faded when he trailed his lips up my neck, took my diamond stud in his mouth, and bit my earlobe gently. I let a moan escape my lips and my body tensed in heated anticipation. He roamed my curves. Sliding his palm over my belly, he moved south and slipped into my panties and over my mound. He stopped suddenly and his eyes widened.

"What the…?"

He spun me around, hooked his thumbs under the

strings of the panties and pulled them down without ceremony, revealing the results of my very first Brazilian wax.

I bit my lip, nervous and shy to be so bare. "Do you like it? I wanted to surprise you."

"Color me surprised." He pushed me back up to my dresser and dropped to his knees, bringing the panties to the floor with him. "Sweet Jesus. You do love me."

My giggle segued into a gasp when he slung my leg over his shoulder and dove into me, licking me, spreading me with his fingers so he could tantalize the sensitive flesh. The man had a brilliant mouth, and everything felt so… different down there. More intense, like I was being touched for the first time. An exposed nerve bared only for him. I shivered at his breath over me. The sensations of his lips and tongue as they tantalized my bare flesh had me trembling.

I glanced to the side, catching our reflection in my floor-length mirror. My face was flushed and my breasts heaved, heavy and tender up against the bra. Watching him eat me with such passion, this flawlessly beautiful man in his flawless tuxedo, pleasuring me like his life depended on it, was possibly the most erotic thing I'd ever witnessed. My heart swelled at the sight of it. Warmth washed over me, spreading like wildfire until I was burning with love and arousal.

My eyes fell shut when he sucked my clit. My body skidded toward the impending orgasm. "Don't stop, please…"

"I'm never leaving. You're too fucking sweet. And now… Fuck." He circled my opening with his tongue and dove inside, fucking me with shallow plunges.

I gripped the edge of the dresser. I was a few strokes away from having no strength in my legs, and prayed I could hold myself up when the time came.

"Yes, like that. Blake, oh my God, I'm going to—"

"Come for me, baby."

The low rasp of his words vibrating on my pussy pushed me over. A short series of thready cries gave way to a wail as he took me over the edge. I shook uncontrollably, out of my mind with the pleasure he gave me. He held my hips tight, effectively holding me up as the tremors faded. I tried to gain my composure, struggling for breath.

He rose and gave me a gentle shove toward the bed. I flopped down, mindless and boneless.

"That was unexpected," I said, my voice light, drunk on bliss.

"Well, you do hate networking, so maybe that'll relax you."

Laughter bubbled to the surface and I smiled, delirious and sated. Propped up on his elbow, Blake lay beside me with a satisfied smirk. I lowered my gaze and immediately recognized the outline of his erection through his tuxedo pants. This situation had become a little one-sided. His grin broadened and he stilled my hand as I moved toward him.

I puffed out my lower lip, disappointed with his refusal. "What now?"

"That can wait."

"Why? We have time." I thought so anyway. I'd lost all concept of space and time in my recent orgasmic blackout.

"Delayed gratification, my sweet. I'll be bored as hell at this thing, so now I can imagine taking these thigh highs off you with my teeth and licking you from head to toe all night. By the time we get home, I'll be ready to do some truly shameful things to you."

My nipples hardened, grazing almost painfully inside the satin of my bra as my breasts swelled with each shaky inhale. Sometimes I was convinced he could make me come with words alone. I loved how dirty and honest he was when it came to sex. And from the sounds of it, he was coming to terms with my openness to his kinky ways. I only hoped he'd take me there in baby steps. I never knew where my limits were until Blake barreled through them.

"What kind of shameful things?" I asked, equally curious and anxious.

"I have a few ideas."

"Do tell."

"Hmm, no, I like surprising you too much. Plus, that'll give you something to think about. Anticipation of the unknown."

"Give me a hint."

His eyes twinkled and he smirked. "Not a chance. Let's get that beautiful dress on you before I lose my mind staring at you in all this lace."

He pulled away but I brought him back to me, urging him down by his black lapels until our lips met. I was still reeling from the orgasm, and I had an inexplicable urge to taste myself on his lips. He kissed me back tenderly, brushing his fingers over my cheek. I got lost again, forgetting time and reality until he backed off gently.

"If you don't let me go, baby, I'm going to make you come again. And then we'll never get out of here because I can't take much more."

★ ★ ★

Guests glided along the museum's hallways in their elegant attire. Blake and I followed, finding our way into an expansive enclosed courtyard. The room alone was breathtaking, with forty-foot floor-to-ceiling windows offering a view of the original building's stone walls lit up against the summer night sky. I'd been to some fancy Harvard gigs before, but nothing like this.

I stopped at the balcony overlooking the party and took it all in.

"Beautiful," Blake murmured in my ear.

"It's breathtaking." I stared in childish wonder.

He circled my waist and pulled me tightly to his side. I turned to meet his eyes. They burned into me with the stormy intensity I'd come to love, to crave.

"I wasn't talking about the view." He brushed his thumb over my lips and planted a chaste kiss there.

My heart did a flip as I breathed him in. The sights and sounds around us ceased to exist for a minute while I reveled in the work of art that was Blake.

A voice broke through my thoughts. Someone called my name in the distance. Daniel, arm-in-arm with Margo, approached our spot on the balcony. Daniel looked dapper in his tuxedo, and Margo wore a flowing emerald green satin gown that suited her slight frame and auburn hair.

I hesitated, unsure how to greet them in public until Margo came close to kiss my cheek.

"Erica, so good to see you. You look lovely."

"Thank you. It's wonderful to see you."

The men shook hands and Daniel greeted me with

a warm smile. An emotion passed over his face that was quickly masked by his perfected smile, even broader now.

"Beautiful, Erica. Landon is a lucky man."

Blood rushed to my cheeks at his compliment.

"Is this vintage?" Margo ran her delicate fingertips over the velvet flourishes of my dress with obvious approval.

"Um, yes," I answered nervously, my gaze darting to Daniel whose eyes betrayed him. In my girlish excitement over the dress, I'd never really thought that Daniel would notice it, let alone remember its origin. But by the pained look in his eyes, he did.

Daniel cleared his throat. "Well, why don't we go mingle and see who we can introduce you to?"

"That would be wonderful," I said quickly, eager to diffuse the awkward moment that only Daniel and I could fully understand.

Margo frowned slightly. "I can show Erica around a bit, sweetheart. Why don't you two get a drink?"

Something passed between them without words. I couldn't place it.

"Right. Let me buy you a scotch, Landon. Maybe I can talk you into making a donation to my campaign."

Blake's lips lifted a fraction. "I don't do politics, but I'll still take that scotch."

Daniel laughed loudly and casually patted Blake on the shoulder. Margo swiftly hooked her thin arm into mine and led us down the broad staircase and into the crowd below.

"How have you been, dear?" She slowed enough to lift two glasses of champagne off of a passing tray and handed me one of the delicate flutes.

"Well. And you?"

"Well enough. The campaign has been stressful of course."

"I can't imagine. Daniel made it sound like things were promising though."

"Numbers fluctuate, predictions shift. We're slipping behind, but he tells me everything can change at the last minute." She shrugged and gave me a half smile.

"There's still time. I'm sure he has the best people working for him."

"He does, I know that. I just worry. He needs all his energies on this effort to pull through ahead."

She held me in her gaze, as if she wanted to tell me more. I waited for her to continue.

"He speaks of you often, Erica. I know he wants a relationship, to make something out of this new development with you. But if you care for him, you'll give him some space until the election is over. He needs to win this, and God forbid if anything came out about your relationship... It could be devastating. Do you understand, dear?"

I swallowed down the last of the champagne, hoping she couldn't see the way her words hurt me. I hadn't pursued him since our last meeting for this very reason. I hoped she understood that he'd invited me, not the other way around. She wasn't being mean, but that didn't lessen the sting of her feelings about my potential involvement in her husband's life.

"Of course. I—I'll keep my distance. Shouldn't be hard since our lives don't exactly overlap."

She took my hand, gave it a light squeeze, and smiled. "Thank you."

Feeling suffocated by her words, I scanned the room,

already wishing I were connected enough to know any of the people around me, until I stopped suddenly on two familiar faces.

"Will you excuse me, Margo? I see a friend."

She nodded. I crossed the room toward Risa, clad in a solid black gown with a dangerously low backline.

"Erica, hi! You look gorgeous."

"Thanks, you too."

She returned my smile and we both looked up to the gentleman I'd interrupted with my arrival.

"Erica, I think you know Max."

"Of course."

"You look well, Erica."

Max gave me a slow once over that ended with a slanted smile. I had forgotten how dashing he could look, his short blond hair and tanned skin contrasting against the bright white of his tuxedo shirt. In fact, I was surprised I hadn't found Risa melted into a puddle at his feet based on her obvious and unabashed approval of the gorgeous men who'd graced our office. If I found her flirting at James's desk one more time, I was probably going to have to say something. For his sake.

"Likewise."

"Risa tells me the site is doing well."

I glanced at Risa and realized, gratefully, that she had no idea what had gone on between us. I hadn't seen or spoken to Max since Blake blew the deal we'd been minutes from finalizing. I'd flown out of the Angelcom boardroom in a tearful rage, unable to really explain what had happened. With that, our working relationship had been effectively severed, since Blake wouldn't have anything to do with him when it came to investments, and vice versa.

"So far, so good. We have high hopes for growth now that we have Risa on the team."

"No doubt. She's been working the room like a pro."

She slapped his arm playfully and laughed. "Well, Max has been introducing me, so I can't take all the credit."

Risa exuded a mix of excitement and bashfulness that most guys probably ate up. She was pretty and came across as sweet. She could get what she wanted though, and I was interested to see how she went about it. Especially with someone like Max. If she could play the high-powered playboy, I'd be nothing short of impressed.

The three of us made small talk until Max's focus shifted from us.

"MacLeod. Good to see you. Enjoying the party?" Max reached out to shake the hand of the other tuxedo-clad guest whose dark brown eyes gleamed when they met mine.

"Working on it."

"Erica, this is—"

"How are you, Mark?" I interrupted Max's introduction and forced myself to hold Mark's steady gaze. Inside, alarms were going off and my heart beat loudly against my chest. But I refused to show him any weakness.

"Much better now," he murmured.

Max grinned, mirroring Mark's lascivious gaze on me. I tightened my grip around my clutch and harnessed all my energies to appear polite and unaffected, keenly aware that my reaction to Mark's proximity would be noted by those around us. Of course the two men would know each other from business dealings with Daniel's firm, but Max was the last person who needed to know about my dark past with

Mark.

I'd known I might see Mark here, and I'd swore I'd keep it together if by chance I did. If Daniel would be in my life, at any point, Mark would continue to make appearances. I couldn't have a panic attack every time he did.

No longer a ghost, Mark had become real. All too real. A tangible creature with a name, a past, with vulnerabilities and weaknesses as real as my own. I tried to remember all this as he shamelessly drank me in.

"How about a dance?"

I masked my disgust at the suggestion. Max and Risa looked at us expectantly.

"Maybe later. I need a refill." I tipped up my empty glass. I'd need way more than a glass to consider the request.

"I'll get you one. Go, dance." Max winked and took my glass.

Max had never given me cause to hate him. Even with Blake's warnings, I had often questioned whether his intentions were as malicious as he'd made them seem. Now I hated him for reasons he'd never understand.

Mark captured my hand and pulled me to the dance floor, his grip tight. I moved mechanically to follow him, swept too quickly into the situation to game plan an exit. He slowed and swung me close to him. A wave of nausea washed over me at the sudden contact of our bodies. I tensed, certain that becoming physically ill on the dance floor would not bode well for whatever I'd hoped to achieve professionally tonight.

"Relax," he crooned, bringing us so close his mouth was at my ear, his breath hot and moist on my skin.

Every place our bodies connected sent shockwaves of

pain through my system. Years of loathing the man and the memories he'd given me were programmed into my brain, telling my body to fight. I clenched my jaw and took a deep breath through my gritted teeth, not because he wanted me to, but because I was determined to get through this without completely freaking out.

"Why are you doing this?" My voice was unsteady. I wished I sounded more in control than I felt.

"Can't stay away. I think I've missed you. So glad I had Daniel invite you. I had a feeling you'd come when he asked."

"What do you want from me? Just let me be, please."

"I think you know."

His mouth brushed against my neck and my whole body froze, panic taking over. My focus blurred with the tears that threatened. Couples all around us smiled and danced, but I couldn't see Blake anywhere. Max and Risa stood beyond the dance floor chatting. They were no help to me now.

He can't hurt you here. Logic's voice was quiet and easily overwhelmed by the loud and alarming thoughts reeling through my mind. He'd gotten to me once, despite a circle of friends and a crowd. I could put nothing past him.

"You know, I can still remember everything about that night."

The only benefit of being so close was that I couldn't see his face. His face, the terrible sneering smile that was permanently embedded in my memory. I shut my eyes, trying to block everything out, but I remembered it all.

"Was that your first time? Must have been. You were so tight. So scared."

I fought the urge to heave and I tried to push away when he seized my wrist in a vise-like grip, pulling our bodies even closer with his other arm.

"I love a good fight, but let's not make a scene at Daddy's party, shall we?"

"Let me go. Please," I pleaded. I started trembling uncontrollably. Ghost or man, I had to get away.

The band slowed to the end of the song.

When I thought I might actually scream, Mark finally loosened his hold and released me.

"Until next time, Erica." He smirked.

I stepped away, relaxing only slightly at the separation. I tried to orient myself on the dance floor. Where was Blake? I needed to get out of here. The music started back up and people began moving around us, talking and laughing. Everything felt like chaos around me.

"Is everything all right?" Daniel came from behind, circling me with Margo by his side.

The reality that Daniel was tied to Mark, this horrible person who'd damn near ruined me for good, was more than I could bear. I turned without answering and left the dance floor, escaping down a hallway that led to the outdoor courtyard.

The courtyard was aglow from the tiny holiday lights wrapped around the trees that lined a brick path. As soon as I stepped outside, I took a deep breath of the night air. I was dizzy, my fingers were tingling, and I knew from experience I was on the verge of hyperventilating. The cool air washed over my skin, which was now covered by a thin sheen of perspiration, a remnant of the past few minutes of sheer panic.

"Erica."

Daniel rushed up to me, his eyes full of concern.

"Are you all right?"

"No." I shook my head and then thought better of my reaction. Reason was slowly returning to me in Mark's absence. "Yes, I'm fine. I'm sorry. I just need some air."

"Here, come this way." He held me gently around the shoulders and ushered me to an empty corner of the courtyard. We sat down on a wrought iron bench. My whole body felt heavy, sluggish. I was being held together by the dress that had just been pressed indecently close to the man who'd raped me.

I dropped my head in my hands. I hated Mark. Truly, and with every ounce of my being. I'd spent years of my life in fear of him. Never knowing when or how he could come back into my life. Now that he was here, the fear gave way to a potent rage. Before, the only person left to blame for my rape had been myself. I'd been too drunk, too naive. Every scenario brought the events of that night back to my actions and how I could have stopped it all somehow. Those days had ended. Mark was as evil as I'd ever imagined him to be and my anger and all the pain I'd felt after that night, because of that night, belonged to him.

Daniel gently swept a lock of hair behind my ear. "Did Mark say something to you?"

His voice brought me back to the present, and when I looked up he was frowning with evident concern. I closed my eyes, pressing my fingers to my temples. Tears threatened and I suppressed a sob. Something about Daniel, the way he looked at me, made me want more than I ever expected from the father I'd never had.

"Erica." His voice sharpened.

"I know Mark," I blurted out, immediately wishing I hadn't.

"I don't understand."

I swallowed hard, trying to hide the emotions that welled as I searched for the right words. I hadn't thought this out at all. Everything had happened so quickly.

"From college. We met before. I... I don't know." I searched his eyes, wishing that somehow he could just know—just understand without me telling him. His face seemed pale and stoic, giving me no indication of what he might be thinking of me.

I wanted the ivy on the courtyard walls to swallow me up and deposit me back into my bedroom, away from these people, everyone who could never understand what I'd been through. Then I heard Blake's voice, like a light in the darkness. He hurried to join us where we sat.

"Erica. I was looking all over for you."

Feeling weak, I nodded silently, pulling myself up to stand beside him. Daniel rose with me, steadying me with his hand at my elbow.

"Blake, I don't think Erica feels well. You should take her home."

Blake frowned and looked between us.

"Of course."

That quickly, Daniel stepped away, disappearing back into the party.

"Baby, are you all right?"

"Yeah," I whispered. "Take me home."

CHAPTER SIX

The music was loud, reverberating through the walls of the house. Even from outside the noise was deafening. I couldn't breathe, I couldn't think. My limbs moved too slowly, my mind foggy from the alcohol. We'd wandered outside. I didn't understand why until he shoved me down onto the grass in a dark shadow of the yard. I couldn't gather the strength to free myself from the weight of his body as he pinned me down. Before I knew it, he was tearing through me like a knife, gritting his teeth as he did it.

I opened my mouth to scream but nothing came out, my voice gone. I was shaking, fighting, blind and voiceless when he called my name.

He knew me. He knew my name.

"Erica!"

Blake's voice invaded the nightmare. My eyes shot open. "You were dreaming."

His hands slid down my arms. Every touch hurt.

"No." I recoiled, struggling to root myself into reality. "Please, no. Don't touch me, I can't—"

I pushed myself away, nearly falling off the bed in my urgency to escape beyond his reach. I stumbled into the bathroom, holding myself up by the sink. The person I saw in the mirror was someone I knew, someone I hadn't seen in a long time. My eyes were tired and dark, my skin flushed from the nightmare. I splashed water on my face, the chill simultaneously cooling me and bringing me back to the present.

Slowly, the events of the night came back to me. Pain crept through me. I'd come full circle. After all my self-assurances that I could handle Mark's reemergence into my life, I was right back to where I'd started. I'd be looking over my shoulder, waiting for him around every corner. Except now the chances of being found were much higher. A sob escaped me and I crumbled to my knees, the floor cold and hard.

Blake stepped into the room and knelt down a few feet away.

"I did this, Blake. I brought him back. All of this is my fault."

"Who, baby?"

"Mark." My voice was a whisper, swallowed by the sobs that followed. I hugged my body with my arms, trying to stave off the pain. God, the pain was so intense, coursing through my veins with every heavy beat of my heart. My stomach writhed at this memory of the physical and emotional torment the man had put me through. I'd forgotten what he could do to me, after all these years. I tried to catch my breath and chanced a look at Blake, afraid of what a mess I was.

He winced, his expression tight with concern and restraint. His hands fell to his knees, fisting anxiously. "Tell me what to do."

Silence fell as I contemplated the request. I could barely hold myself together as it was.

"Do you want me to leave?"

"No," I rushed. "Please, don't leave. I... I don't want to be alone."

I suppressed the next wave of tears that threatened at the thought of not having him with me. I wanted to reach out to him, to remind him how much I needed him, but I was firmly cocooned inside myself, unwilling and unable to let anyone close in my current frame of mind. Still, the thought of going through this alone was unbearable.

"Then I'm not going anywhere." He shifted, leaning back against the bathroom wall, studying me intently.

The sound of his voice washed over me and I relaxed a little. I took a deep breath and wiped away the errant tears.

"Talk to me," I said.

"About what?"

"Anything. Tell me something...happy. I want to hear your voice."

His face relaxed, his eyes softening with it.

"Our story is the happiest one I know. I never thought I'd meet someone like you. You're beautiful, smart. And strong. God, you're so strong. Sometimes it blows me away."

The tears came again, like my body was purging itself of all the emotions I'd built up. I loved Blake so much. He couldn't possibly understand how much. Under the weight of everything, I felt anything but strong, but to know he saw strength in me gave me a glimmer of hope that I could get through all this somehow.

"You're killing me. Seeing you like this, Erica, it shreds me. Tell me what to do. How can I fix this?"

I laughed weakly. "You can't fix me, Blake. But thank you for wanting to."

I took another breath, determined to get myself off the floor. I rose, appalled at the vision that looked back at me in the mirror. My eyes were puffy and red. I looked as devastated as I felt. I splashed more water on my face and toweled off before returning to the bedroom.

I fell heavily onto the bed, curling up with the blanket that was unnecessary on the warm night. I needed the comfort of being wrapped up because I knew I couldn't handle Blake's hands on me right now. My heart wanted it, but I was too raw, too scared of what anyone's touch could do to me. He joined me and we faced each other, as far from one another as we'd ever been in a bed we'd shared.

"I'm sorry," I whispered.

"You have nothing to be sorry for."

"You shouldn't have to deal with this."

"Neither should you, but here we are. And I'm not going anywhere until you tell me to leave."

I reached across to find his hand. We fell asleep that way, hand in hand, the simple touch enough to remind me that we still had each other.

★ ★ ★

I woke up to an empty bed, the smell of breakfast wafting into the room. My smile faded when I rose. My head was throbbing as if I'd spent the night drinking instead of crying.

I slipped on my comfy sweatpants and joined Blake in the kitchen. He turned from the stove where he was scrambling eggs.

"How are you doing?"

"Better." I settled into one of the seats at the island.

He poured me a cup of coffee, adding copious amounts of sugar and cream, just the way I liked it. I thanked him and took a sip, feeling a little more ready to start the day.

He made two plates for us and ate his standing on the opposite side of the island. He maintained the distance that I'd needed the night before.

"Do you want to talk about what happened?" he said quietly.

I'd been so wrapped up in my horror last night, he hadn't had the first idea what had spurred it. I hadn't wanted to tell him, to worry him, but he'd ridden the night out with me. He'd been there for me the way no one ever had. He deserved answers as much as I didn't want to give them.

I sat back in the chair and looked outside at the bright morning sky. Sunshine already poured into the apartment through the large bay windows of the living room.

"I ran into Mark last night." I looked back to him.

The muscles in his face tightened, and his entire posture changed, as if Mark was there and he was ready to fight.

"What did he say?"

I swallowed, searching for the right words. Mark had been vague but his intentions were clear when he'd held me in the dance. I knew that now. "He implied that he... still wants me."

Blake dropped his fork on his plate. "Why didn't you tell me before? I had no idea."

"I didn't want to upset you. I know how you are. You'll worry, overreact."

"Goddamn right, I'm going to worry. Jesus, Erica. I need to know these things." He took a deep breath and shoved a hand through his hair. "I'm going to get you a security detail, starting today."

"No, Blake. Seriously, this is what I mean. You're

overreacting."

"When someone threatens to rape my girlfriend, I'm going to react. You can call it whatever you want, but I'll be damned if he's going to get anywhere near you."

"Hiring a bodyguard to watch over me day in and day out is overkill. I'm not living under the shadow of this threat for the rest of my life. I can't live like that. I *have* lived like that, and I can't do it anymore."

"What about last night? I've never seen you like that. You were completely inconsolable." His hands fisted on the counter. "I couldn't even touch you."

"It's not usually that bad." Months had passed since I'd had that same nightmare. Being in close contact with Mark had made the memory new again, the wound fresh. I shivered at the thought of it, toying with the food on my plate. My appetite had disappeared, replaced by a knot in my stomach created by the truth in Blake's words. I would need to wrap my head around the fear Mark had planted, and I hadn't quite figured out how I was going to handle that yet. But I was pretty sure that employing a full-time bodyguard wasn't the way to go.

"If we do this, he wins. Can you at least try to understand that?"

"I think he wins if he figures out a way to get you alone again. Tell me that isn't something that worries you."

I winced at the thought. "I was an easy target before. Christ, I was almost unconscious. He's just trying to scare me now, and I'm sure that's what he's getting off on. Between you and Daniel, I don't see how he could realistically come after me." All rational reasonable thoughts, but I barely believed them.

"Well I'm going to make sure he doesn't."

His jaw tightened and bulged. Determination was written all over his face. I hadn't seen that look since he imploded my business deal with Max.

"What do you have in mind?"

"You should stay home today, Erica. It was a long night. You need to rest." His mouth was set in a tight line.

I waited for him to look at me, but he made quick work of cleaning up the mess in the kitchen.

"Stop changing the subject."

"I'm not. You look like you've been to hell and back. You should take a day."

"Thanks," I muttered, pushing away from the table.

Disappearing into my room, I heard him call me back before I shut the door behind me. I'd wanted to resolve the distance that had come between us last night, but I was too tired and emotionally drained to fight with him now.

By the time I'd showered and dressed, Blake was gone. Uneasiness settled over me as I pulled my things together for work. He wasn't going to let this go. Nothing would sway him when he'd set his mind to something. When it came to my safety, he wasn't going to leave anything to chance.

I cursed myself for falling apart last night, but the thought of having to go through it alone, like I had so many times before, seemed far worse. I'd become used to being vulnerable around Blake, showing him my scars, my past. When I did, he didn't judge me, and somehow that gave the pain less power over me.

I had grabbed my keys and my bag and was heading toward the door, when Sid walked in. He looked as haggard as I likely did, pale despite his dark coloring with tired circles under his eyes.

"You're just getting in?"

"Yeah." He rubbed his neck and dropped his bag on the floor. "All-nighter keeping the site up. Great fun."

"Is everything okay?"

"It's fine for now. Chris is taking over until I can get some rest."

"I'm sorry, Sid. I'm going to take care of this. I swear it."

He shrugged, looking too exhausted to put stock in my words, and shuffled back to his room.

★ ★ ★

I made a beeline for my office, not bothering with hellos. Risa didn't take the hint and peeked around the partition, looking bright-eyed and perfectly put together as usual. I didn't have the energy to deal with anyone's issues or questions right now, but before I could tell her to give me a minute, she sat down in a chair facing my desk.

"I have big news." She grinned, her black shoulder-length hair framing her face.

I raised my eyebrows, already feeling agitated. Only something truly monumental could shift my focus this morning.

"What's that?"

"I got a meeting with the marketing director at Bryant's about a potential sponsored account with us."

Bryant's was one of the largest clothing retailers in the Northeast. Getting a meeting with them was in fact monumental enough to get my attention.

I shook my head, unsure if I fully understood her. "How

did this happen?"

"Max. He has the connection. I let him know who we were looking to connect with and he offered to put me in touch. I got right through to the people at Bryant's this morning, and we have a meeting set up for tomorrow morning."

"Wow, that was fast."

"I know, but I figured we should take whatever they had available. The sooner, the better, right?"

"Absolutely. Send me the details. We'll meet with them together."

"Do you want to go over some options we can pitch and I'll pull together a presentation with those?"

I pulled my thoughts together and blew out a slow breath. My mission for the morning had to go on the back burner. "Sure. What have you got?"

CHAPTER SEVEN

By noon, Risa and I had locked down the presentation, leaving me to my original plan for the day. I headed down to Mocha to caffeinate for lunch. I found a table and pulled out my laptop, figuring I'd take advantage of a short change of scenery.

"Hey. Mind if I join you?"

I looked up to find James pulling out the chair across from me. He looked fresh in a black button-down rolled up at the sleeves and dark blue jeans, his wavy black hair perfectly mussed. No wonder Risa was all over him. He was definitely handsome in a bad boy kind of way. Built well with a killer smile and bright blue eyes that were like tractor beams, he locked me in every time. Something about his eyes made me feel like we'd known each other longer than we really had.

"Sure."

"You look like you're on a mission."

I chuckled softly. "I *am* actually."

"Can I help?"

I considered his offer for a moment. What did I have to lose by getting a little help? I started in on my plan.

"You know the hacker group, M89, that is attacking the site, right?"

He grinned. He'd been in the trenches with Sid and Chris for the past week, so he probably already knew their history better than I did.

"Okay, right. So this group isn't the original M89, but there has to be a connection between someone in the original group and whoever is heading it up now. They were all based in Boston a decade ago, so I figure it shouldn't be too hard to track where they're all at now and see where that takes us." I omitted the information about Cooper. I didn't want to shed any light on Blake's connection to the group and Cooper's suicide.

"You're going after these people yourself?"

I remembered Sid's defeated look this morning. "What choice do I have?"

"What if that just exacerbates the situation?"

"I have a hard time imagining a scenario more damaging than the one we're dealing with right now."

He pursed his lips and nodded. "Agreed. What can I do?"

I shared with him the names of all of the original M89 members that I needed to research. We split the names, and when we returned to the office, we set to work tracking down anything we could find on them.

To my surprise, I found a professional history for all of those on my list. Everyone seemed established with a career, though many were now based on the west coast working for technology companies in the valley. I studied their photos carefully, as if somehow their faces could tell me something I didn't already know. Which one of them hated Blake enough to sabotage us this way?

I jumped when my phone rang.

"Blake, hi," I said.

"How's everything going?"

I glanced at the names written in my notebook and shifted my thoughts back to where we'd left off this morning. "Fine."

"Listen, I have to go to San Francisco to take care of some business. I'm flying out tonight on the red-eye."

As annoyed as I'd been this morning, a pang of regret coursed through me. I tried rubbing the frown from my forehead.

"That's sudden."

"Something came up. I know this isn't a great time. I don't really want to leave you right now, Erica."

I sighed. "I'll survive."

"I'm confident of that. Have you met Clay yet?"

"Who?" I frowned again.

"I guess not. He's hard to miss."

"Who the hell is Clay?"

"I've hired him to taxi you between work and home. He'll be outside the office when you need to leave tonight."

"Shit, Blake. We talked about this."

"We did, and this is what needs to happen, at least until I get back."

The coffee at lunch had given me just enough energy to be outraged.

"Have a great trip, Blake." I hung up and shut off my phone. I couldn't deal with his controlling shit right now.

James came in then, stopping short when he saw me.

"You all right?"

I straightened and tried to put Blake out of my mind. "I'm fine. What's up?"

"What have you found so far?" He took a seat and lowered his voice as he spoke.

Not like researching the hacker group we'd all become so familiar with was a big secret, but I didn't want people to know I was on a wild goose chase to actually hunt them down. Thankfully, he already seemed to pick up on that.

"Some enviable LinkedIn profiles. Seems like everyone has moved on and is doing well. Upstanding citizens as far as I can tell. What about you?"

"Same with mine, but there are two people you missed from the list."

I hesitated, waiting for him to continue.

"I'm assuming you know Landon was involved."

I nodded silently.

"Okay, and then there was Brian Cooper."

"He's dead," I said flatly, betraying what I already knew but had failed to share earlier.

He hesitated a second, no doubt registering that fact. "Right. Well, he was survived by his mother and his brother, Trevor."

"Did you find something on them?"

"His mother lives about twenty minutes from here."

"I doubt she's spearheading a hacker group. What about his brother?"

"I can't find anything on his brother."

"How is that helpful?" I regretted the way that came out. I was tired and edgy, but taking it out on James when he was only trying to help was unnecessary.

"Don't you think it's a little odd that every other person on this list has a glowing resume and the twenty-five-year-old little brother of their former partner in crime has absolutely no professional associations, no Internet presence, no profiles, nothing?"

"Maybe he learned a hard lesson from his brother and decided not to waste his life online like the rest of us."

He tilted his head, looking as unconvinced as I felt.

"Fine. So we have no idea where he is or what he's up to." I clicked my pen as I pondered my next move. A part of me worried about the road I was going down, but things couldn't get more fucked up than they already were. Might as well go all the way down the rabbit hole. "Get me the mother's address."

"You going to see her?"

"That's the plan."

"Let me come with you. Could be totally harmless, but you shouldn't go alone."

The protective tone of his voice took me by surprise. I silently wondered if I had damsel in distress tattooed on my forehead, but in truth I wasn't wild about going on this venture by myself either.

"It's okay. I can handle this."

He didn't look any more comfortable with my solo plan, and I couldn't help but give him points for caring. Still, I wasn't getting him any more involved in this mess, especially if it meant outing Blake's association with Cooper's death.

"Don't worry, James. I won't be alone."

★ ★ ★

I stepped out onto the street and came face to face with an imposing man standing guard by a black Escalade parked at the curb.

"Ms. Hathaway."

He took a step in my direction and I resisted the urge

to take a defensive step back. His sheer size took me aback. This man had been hired to protect me.

"Hi, Clay." I shook his hand, which engulfed my own. He was well over six-feet tall, and his black T-shirt strained over his enormous muscular arms. He looked every bit the part of a bodyguard, except for the kind light gray eyes that contrasted beautifully with his dark skin.

"Mr. Landon has instructed me to escort you wherever you need to go."

I suppressed the urge to take my irritation at Blake out on him. Not that I really could. "Perfect. I need a ride to Revere."

He nodded and opened the back door for me. I hopped in and gave him the address, hoping against hope that Clay wasn't under orders to report my whereabouts to Blake too.

A short while later, Clay pulled up to a large colonial-inspired home in an impressive new development. Unlike their well-kept neighbors though, whoever lived here didn't spend much time maintaining appearances. The grass was tall and weeds thrived through the cracks in the path to the house. No flowers adorned the yard and the flag that hung was tattered to shame.

"Would you like me to come in with you, Miss Hathaway?" The depth of Clay's voice startled me.

"No, I don't think that would be a very good idea. Just wait here. I shouldn't be long."

I walked up to the front door, steeling myself for an awkward visit with the Cooper boys' mother. I rang the bell and waited patiently. After ringing it again with no answer, I knocked loudly on the off chance the doorbell was broken.

Finally the door opened, and before me stood a young

man with long black hair that fell over his eyes. He was ghostly pale and not much taller than I. My breath caught, but I kept my composure.

"Is Ms. Cooper home?"

"What do you want?"

"It's a private matter. Would you mind if I came in?"

He eyed me cautiously before finally moving away from the door, leaving it open for me to enter. I followed him in, stepping into a dark living area. Every curtain was closed. Only the persistent sun peeking through the edges of the blinds lit the room. Other than the general clutter, the house seemed new.

The young man made a half turn toward a hallway at the end of the room before stopping to stare at me.

"What did you say your name was?"

"I didn't." Adrenaline rushed through me, giving me the courage to speak again. "You must be Trevor."

His eyes narrowed. "Who are you?"

"Erica Hathaway. You know, the one whose business you're trying to destroy?" I had no proof that he had any such intention, but he was the best lead I had, and if he was involved, I probably wouldn't be getting very far with a polite line of questioning. "But I have a feeling it's not me you're really interested in."

"Get out." He grimaced and walked toward me.

I stood my ground. Worst-case scenario, I was pretty confident I could hold my own. Plus, I had Clay. I held up my hand to stop him.

"Not so fast. We need to talk."

He stopped short in front of me.

"I'll call the cops," he said through gritted teeth.

I laughed, genuinely amused by the threat. "Go ahead. I'm sure they'd be very interested in the contents of your computer."

He didn't blink.

"You've been terrorizing my site for weeks and you've made no demands."

"What site?"

I frowned at his question. "Clozpin."

The corner of his mouth lifted in a satisfied smirk that solidified my suspicions. That little shit. I'd had no intention of coming face to face with the person hacking our site, but now that I was, anger rushed over me.

"What the fuck do you want?" I yelled, no longer able to control myself. I was the worst negotiator ever.

His smile disappeared, replaced by a haunted seriousness.

"Tell Landon I want my brother back."

I stilled, uncertain where to go from here. I hadn't expected this. I thought I'd be appealing to Brian's mourning mother for information about Trevor. I hadn't thought beyond that.

"You need to make peace with what happened," I said in a more controlled tone.

"You need to leave."

Fine. Maybe I couldn't appeal to him on a personal level, but what he was doing was blatantly illegal.

"I can have you investigated. Everything you're doing will be exposed." I hesitated over what I'd say next. "You'll end up just like your brother if you don't stop this now."

He sneered and took a step closer, bringing his face inches from mine when a voice called his name from the back of the house. Like a startled animal, he jumped back and looked in the direction of the noise.

"Get out."

I dug in. "I'm not going anywhere until we figure this out."

He rolled his eyes and disappeared at the sound of a crash in the hallway. "Ma. Are you all right?"

"Yeah. Who th' *fuck* is in there?"

Ma sounded like she'd swallowed a box of nails soaked in vodka. The loud rasp of her voice made me reconsider my decision not to leave.

I scanned the room quickly, desperate to find something, anything, that could help me get to the bottom of this. The dining room table was covered with paperwork and mail. I pushed through some of it until I spied a piece that had been opened. A check in the amount of over ten thousand dollars made out to Trevor. The envelope below it showed it had been sent from an investment firm in Texas, a name I didn't recognize.

I heard Ma stumbling through the hallway, their voices getting closer and louder.

"I don't want no fuckin' strangers in this house. How ma'y times I gotta tell ya?"

"I didn't bring her. She just came in. She knows Blake."

I froze for a second. Fucking Trevor had dimed me out to his crazy mom. I left the check on the table and stuffed the envelope into my pocket just as they emerged into the living area. Ma was a heavy-set woman in her forties dressed in a tracksuit. Her blond hair was dyed with grown out roots and matted slightly. Her eyes were wide and bloodshot as she jerked out of his grasp. I took a few steps back as she approached, shaking her fist at me.

"Lil' bitch. You think you can come here, waltz right in. You tell Blake he can come here and face me!" Her eyes were glossy and crazed with emotion.

She lunged at me and I back away quickly. She lost her balance and stumbled. Trevor rushed to her and she cursed again, swinging her arm back at him.

I couldn't talk to either of them. The situation was spiraling beyond my control so I slipped out the door and ran down the path toward the Escalade.

Clay jumped out and opened the door for me.

"Drive," I ordered, glancing over to see Trevor's mother making her way down the path, Trevor chasing behind her. She was hurling slurred expletives that I couldn't make out as Clay pulled away, leaving them in the rearview.

★ ★ ★

"Do you want to tell me what the hell you're doing?"

I could tell by the quality of the call that Blake was calling me from the plane. That he'd bother while he was still in the air was a testament to his hyper concern over my safety, but I bristled at the fact he was scolding *me* when he was the one who'd got us into this mess.

"Blake, for once in your life, shut up and let me talk."

"I've only been in the air a few hours and Clay's telling me you're getting chased out of someone's house."

"I'm getting to the bottom of a situation that you have been ignoring for far too long," I snapped. "You can hear me out before you start flipping out."

I was still high on adrenaline, ready to fight with anyone who crossed me. If Clay hadn't already dropped me off, I would have strongly considered giving him a piece of my mind for tattling on me to Blake. I'd be like a Chihuahua barking at a bullmastiff, I realized, and filed that scenario under never-going-to-happen.

"Brian Cooper's brother, Trevor, is running M89."

He paused. "How do you know that?"

"Before his bat-shit crazy mother came onto the scene, he basically admitted it to me. And that they'd both be eternally happy to witness your ruin. You might be right about the not negotiating with terrorists thing. He didn't seem open to making peace."

"So you've probably just pissed them off more is what I'm hearing."

"What he's doing is illegal. Can't we just call the police and get his things confiscated?"

"He's running a virtual operation. If you think he doesn't have fail-safes in place to cover his ass, especially after what happened to Brian, you're crazy. Now that he knows you're onto him, I wouldn't hold out much hope for the authorities resolving this for you."

I muttered a curse under my breath before I remembered the envelope. I pulled it out of my pocket to study it again. "Have you heard of AcuTech Investments?"

"No, why?"

"He's getting checks from them. Like, huge checks."

"Send me the info. I'll look into it while I'm out here."

"Okay." I calmed down a bit and immediately regretted that Blake was already hundreds of miles away. The past forty-eight hours had been intense in more ways than one, and we'd done nothing but bicker through most of it. "How long will you be gone?"

"Hopefully just a couple days. We'll see how things go."

"I miss you." I worried my lip and fought to keep my voice even. Blake hearing me upset would only add to his frustration at being gone.

He sighed on the other end of the line. "I know, baby. I miss you too." His voice was lower, softer. "Can I ask you a favor?"

"Sure," I said quickly, anxious to occupy my thoughts with something other than missing him terribly.

"Can you check in with Heath while I'm gone? Maybe grab lunch or something. I'm sure he'll be fine, but he hasn't been back long. I want to make sure he stays on track."

"Of course."

"Thanks. I'll call you later, okay?"

"Okay."

"No more crazy stunts either."

"Yeah, yeah," I muttered. I hung up, collapsed onto the bed, and gave myself over to sleep before the sun had even gone down.

CHAPTER EIGHT

Risa seemed confused when we climbed into the back of the Escalade. We both wore tailored black suits and heels, and for once I felt I'd put as much effort into pulling off a look this morning as she did.

"Who's he?" she whispered as Clay settled in behind the steering wheel.

I had failed to mention that we'd be chauffeured by my security detail. "This is Clay. He's my bodyguard slash babysitter." I made sure he could hear me from the backseat. "He makes sure I stay out of trouble. Isn't that right, Clay?"

"Yes, ma'am." He pulled out smoothly onto the busy street and steered us toward our destination.

I caught the hint of a smile in the rearview mirror. I grinned in reply though I wasn't sure if he saw it. That was as much of a scolding as he was going to get from me. Bryant's office was out of the city, so I sat back and sifted through the emails on my phone to kill time.

"Oh, no."

Risa stared down at her phone, her hand cupped over her mouth. My heart sank, hoping she didn't have bad news about the site.

"What?"

"Breaking news. Mark MacLeod was found dead in his apartment this morning. He was the one you were dancing with at the gala, wasn't he? Max's friend?"

I stared at her blankly, my jaw agape and no words coming out. What could I say? I shut my mouth and made an effort to mask the panic. My mind spun, trying to make sense of the news.

"What happened?" My voice wavered. I swallowed hard, pressing my damp palms to the seat.

She scrolled through the article for a few more seconds. I wanted to rip the phone out of her hands to read it myself but refrained. "Apparent suicide but they aren't saying how. Says a toxicology report is pending."

Mark was dead. Dead. I silently repeated the fact over and over in my mind, willing myself to believe it.

The worst nightmare of my life was gone forever.

I stared out the window, trying to grasp the magnitude of the news Risa had just shared. I waded through the emotions that flooded me. The relief was unmistakable. No longer would I live in constant fear of the man, dreading how his presence would color every moment spent getting to know my father.

As these realities slowly dawned, a heaviness lifted. As if I'd been given a gift, a prayer answered. Tears welled, and I bit my lip to still its quivering.

"Did you know him really well?" Risa's voice was quiet and laced with all the appropriate sympathy one should have in a moment like this.

What she didn't know about the truth of the matter could fill volumes.

I cleared my throat and straightened. "No. I'd met him briefly before through Blake's investment firm. I think he had a thing for me, but I barely knew him. It's shocking... Sad."

Was it? This wasn't a tragic accident, and as relieved as I felt, I couldn't shake my uneasiness. Mark had killed himself, but why? With everything he had going for him, I couldn't understand it. Mark seemed to take special interest in tormenting me emotionally since he'd come back into my life. What else could be at play? I knew nothing about him except the personal hell he'd created for me.

Clay dropped us off at the building entrance a minute later. Risa and I made our way to the elevators as I tried to regroup emotionally.

"Are you okay? I think I could probably do this meeting on my own if you need some time."

I punched the button to go up. "I'm fine. Let's do this."

She took a deep breath and smiled. Normally I would have been nervous, but nothing seemed as important next to the news I'd just heard.

Our meeting with Bryant's marketing director was mercifully quick, which was good because I was having a really difficult time concentrating on anything the man said. He didn't have a lot of time blocked out for us, so I let Risa take the lead presenting the details of our proposal. She was appropriately concise and delivered well. Whenever she hesitated or stumbled, I chimed in. Between the two of us, we made a pretty compelling pitch. The director seemed satisfied and said he'd run it by his team and get back to us as soon as he got approval.

On our way back, Risa released a heavy sigh in the car and relaxed back onto the headrest.

"Were you that nervous?"

She smiled. "Kind of. I'm really glad you came."

"Me too. We made a good team."

I held out my hand for a fist bump, which she met with a laugh. I was anxious to keep the mood light and our conversation focused on work. I couldn't handle any more questions about Mark right now.

"Definitely. Whether this goes through or not, I think I can definitely use this as a stepping stone to connect with some other retailers. Maybe Max has some more connections."

"Maybe." I wasn't sure about overusing Max's resources, but he seemed willing. I had nothing to lose by letting Risa work her magic with him.

As soon as I got back to the office I slipped into Mocha. I pulled out my laptop and searched the news. Details of the story were slowly being released to the public. I got halfway through the article I was reading when my phone rang, Alli's face lighting up the screen.

"Hey," I answered.

"Oh my God, have you been following the news?"

"Yeah."

"I'm in shock. Does that seem like him, to just off himself?"

I blinked and stared at the photo of Mark on the screen. A portrait of him taken for the law firm, looking professional and more than ready to take on corporate America. The smile that made me sick to my stomach was plastered all over the news.

"I'm not sure," I admitted. "I saw him two nights ago at the Spirit Gala. He came onto me, totally freaking me out. I wouldn't have guessed something like this could have happened."

"Well, it's not like you knew him well."

"You don't think it has to do with me, do you?"

"Jesus, are you blaming yourself for this, Erica?"

"No, but—"

"Okay, you're going to stop that shit right now. Mark was a terrible person. You should be happy he's gone and out of your life now. Good riddance."

"I don't know. I guess I'm in disbelief." I had a hard time celebrating anyone's death, even someone I loathed as much as Mark. Daniel and Margo would probably be beside themselves with grief right now. "Says he didn't even leave a note. Doesn't make sense."

"What would he have written? A confession of all the horrible things he'd done?"

Simone brought over my usual latte without my even asking. I mouthed a thank you to her and stirred it slowly as I contemplated Alli's words.

"I guess you're right. I'm still trying to wrap my head around all this."

"Try to think of it as a chapter in your life closing. You can finally move on now."

I shook my head, knowing full well that his death could never erase what he'd done to me.

★ ★ ★

I forced myself to finish writing the Bryant's contract, though Mark's death barely left my mind as I pushed through work. I was about to give in and check the news again when Risa popped in.

"How's it going?" She beamed in front of me.

"Almost done with this. How about you?"

"I was able to book two more meetings with retailers next week."

"Wow, you're on fire." I raised my eyebrows, genuinely impressed.

She smiled broadly, and then her expression became more serious. "Have you been following the news?"

I stayed focused on my screen. "No, what's new?" I couldn't help but ask.

"They said he shot himself. His blood alcohol level was twice the legal limit."

I closed my eyes, fighting the vision of what that scene must have looked like. Of all the ways to attempt to end his life, he chose the one he was guaranteed not to survive.

"Funeral services will be on Sunday. Do you think you'll go?"

"Risa, I told you I barely knew him," I snapped. Bloody hell. I really wished she would mind her own goddamn business. I wanted nothing more than to be alone with my thoughts, and she was in the front row trying to read them.

"Okay, sorry. I thought you'd want to know."

"Now I know, thanks." I started typing up the last of the terms into my open document, hoping she'd take the hint that I was busy.

She did and left wordlessly. I relaxed again, immediately regretting that I'd been so rude. My head was so messed up, and the one person I really needed wasn't remotely close.

I waited until after five when everyone had left to call Blake. I heard him talking to someone when he picked up.

"Blake."

"Hey."

"Mark is dead," I said, my brain working hard to believe

the words. I still couldn't believe it.

There was silence on the line as I waited for him to respond, to ask me how and when. Surely he'd have as many questions as I did. If anyone hated Mark as much as I did, it was Blake.

"I know."

"What do you mean?"

"I saw it in my news feed. I'm sorry, I wanted to call but I've been tied up in meetings all morning. Hang on a second."

"Okay." My voice was quiet, my throat tight with emotion. I wanted to be angry with him for not calling, but all I could think about was how much I missed him. The noise was muffled on the other end, and then the voices in the background disappeared.

"Are you okay?" His voice was softer.

I drummed my fingers on the desk, wondering how to put into words how completely not okay I was. "When are you coming home?"

He sighed on the other end. I winced. I was becoming the emotionally dependent girlfriend that he probably really didn't need. Not to mention the kind I never thought I'd turn into.

"Sorry, just do what you need to do there, Blake. Don't worry about me, okay? I'm fine." I bit back the tears that threatened, trying to sound as unaffected as possible.

"I'm coming back as soon as I can."

"I'm fine," I repeated, willing both of us to believe it as I wiped away the tear that fell down my cheek. "I'm just kind of a mess right now, but I'll be fine."

I heard the voices in the background again and he

muttered a curse under his breath. "I'll call you tonight, okay?"

"Sure."

I hung up and let my head fall into my hands. Why did I need Blake to put me back together? What had changed in these past weeks that I needed him like I needed my last breath? I couldn't make sense of it, or of the insane thoughts I was having about hopping on the next red-eye to San Francisco to see him.

"You look like you need a drink."

James was standing by my desk. He looked great as usual in a black graphic T-shirt and dark blue jeans, but the worried look on his face was what caught my attention. I wiped my eyes quickly, suddenly worried about the state of my mascara after a day like today.

"I thought everyone was gone."

"I had to wrap something up here. I figured we could catch up."

I straightened and silently hoped that he hadn't heard my exchange with Blake.

"Maybe later. I should head home." I piled up the papers that had accumulated on my desk over the course of the day.

"On a Friday night? I thought you'd be celebrating the new account."

"Well it's not final yet. Plus I still have work to do. I need to figure out the direction for the ad campaign we're planning."

"How about you toss some of that work my way and let me take you out for a drink. I'll come in tomorrow if I have to."

I shook my head. "I don't expect you to do that."

"I want to. Come on, there's a cool dive bar down the street. Unless you're more into those fancy martini bars?"

I lifted my lips. He had one thing right for sure. I could use a drink. Having someone to talk to, even if it wasn't about my solidly heinous day, was pretty appealing too.

"Fine. One drink."

★ ★ ★

James delivered on his promise for a quintessential dive bar. Dark and sparse on decor, the place attracted a local crowd. Most were casually dressed, so I stood out with my suit. Maybe a martini bar would have been better based on the double takes I was getting.

We found two seats at the crowded bar and each ordered a drink. I tried to ignore the news scrolling on the one television mounted on the wall.

"Are there any new developments?"

I panicked slightly. "What do you mean?"

"With the Cooper kid?"

"Oh, yeah, he's definitely our man." I thought back to the scene at the house and resented that I couldn't tell him the whole truth. He'd made a good find with tracking down Brian's family, and I silently wondered if he might have any other ideas about getting to the bottom of this situation.

"You're kidding. You met him?"

"I swung by the mother's house last night. He lives with her, so I ended up meeting them both."

"Is he going to back off?"

I shook my head and thanked the skinny blond bartender who had delivered our drinks.

"So how does Landon tie into this?"

I took a sip of my drink, savoring the bite of the liquor. "Let's just say that the original group didn't break up on good terms. Trevor is holding a grudge against Blake, and based on how last night went, that's not going to change any time soon. That grudge has spilled over onto our company due to his involvement with us. So I'm basically at a dead end again unless I can figure out a way to reason with Trevor somehow."

James rested his elbows on the bar, circling his beer with his hand and showcasing his strong arms and the tattoos.

"Maybe I could reason with him."

I laughed. "I'm sure you'd have no problem strong-arming him, and at this point I'd probably try anything if I thought it might work. Unfortunately I'm not sure it would do any good. Blake doesn't seem to think he'll be easily deterred."

"What's with you and Blake anyway?"

He took a sip of his beer and looked up at the television, as if he weren't too concerned with the answer. Before I could reply, someone yelled my name from across the room. Dressed in a backless black top and ripped up boyfriend jeans, Simone marched up to us.

"Woman, I didn't know you came here!"

"I don't," I said, immediately happy to see her face outside of the café. She looked carefree, her red hair loose and falling over her shoulders.

"This is my place!"

"You own this place too?"

She laughed loudly, attracting the attention of nearly every red-blooded man around us. "No, this is like, where I come when I'm not working or sleeping."

"Oh, cool. I like it."

She wrapped her arm around me and paused when she saw James.

"Hey, you." Her eyes narrowed suggestively.

He smirked. "Hey."

"Simone, this is James."

"My pleasure. You guys wanna play some pool?"

James looked at me to gauge my interest and I shrugged. "Not my best game, but I'll give it a go."

"Whatever, you're probably a fuckin' shark."

Simone's Boston accent was coming out thicker than usual. She had clearly gotten a head start on me in the drinking department. Still, she was undeniably entertaining. If she was a character before, she'd be a downright show-stopper now.

James put our name in for the next table and was talking with the people playing while Simone and I stayed back.

Simone propped herself up on James's seat. "Let's get you a real drink."

"I'm drinking whiskey. Doesn't get much more real than this."

"I'm talking 'bout shots."

"Uh, I'm not sure about that."

"We'll just do one." She pursed her lips and waved to the blonde who was now ignoring us. "Hey, blondie. Two red-headed sluts."

I rolled my eyes. "Subtle, Simone."

"What? I'm the red-head and you're the slut."

"Excuse me?" I looked around self-consciously, hoping no one had caught that.

She downed her shot without answering me and I followed suit. She immediately ordered two more rounds. I'd barely eaten anything today. I was running on coffee and the munchies I had hidden in my office drawer. I needed to slow down or pay for it later.

"What's going on with him? I thought you were with the investor guy." Simone nodded in James's direction.

"Nothing's going on with James. We were just having a drink. And I *am* with the investor guy. So don't get any ideas."

"Don't worry. Not my type. That one, however, is more my speed. I'd like to get a better look at that ink." She bit her lip.

"Go for it. He's a really nice guy." I tossed back one of the two shots the bartender had set in front of me. Blake was thousands of miles away and I'd had the day from hell. Maybe I needed a couple shots to take the edge off.

"I would, honey, but he hasn't taken his eyes off you since I got here. I know that look when I see it."

I frowned and spun in James's direction with no discretion. Our eyes met and he quickly averted them and leaned against the pool table to watch the next play.

Shit.

"That's ridiculous." I turned back to the bar and tossed back the third shot.

★ ★ ★

I wasn't as bad at pool as I'd originally thought. Despite my significant buzz, I was making some decent shots. Simone had partnered with someone from the winning team of the last game, and James and I were ahead after the first few rounds. I leaned in for my next shot, but before I could take it, a hand slid across my lower back, warm through the thin fabric of the shell blouse I was wearing. James leaned in next to me, his body too close. Unprofessionally close.

"Aim for the left pocket."

His breath brushed against my neck and my whole body tensed. I closed my eyes a second, wishing he were Blake. God, just for a few minutes. I missed him so much. When I opened them, I caught Simone looking at me with a smug told-you-so look on her face. I shifted my angle, took the shot, and the ball sank into the pocket. I stepped back and wobbled slightly on my heels. James was there, stilling me with his hand at my waist.

"You all right?"

"I'm fine." I smiled and took a self-preserving step away. I needed to get a handle on this situation before James got the wrong idea. I was about to start scolding myself for having drinks with an employee, when a familiar face emerged from the crowd beyond the pool tables.

"Uh-oh," I murmured.

"What's wrong?" James asked.

Heath walked up slowly, his hands in his pockets, until he stood directly in front of us. He gave James a hard look before turning back to me. My eyes went wide as I replayed the past few minutes over in my mind, including James's brief and suggestive tutorial on playing pool.

"I'm in trouble, aren't I?"

Heath answered with a tight smile. I grabbed my purse and fished out my phone seeing that Blake had called at least a dozen times. *Fuck.*

"I have to go." I glanced quickly to Simone and James, eager to connect with Blake and explain this all away.

"Do you need a ride?" James stepped forward.

"No, she doesn't."

Heath nearly leveled him with his stare, his jaw ticking in a way that made me seriously wonder if he were somehow channeling Blake right now.

"Come on. Let's get out of here," he said, his voice more forgiving toward me.

My eagerness came to a skidding halt. My face heated. Heath would be here under strict instructions from Blake. The thought of being escorted out of the bar at Blake's bidding humiliated me, and my dignity wasn't having it.

"I'll be out in a minute." I raised my eyebrows at him, daring him to challenge me.

He paused and finally agreed with a slight nod.

"Who the hell was that?" James grimaced in the direction of the exit that Heath had just left through.

"Blake's brother."

"A little protective, is he?" Simone walked up and leaned against the pool table beside me.

"Sometimes," I lied.

"You really leaving me?" Simone gave me a pouty look.

I smiled. "Yeah, I'm wasted anyway. I need to go pass out before I get stupid."

"Lame."

"Shut up. James will take care of you, right?"

James smiled politely, but disappointment shadowed his gaze. Simone leaned in for a hug. When she let me go, James pulled me close and pressed a quick kiss to my cheek.

"Good night."

I turned out of his embrace so quickly I almost lost my balance again. I headed out of the bar without a goodbye.

Clay drove Heath and me back to the apartment in silence. I wanted to read them both the riot act, but it wouldn't make an ounce of difference when Blake controlled everything they did. They were no different from me.

I stepped into the apartment and slammed the door behind me before Heath could say good night. Cady, our downstairs neighbor and Blake's personal assistant, sat next to Sid on the couch watching a movie. They were curled up closer than I'd ever seen them. I waved and said hi before disappearing into my bedroom.

I fell down onto the bed and wished the walls would stop moving a bit before I made the call. I cursed and pulled up his number.

"Erica." His voice was a potent mix of panicked and pissed off.

"You rang?" I decided to keep the mood light and go with that.

"I'm beginning to feel like a broken record, but what the fuck?" Blake's mood was decidedly not light.

"I was having a drink with a friend. It was loud. I didn't hear my phone. Stop overreacting."

"Was your friend the one with his hands all over you? Or was that someone else?"

I clenched my teeth and breathed through the string of curses that ran through my head. Heath would be hearing from me about this.

"You must be referring to James from work, and no, he did not have his hands all over me. We were playing pool. He was showing me a shoot. A *shot*. He was showing me how to shoot." I groaned out loud. My slurring wasn't helping my case.

"That's a really great mental image you've just given me."

"Stop being so jealous," I mumbled, already too tired to fight.

"Are you home now?"

"Uh-huh. In my bed. Thinking about getting naked too," I teased, hoping he would take the bait so we could stop bickering.

"Horny, are we?"

"Oh, we could Facetime. Are you on Wi-Fi?"

He laughed and I smiled, relieved that he wasn't as mad as he seemed.

"I've got a dinner meeting with one of the partners on the project I'm working on out here. As much as I'd love to blow it off for phone sex with you, baby, it'll only keep me out here longer if I do. And I don't think either of us can afford delays. Agreed?"

I pouted and slumped back onto the bed. "Agreed."

"I need you to do two things."

"Great. What does the master of the universe decree?"

"Drink a bottle of water. Drink the whole thing and take four ibuprofen. Sounds like you're going to need them."

"Yes, sir," I groaned, ready to hang up and make my way to the kitchen.

"Hey."

"What?"

"I love you, Erica."

"I love you too."

CHAPTER NINE

Someone was knocking on my door.

"What do you want?" I groaned from under the covers.

"Rise and shine. I thought you could use some breakfast."

I peeked out from the duvet. Heath looked fresh and peppy, holding a tall iced coffee and what I hoped was a box of donuts. Only caffeine could get me vertical this morning.

I sat up slowly. I didn't feel quite as terrible as I should have, thanks to Blake's late night hangover prevention advice. I reached for the coffee and leaned against my headboard. Heath sat down at the foot of the bed, eyeing me tentatively. He was probably waiting for me to lash out at him. If I'd felt better, I might have.

"I hate you, you know?" My voice was hoarse, which detracted from the intended impact of the words.

"I know. I was sort of hoping this could be a peace offering."

I grimaced at the memory of James's subtle advances, and worse, that Heath had likely witnessed it all.

"For the record, there's nothing going on between James and me. He was getting too friendly maybe, but he works for me. If someone needs to set him straight, I'd like to be the one to do it."

"Honestly, it's none of my business. Blake was grilling me about who you were with, and I wasn't going to lie to him. For what it's worth, I'm sorry. Blake's hauled me out of more bars than I can count. They weren't my finest moments either."

I cast my gaze down at the blanket, picking at a tiny feather poking through the white fabric. "I'm sorry he put you in that position. I suppose if I had been more reachable, even though Blake is completely crazy, that whole scene could have been avoided. A bar is probably the last place you really needed to be last night."

"Don't worry about that. My sobriety isn't that tenuous. If it were, I doubt Blake would have sent me in there. I think he just thought I was a better option than Clay." His lips curled into a smile.

I laughed at the thought of Clay, who was one of the largest men I'd ever seen, negotiating with James about who was giving me a ride home. Talk about mortifying.

"Good call." I took a long sip of my coffee, feeling my brain come back to life a bit. "Heath, how do you deal with Blake?"

"Don't you mean, how does he deal with me?"

I laughed quietly. I could have easily said that not so long ago, but Heath had changed so much. He seemed like the reasonable one somehow, and Blake was the impulsive one of the two. "I don't know. It's like we said that night in Vegas, how everyone sort of orbits around him. I don't know how he does what he does, or why he even wants to sometimes.

"Erica, I owe him my life at this point. After everything he's done for me, I'm willing to defer to just about whatever he thinks is best. If that's helping with the business, moving here, whatever he needs. God knows, I'm not so great with making decisions."

"You're thinking about moving here, permanently?"

His gaze met mine. Clearly he hadn't meant to tell me that.

"We've talked about it. I've slipped up so many times in New York, and I have a lot of support here between Blake and my folks. I need to talk to Alli about it though. She's the most important person in my life right now. I want to know that we can deal with that before I make a decision."

I didn't imagine Alli would take it very well, but I wasn't about to test their already complicated relationship by butting in. "Don't worry. I won't say anything. I'm sure she'll come to me when she wants to talk about it."

He seemed relieved. "Thanks."

"Do your parents live close?" I couldn't help but linger on the mention of them.

"About half an hour north of the city. They don't usually come into town, but when I'm around, we try to do dinner once a week."

"Oh." I tried to hide my surprise. Of all the time Blake and I had spent together, I had no idea his parents were so close or that he regularly saw them. That he hadn't mentioned either to me stung a little. Naively, I'd never thought much about the rest of his family outside of Heath and Fiona. My own family was decidedly far from normal, if present at all. Heath made it sound like they had something more stable though.

"What are you up to today?" Heath grabbed my attention again.

"Who wants to know?" I teased.

"Hey, I'm off the clock now. Was just making small

talk."

"Show me you mean it, and give me those donuts."

★ ★ ★

In a perfect reflection of my hung-over state, the day was overcast and dreary. Not wanting to be caught in weather, I let Clay drive me to the office. I was starting to pity him since he hadn't gotten a day off since Blake had put him to the task of taxiing me around.

I skipped my usual stop into Mocha. I was already powered up and I wasn't sure if I could handle a debriefing from Simone just yet. I settled in at my desk. A text dinged on my phone.

James: You alive? I'm headed into the office in a bit.
Erica: Have officially risen from the dead. Already here. No rush.

I should probably talk to James about last night. Maybe I could get away with avoiding it altogether. I mean, we'd both been drinking. People make all manner of bad choices under those circumstances. At the end of the day, keeping things professional at work was probably just as important to him as it was to me. He wanted to keep his job, after all.

I checked my email and found my way to the news. The details surrounding Mark's death were too compelling to resist. I felt like a driver passing the scene of a terrible accident and I couldn't look away. They had new photos of Daniel and Margo, looking as grieved as I expected them to be, trying to avoid the paparazzi's cameras. My heart ached for them, as twisted as the sentiment was for me. My sympathy had become partial and conditional.

On impulse, I picked up the phone and scrolled through the numbers until I landed on Daniel's. I took a breath and made the call, fully expecting it to go to voicemail. All I wanted to do was let him know they were in my thoughts, which seemed like the appropriate thing to do under the circumstances. I was his daughter after all. I didn't want him to think I didn't care, even if Margo wanted me to keep my distance.

I was shocked when Daniel picked up.

"Hi." I struggled with how to proceed. The usual *how are you* line wasn't going to work here. "I know this probably isn't a good time. I just wanted to let you know that I'm thinking about you and Margo. I'm so sorry."

He was silent for what seemed like a long time. "Do you think we could meet today?"

I resisted the urge to agree immediately. Margo's words echoed in my mind. "Today?"

"Can you meet me at Castle Island in an hour?"

He sounded different somehow, less guarded and curt. The casual tone should have been welcome, perhaps, but it worried me. I bit my lip, wishing I knew what he was thinking.

"Okay," I agreed.

"Do you need a ride? I can send a car."

"No, I'm good. I'll see you in a little bit."

I hung up and texted James that I was heading out for a while. An uneasy sense of urgency compelled me as I exited out the back and onto the cross street where I hailed a cab. Blake would be furious if he knew I was trying to slip under the radar, but I didn't want to have to explain to Daniel why I was traveling with my brawny bodyguard.

The rain had subsided, but a heavy fog had settled over the bay as the cab pulled up. I paid the fare and stepped out. A sole black Lincoln was parked nearby. Otherwise the usually busy beach stretched along the loop was bare due to the weather.

As I approached, an orange-haired brute of a man stepped out of the driver's side. His eyes were impossibly light, barely blue, and freckles scattered thickly across his face.

"He's down there," he said, gesturing toward the path that began the full circle around the bay, the end of which had disappeared in the fog.

I started down the path, searching for Daniel's figure as I gained visibility. He finally came into view. In khakis and a brown bomber jacket, he stood overlooking the glassy water of the bay, the patchy view of the city skyline ahead.

He smiled faintly as I approached. Despite his casual dress, he seemed even older than I'd remembered. The gray in his hair more obvious, and the lines of his face more defined.

"Thanks for coming out."

"Of course." I felt uneasy though I wasn't exactly sure why. Maybe I had underestimated how awkward this might be.

He reached into his jacket and pulled out a shiny engraved flask. He twisted off the top and offered it to me. I shook my head. He brought it to his lips and drained a good portion of it. Breath hissed out through his teeth, permeating the air with the peaty smell of scotch. The good kind.

"I'm so sorry, Daniel." I reached out and touched his shoulder. He replaced the flask in his jacket and covered my hand with his own. He turned and sat down on one of the granite slabs that provided a barrier between the path and the water below. Keeping my hand in his, he pulled me down so I was seated beside him.

"You don't need to do that."

"What do you mean?"

"You don't need to say you're sorry, Erica."

I frowned. Was he trying to be strong? "Daniel, I *am* sorry. I don't like to see you hurting. I can't imagine what you must be going through. I wish I could do something."

A wave of guilt rushed over me. Would I bring Mark back if I had the choice? As sad as I was for Daniel's loss, I was unmistakably grateful for my own. I couldn't bring myself to empathize with him the way I would have under very different circumstances. I was a walking contradiction. But Daniel was my father. We had a sad excuse for a history, but he needed as much support as I could give him right now.

He shook his head and released my hand, diving back into his jacket for the flask. After he'd emptied it, he turned to me. His eyes were bloodshot as they burned into mine. From the alcohol or from emotion, I couldn't tell, but his expression appeared unmistakably haunted.

"I don't know how it happened, but almost from the moment you walked into my life, you became my pride, Erica. I never really knew what that felt like before until you. That's pretty depressing, isn't it?"

His words robbed me of air. I swallowed hard and drew

in an unsteady breath. He brushed my hair back lightly from my face. The tenderness in his gesture made my heart twist.

"What about Mark?"

He turned his focus back on the horizon, the empty islands beyond. "No amount of parenting could help Mark. I don't know. His father passed away unexpectedly, and by the time Margo and I got married, I already felt like he was too far gone for me to really help. There was a darkness that lived inside the boy, and for a long time I thought I could channel that into something. Christ, corporate America is full of cold, heartless bastards, but he couldn't even seem to play by those rules. With everything we'd given him..." He sighed and shook his head. "He wanted for nothing. *Nothing.*"

The way he emphasized the last word, I didn't doubt it.

His expression brightened slightly. "And then there's you. You had none of my money or influence. None of the opportunities, but still here you are, so driven and everything I could have wanted for you. And you're mine." He smiled softly. "That's the best part."

I struggled to rein in my emotion, but I was drowning in his words. Could he really mean everything he said? Was this the booze talking? He seemed to be reading from the script of everything I'd ever wanted him to say. I'd waited years to hear those words from him, before I even knew who he was or what he'd meant to my mother.

"And to know that the son I gave everything to…hurt you." The muscles of his jaw tightened as he looked away again.

"You knew?" My voice was too quiet, almost disappearing in the ocean breeze that blew across us.

"You were so upset at the gala. I could see it all over your face. I confronted Mark about how he knew you the night of the gala, and he admitted everything. He was pretty pleased with himself, actually. He let me know that if I planned to get in the way of him pursuing you, he'd out the truth about our relationship. After everything I'd put into this campaign, he wanted to barter with me. Keep you safe or keep the campaign safe." His face twisted into a bitter snarl. "He can't hurt you anymore."

I froze, paralyzed by the words I'd tried to comfort myself with the last time Mark had held me captive in his arms.

"I don't understand. He...he killed himself." The last sentence sounded more like a question, because nothing seemed certain anymore.

"Certainly looked that way, didn't it?"

An eerie silence fell between us. I shook my head, unwilling to believe what he was implying. He couldn't have. I stood and took a few unsteady steps away before facing him again.

"Daniel, what are you saying?"

"I think you know."

"No...my God. You couldn't have...not for me."

He frowned. "Yes, for *you*. I did what had to be done, goddamnit. He was threatening you. Blake was threatening me. We're all better off without him, trust me."

He stood and fished a pack of cigarettes from his jacket. He lit one and took a long drag.

"What do you mean, Blake was threatening you?"

He shook his head and laughed a little. "I should have known better when you introduced us to him. You can't keep secrets from a man like Landon. Seems that having an election to win is a vulnerability that my enemies are more than willing to take advantage of."

"Blake's not your enemy." I had no idea what had gone on between him and Blake, but Blake knew how important my relationship with Daniel was. He wouldn't purposefully hurt him, even if he thought it was for my sake. At least I didn't think so.

Seriousness darkened his gaze and he took a step closer, pointing at me. "Anyone who wages threats, Erica, is an enemy, no matter their intentions. He came to me the day after the gala, letting me know, under no uncertain terms, that I was to get Mark out of your life. Ship him off somewhere, to our New York office, a desert island. He didn't care much, as long as he was away from you. He said if I didn't, he'd compromise the campaign. I'm not the type of man you make idle threats to, but I'll admit I weighed my options." He blew a billow of smoke out the side of his mouth. "Now you're safe, the campaign's safe, and Blake's satisfied for the moment. Everyone wins."

"You...killed him?"

"I did what needed to be done." He raised his voice, directing his venom at me. "Don't act like you aren't fucking thrilled to have him out of your life." He rubbed his forehead and took a breath. "Margo, God love her, is the only one suffering right now, but she wanted me to win more than anyone. Now we will."

"What do you mean?"

He shrugged and took another drag. "The numbers are already going up. Mark's death has painted me as a human relatable candidate. As soon as they close the investigation, which should be soon, the race will be in the bag. We can't lose."

I couldn't take another minute of it. The warmth I'd seen in him earlier had vanished, replaced with a smug and calculating man whose only concern was the shortest route to success. I had no idea how his love for or pride in me fit into this scenario, and I didn't want to know.

I started to make my way back toward the promenade. Daniel called my name but I kept walking briskly into the thick fog until I saw the end of the path.

I couldn't think straight anymore. Mark was gone. Heaven help me, Daniel had killed him. For me, or for the campaign? Who could do it, for any reason? Clearly I was in way over my head, because this all made sense to Daniel.

The orange-haired man met me at the end of the path, blocking most of the way with the width of his frame. He was no Clay, but he was not to be trifled with. I slowed as I came near.

"Mr. Fitzgerald needs to speak with you. Wait here."

I turned back. Daniel emerged out of the fog toward me, no love in his eyes. I slipped past his man and only made it a few steps before he grabbed me by my shirt and yanked me back toward the car where Daniel met me.

"Let her go, Connor."

He released me on command and I backed slowly towards the car, trying to create as much distance between them and me as I could.

"You didn't let me finish."

"What more is there to say? You killed your son. You want me to congratulate you?"

"He wasn't my son. But by God, you're my daughter.

You're a Hathaway on paper, Erica, but as far as I'm concerned you're a Fitzgerald."

"What do you mean?"

"A few more months and I'll be in the governor's seat. Then before you know it, we'll be in Washington working our way up, and you're going to help me get there."

"How could I possibly do that? I know nothing about politics."

"Get your business profitable and sell it, or don't. I don't really care, but I'm bringing you on to lead my online campaigning efforts. You're smarter than anyone I've got."

I gasped. He couldn't mean this. He couldn't have crafted this entire plan in his head and thought that I would celebrate with him. I waved my hand, dismissing the suggestion. "No. I'm not having any part of this. I like my life just the way it is, thank you."

His face twisted into an unpleasant sneer. "That's right. I almost forgot about our friend, Landon. He won't let you give up so quickly, will he?"

"I doubt it, since he's invested four million dollars in the company."

"Pay it back."

"What do you mean? I can't pay it all back yet, even if I wanted to. I've already started investing it."

"I'll help you pay it back."

"This is insane, Daniel. Maybe we should talk about this another time, when things aren't so complicated. You're asking me to give up everything I've worked for."

"That's not all you'll be giving up."

"What do you mean?"

"Landon. He needs to be out of the picture."

The blood drained from my face.

He laughed. "Well, not completely out of the picture. As long as you work with me, Erica, I'll be satisfied if you just remove him from your life. That way I won't need to remove him in a more permanent fashion."

I fisted my hands, tensing against the anger that rushed over me. He couldn't be serious. "Blake isn't a threat. He loves me. You're deranged if you think I'd leave him just because—"

His nostrils flared. Without warning he lifted his arm and backhanded me against the car. I fell back with a thud, catching myself before I dropped to the ground. My shaky hand went to the place where he'd made contact. The sharp pain of it paled in comparison to the shock that he'd done it, and without hesitation. I pulled myself up slowly, too afraid to look at him. I had to get out of here but before I could even think about my next move, he brought his face inches from mine. I swallowed hard and pressed back against the car trying to still my rapid breathing.

"That's a warning."

I shivered at the unforgiving tone.

"I run this fucking city. I don't care how much money Landon's got, *no one* threatens me and gets away with it. You'll do this or I'll fucking kill him. He wouldn't be the first to cross me, and I doubt he'd be the last. I protect what's mine at all costs, and right now he's in my fucking way."

I recoiled at the venom in his voice. I was too stunned, too scared to speak. I chanced a look at Connor who stood apathetic and emotionless a few feet behind Daniel. My chances of getting out of this situation on my terms were quickly dwindling. I fought the tremble that coursed through me. I was trapped.

Cautiously I tilted my head up to Daniel, trying to read him. He stared back with a smug glitter in his eyes.

"You wouldn't," I challenged, my jaw resolute.

He lifted his hand and I flinched back. I opened my eyes when he brushed his knuckles over the stinging flesh of my cheek, a surprising act of tenderness after what he'd just done and said.

"I certainly would, Erica. Don't doubt it." His voice was low, deliberately slow, his breath spiked with alcohol. "You're smart so it won't take long for you to learn how things work in this family. If you care for him, you'll stay away from him. We don't need any more accidents. Do you understand?"

Fear sliced through me, his words chilling my blood. When he put it like that, nothing had ever been more clear. I swallowed before answering, trying to keep my voice steady.

"I understand."

CHAPTER TEN

"Let me out here."

Connor slowed to a stop a few blocks from the office. I reached for the handle. Daniel caught my wrist, preventing me from exiting the vehicle, which was all I'd wanted to do for the past twenty minutes. I'd loosely considered jumping out of it while we were driving, but thought better of it.

"I know you're going to think I did this for the campaign, but I did this for you. For us. I made a sacrifice, and now you need to make one."

I stared blankly out the window. After all of that, he wanted my blessing, my forgiveness? That he did was almost laughable.

"Look at me."

I closed my eyes a second before facing him.

"He's too close to all of this, and I can't take any more chances. Try to understand what's at risk before you decide to hate me."

I caught a glimmer of regret in his eyes. Maybe he was sobering up, but the part of me that might have softened at his words before had been silenced. Only days ago, I'd longed to know him better. Now I'd gotten a glimpse of who he really was—a dark and violent man under the suits and the clout. I'd seen too much, and there was no going back now.

"Can I go now?" I wasn't sure how much longer I could

survive in his proximity. I longed for the muggy summer air outside the car, to be free of him and his goddamn henchman. His threats and his warped brand of paternal love were suffocating me. The urge to scream simmered below the surface. If I didn't get out of the car soon, I was going to boil over.

Finally he released me. I left the vehicle as gracefully as I could when I wanted to scramble out and run as hard as my legs would take me. Instead, I kept a steady normal pace back to the office, never looking back.

When I arrived, James was there. His gaze was glued to his computer screen. He stood and came closer when he saw me.

"Jesus, are you okay?"

I hadn't been crying, but my face felt hot and swollen. I looked to the floor, self-conscious and all too aware of the heated skin where Daniel had slugged me. I hoped it didn't look as bad as it felt—physically, anyway. Nothing could look as terrible as I felt on the inside.

"I'm fine," I insisted. I considered staying, working through whatever he'd put together, but I couldn't think straight. Not a chance. "We'll need to pick this up on Monday. Thanks for coming in though."

He was silent for a moment. He touched my chin, lifting my eyes to his. His were surprisingly intense. I'd never been this close to him in good light to really see them, but they were a deep fathomless blue with specks of gray. He brushed the heated flesh gently with the back of his hand, his expression unreadable.

"Who did this to you?"

I stepped back, suddenly panicked by the contact.

"Nobody. It's nothing. I'm fine."

I retreated to my office. My hands were trembling so hard I could barely grasp my things as I shoved them into my shoulder bag. James appeared the second I finished.

"Erica."

"See you Monday," I said quickly as I passed by him, leaving before he could say anything more.

★ ★ ★

I walked for blocks until my feet wouldn't take me any farther. I settled on a bench in a park nestled in the middle of the city. The streets were quiet. The clouds had begun to clear and the sun was thinking about coming out again. Unfortunately, that did little for my spirits.

Daniel's threat played on repeat in my mind. If we were gambling with anything but someone's life, I might have considered calling his bluff. But he'd killed Mark. He'd even gone so far as to make it look like a suicide, and the cops, even if they weren't being paid off, would probably buy it. Daniel wouldn't have done it any other way. Case closed, someone's life snuffed out. Not that Mark's life was the most honorable, but who was Daniel to decide? He'd killed his own stepson.

What was keeping him from doing the same thing to Blake? He was right. Blake could buy and sell Daniel. But Daniel had power and an impressive network of connections built over generations. I didn't doubt his ability to make someone disappear if he decided it needed to happen. The only thing I doubted was whether he could do it knowing how much Blake meant to me. That depended heavily on how much I meant to Daniel. On one hand, he'd all but told me I was his pride and joy. On the other hand, he'd backhanded me into a car and seemed to take smug pleasure in exerting that kind of control over me. I wouldn't call that love.

But I had to do something and find a way out of this mess that kept Blake and me together. If I could buy us some time, I could get closer to Daniel and make him understand that Blake wasn't a threat, wasn't his enemy. If I could do that, Blake and I could have a future. Somehow I needed to convince Blake to give me that time, though, and that wasn't a conversation I could imagine right now. We fought and bickered and meddled, but we wanted to be together. We were closer than we'd ever been. Now I needed to put distance between us. If I didn't... I couldn't even think about what could happen if I didn't.

And who could I talk to now? I couldn't trust Alli because she was so close to Heath. Marie would worry too much, or worse, go to the police. Anyone who knew Daniel had killed someone, even if it was supposedly for my benefit, would be another person whose life was at risk. I had to carry the burden of this terrible truth alone, at least for now.

I wasn't sure when to expect Blake back from California, but the first order of business was getting out of the apartment before he did. I called Marie.

"Is everything okay?" she asked.

"I need to talk to you about Daniel."

She was silent on the phone for a moment. "What about?"

"I want to know what went down between him and my mother. Everything you know."

I heard her sigh, and I could tell right away that she wasn't going to make this easy for me.

"Erica, you're talking to the wrong person. Your mother was the one who knew him, not me."

"And you knew her. You were the closest person to her when they were together."

"So what? They had a brief and passionate love affair, and then they went their separate ways. That's the whole story. I don't know what you want me to tell you, honestly."

I closed my eyes and thought of my mother. Her face. Her pretty blond hair and her smile, the way she'd held me when I needed comfort the most. I needed her now, more than ever. My throat tightened with emotion, and I took a deep breath to snap myself out of it. Crying over this would get me nowhere. My mother was dead and my father was a sociopath. These were the facts of my life.

"Can I come stay with you for a little while? Maybe a couple weeks until I find a new place?" I finally said.

"Of course. Do you need me to come get you? You're worrying me." Her tone had shifted from defensive to caring. Getting her to believe I was fine would be easier than convincing Blake that we needed to end our relationship, though.

"No, I'll manage. Don't worry, okay?"

"Okay, I'll be here."

I hung up and started the long walk back home.

★ ★ ★

I spent one last night in the apartment. I was exhausted by the day's events and I needed to sort through my thoughts before I could face anyone.

But sleep was little relief from the day I'd had. In sleep I was as tortured as I had been hours ago. I jolted awake, frantic that something had happened. A cold sweat chilled my skin. I pulled the blanket tightly over me. The fiction of my dreams had me believing my worst nightmares. That Daniel had followed through on his threats. That Blake had disappeared. Gone, irrevocably gone. I curled my knees close to my body and willed myself back into reality. Blake was safe, but only if I could keep him safe.

The weight that somehow I had brought this on myself, on all of us, settled over me. Because I had, hadn't I? Any way I thought about it, all this came back down to me. Mark was dead and his poor mother would never know the truth. Despite Blake's attempts to keep me safe, from Mark and then the truth, he was now in Daniel's cross hairs. And I was headed into a future so unknown to me, I couldn't begin to fathom it. A life at Daniel's side, if he had anything to say about it. I couldn't imagine what it might be like to belong to his life of politics and greed and manipulation. A life that Mark knew all too well, no doubt.

I clung to the vision of the life I had hoped for. One I couldn't see clearly before, maybe out of fear of what it really meant. One where Blake and I had a future, a real life together. One where we belonged together and no one was threatening to take that away from us. I dared to think of marriage, of building a family together. Then the tears came, exhausting what was left of me until I fell into another restless sleep.

Daniel emerged out of the fog. He'd found me, hunted me down. He could because Blake was gone, forever. Over and over the scene played out until I felt I'd never escape. I thrashed in and out of consciousness, trying to purge the terrible thoughts from my system. Then the chill was replaced by a sudden warmth. Weak with relief, I relaxed. I felt Blake all around me, hushing away my cries. My lover. The power of our love together could surely countervail Daniel's threats and the uncertainty that I now faced. He could make it go away, somehow... In my dream, I tried so hard to believe that. I clung to the promise of it.

But he wasn't a dream. Blake was with me, loving me with his touches, kissing away the worry. In the dim light of the room, I opened my eyes into his. So familiar and yet so foreign, the eyes that looked back at me were loving, filled with worry. Scooping me into his arms, he kissed me, deeply and passionately. I kissed him back, desperate to have him with me again. I inhaled him, unable to believe he was real.

"Another nightmare?" he whispered.

I shook my head. *No. My life is the nightmare now.* I held my lip between my teeth to keep it from quivering. He didn't know. He couldn't know.

He released it with his thumb and lowered his mouth to mine again. He was flush against my side, still fully dressed from his travels. Thoughts raced through my mind as I tried to separate dreams from reality. The relief that he was with me again was quickly overwhelmed by what that meant. I clung to him, gripping his shoulders as if he might leave again. I had to keep him close.

"Missed you, so much." He kissed my neck, my jaw, then my lips again, as if he couldn't get enough of me but couldn't decide where to start. "Can't stay away from you like that anymore."

The love in his voice, cracked with emotion, shredded me. If only he didn't love me, everything would be easier. I could mend my own heart and put myself back together the way I always had before. But the thought of leaving, that he might feel a fraction of what I would at the separation, was unbearable.

He slid a hand under my tank top, palming my breast, plumping it in his hand and thumbing my nipple. He pinched my nipple and I gasped, arching off the bed.

"Make love to me, Blake. Please, I can't wait anymore."

I let my hands roam, remembering every plane of his body, the hard batch of muscles leading below the band of his jeans. I crashed my lips into his and wrapped my body around him in every way possible. The intensity of what I felt for him shot through every limb as I scrambled to remove the layers of clothing that separated us. Nothing would make sense now. I just had to love him tonight, to give us that much.

He stripped down, and seconds later he lowered onto me, covering my body with the heat of his own. The sensation of his skin on mine overpowered me. I'd never wanted him more, loved him more. I slid my hands over his chest and down his body until I reached his erection, the satin skin burning in my grasp. I couldn't wait a minute longer to have him. I guided him into me and he pushed deep with one thrust.

A hoarse cry left my lips with the rush of him filling me. Nothing had ever felt so right. We stayed that way for a long time, holding each other tight, as if one of us might disappear at any moment.

"Now I'm home. Right here."

He rocked into me, impossibly deep, and I arched into the movement, loving every slow thrust of our bodies connecting. I wrapped my arms and legs around him until we were touching everywhere, fully entangled.

He held my cheek in his palm, trapping me in his gaze. I couldn't. I closed my eyes and turned away. I was afraid of what he'd see if he looked too hard. He forced me back to him and kissed me, thrusting deeper as he did. I gasped and shuddered, reveling in the familiar waves of heat saturating every cell of my being. Every limb hummed.

I tried not to think about the other side, the long fall from the earth-shattering bliss he gave me to the darkness of a life without Blake. I tried not to think about it, but the cold, hard reality of it crept in. Time ticked by, my body refusing the climb, evading its addictive pull. If only I could suspend this moment—our bodies impossibly close, slick with the heat of our passion, a never-ending state of being. I could live with that, never reaching the top, if it meant we never had to come down.

I turned away, staring into the near blackness of the room, my thoughts too far from us. He turned my face back to him, his own expression strained, his skin tight and flushed.

"Goddamnit, what's going on?"

I stumbled, trying to find the words. "I'm sorry. Don't stop, please."

"What are you thinking about?"

"Nothing. I don't want to think about anything but you."

He stilled. Then without warning, he pulled out of me and left the bed. He rustled through his travel bag by the door. How he could see anything in the darkness of the room, I wasn't sure.

"What are you doing?"

"Putting you in a better frame of mind."

The bed dipped under his weight again.

"I did some thinking while I was away, baby, and I think you need this as much as I do. We'll start slow though."

My breath caught as he stretched my arms above me, encasing my wrists with two soft leather cuffs, looping the connecting strap around a rail on the headboard.

"There. That's better. You okay?"

"What are you going to do?" It was a quiet plea. A part of me was afraid of what he might do, but I needed something and soon.

He grabbed my hips and tugged me lower until my arms were fully extended above me. My breath hitched, my muscles tensing with the position. He planted a wet kiss between my breasts, and I sighed. Moving to one and then the other, he teased the tips with warm strokes of his tongue. My nipples were hypersensitive, almost painfully hard, jutting out shamelessly for his slow torture. He bit down gently and my body jerked from the pleasure that shot through me.

He continued to roam with one hand while the other slipped between my thighs to the apex of my desire. He teased my clit, tracing my opening, and then back again, my core quickening with the motion.

When I thought I couldn't take much more, he withdrew and flipped me to my belly, my arms tautly outstretched. The cord of the cuffs twisted around the rail, increasing their tension on my wrists.

He licked up my spine, causing me to quiver. His thighs straddled mine as his hands glided smoothly over my skin, down my back, squeezing my hips and the top of my ass.

"Mmm, I missed this. Thought about making your ass pink every night I was gone."

I bit my lip. I knew what was coming and went wet with anticipation, the ache between my legs throbbing now.

"You weren't too well behaved while I was gone, were you?"

I shook my head as much as I could.

His palm made hard contact with my ass. I jolted at the shock of pain. Then an unexpected wave of pleasure warmed me.

"Someone else had his hands on you. We're not going to let that happen again, are we?"

I winced at the memory of James.

"Erica, answer me." His voice was hard and clipped, his hand falling hard on the same spot.

"No, I promise," I moaned, acutely aware of the wetness pooling between my thighs.

He continued to punish the same spot until my head buzzed with a heady mix of adrenaline and inexplicable desire. These weren't gentle playful slaps. They were hard and loud, echoing through the room, each one landing with a sting that had me tensing anxiously in anticipation of the next. They fell so solidly across my skin that I swore I was being punished.

I wanted to be, so I let myself believe it. I convinced myself that Blake was punishing me and I was letting him. For making him so jealous, for letting James get too close. And for what I was about to do to him, to us, I deserved it.

"I want to hear you." His hand made contact once more, smarting the skin that was nearly numb from the endorphins now. "I want to hear those helpless little moans you give me. To know what I'm doing to you is making you crazy inside that tight little body of yours."

I didn't make a sound, my cries burning in my throat.

"Erica," he snapped. The edge in his voice sobered me.

"More," I cried. "I want more. Harder." Inexplicably, I did.

He exhaled harshly. "Are you sure?"

I lifted my hips into his grasp and gripped the rail tightly. "Blake, please," I moaned, overcome with a craving for the pain that I so deserved.

He left the bed, and I heard movement next to me before the sound of clothing dropping back down to the floor. He was over me again, straddling me.

The broad curve of a leather belt followed his touch, cool against my burning skin. My palms went damp with fear and lust, slipping on the rail. A slow tremble worked its way through my body. My chest heaved, and I fought for breath as I waited.

"Tell me if it's too much," he murmured. "Use your— just tell me to stop, okay?"

I arched off the bed, my body asking for more before my mind could make sense of it. Whatever pain came at the other end of this I'd earned or was about to.

"Just do it."

I heard the sharp crack of the leather on my skin before the pain caught up to my mind. My jaw dropped in a breathless cry when the pain pulsed through me. *Fucking fuck, that hurts.*

He paused, waiting for me to speak. When I didn't, he released another lash. I bit the pillow beneath me and suppressed a scream. Undeniably, it hurt. My entire body tensed against each blow. *Why are you doing this?* Tears stung my eyes, my throat thick with pent up emotion. *You deserve it. You did this. Take it. Take it all.*

"You okay, baby?"

"Do it, just fucking do it," I croaked, my voice jagged with the need to cry.

He hesitated a moment, then slapped the belt with measured precision. Again and again, he spread the sharp licks over my ass and my thighs. Somehow, the pain cut right through the shadow of misery that had fallen over me. I sobbed into the pillow. The tears spilled over, saturating the fabric, cleansing me, breaking me down.

I relished the punishment, welcomed the physical manifestation of everything brewing inside me. Everything was releasing. My body went lax, even as he continued, as if I'd been broken down completely, stripped down to the most bare, raw state I could imagine. I couldn't possibly understand why, but something felt terribly right about all of it.

When my sobs slowed, he stopped and tossed the belt off the bed. He kissed my back gently, his fingers feather-light against my skin, soothing the pain. The warmth of his body covered the back of mine. His erection lay heavily on my bottom, the weight of it almost too much on the pained flesh there. The pleasure and the pain. He was a master at delivering so well on both. Now I needed pleasure. I was ready for it.

"You took that really well. I know it wasn't easy. I'm

proud of you."

My heart ached at the comfort that washed over me at the sound of his voice. Soft with affection, his tone was a welcome shift from the commanding character who'd just thoroughly punished me. "I'm going to fuck you now, and you're going to come when I tell you. If you don't, I'm going to punish you again. Do you understand?"

I whimpered an affirmative. Though softly rendered, his threat was heard.

He kissed between my shoulder blades, his teeth grazing my skin. I shivered, my nipples tightening at the sensation. He turned me back over again and nudged my legs apart so he could nestle between them.

Lowering down over me, his hand went to my hip, the other brushing the tear-soaked hair from my eyes. He wiped away the tears, and the lust that hooded his eyes changed. The corners of his eyes wrinkled with concern.

"I'm so sorry," I choked, so overwrought with emotion I thought my chest might burst from it all. He'd never know how sorry I was.

The tight lines around his eyes released and he caught my mouth in a slow, deep kiss. He pressed the flared crown of his erection into me, barely penetrating.

"I'd be lying if I said I didn't want you to be sorry, Erica. I can't tell you what it does to me to see you like this, giving yourself over to me."

"Please," I moaned, arching into the contact, desperate for him.

My breath caught as he rooted himself fully and abruptly. The sensation was searing and overpowering, a potent rush of pleasure over my pain.

"Oh, fuck," I cried.

"Erica," he murmured. "I need this. I need you."

Something snapped, between his words, the restraint, and his thick penetration. A consuming hunger overwhelmed me, and I clenched around him helplessly. He withdrew to the tip and shafted me fully again. I wrapped my fingers around the rail he'd tethered me to and a hoarse cry escaped my lips.

"That's it, baby. Let it all go."

The low rasp of his voice coaxed me to the edge. Except the cliff had turned into an avalanche and I couldn't escape now. A few more thrusts and I was gone, helpless to fight the feeling. The orgasm was coming for me, like it or not. I was lost in the world he'd created for me, as drunk on the pleasure as I was starving for more.

He buried himself deeper, his hips slamming into mine with forceful drives. He pumped into me, his cock growing impossibly larger as he did. He nipped at my earlobe, sucking it, then grazing it again with this teeth.

"*Mine. You're mine. Just like this. Your body, your heart. Every part of you.*" Whispering in my ear, he never let me forget it, not for a second.

"I'm yours." The tears came again as my body gave up the last of its resistance.

"Come now, baby. Give me everything."

The leather of the cuffs bit into the skin at my wrists as I struggled against them. Stretched tight and spread wide, I was completely at his mercy. Every muscle strained and I came apart. My thighs hugged his hips as my sex spasmed in climax. I fell hard, shaking uncontrollably, tensing as the orgasm ripped through me, his name on my lips. For a split second, a heaviness lifted and nothing else mattered.

"Erica," he groaned.

His body jerked against me. His hands gripped my hips fiercely as he found his own release.

He tensed, then sagged against me. His body was slick against mine as he exhaled roughly.

He untied my hands and massaged the reddened skin of my wrists. Then he captured my mouth in slow, breathless kisses, brushing away the last of my tears. We were both spent, stripped down by the experience. With my last shred of energy, I wrapped my arms around him, hooking my leg over his hip. I needed the reassurance of our closeness. I couldn't let him go yet.

We lay that way, wordlessly, for a long time. The intensity of what we'd done settled over me, and my mind spun over what it all meant. In the face of what tomorrow would bring, maybe it didn't mean anything at all.

"I'm sorry," he whispered finally.

"I love you," I breathed, before falling into a deep, dreamless sleep.

CHAPTER ELEVEN

Come up for breakfast when you wake up.
Love,
Blake

I dropped the note back onto the pillow and fell back on the bed. I stared up at the ceiling, wishing the answers were written there. I still had time.

I made my way to the bathroom and tried to tame my totally fucked hair. Fingertip-sized bruises marked my hips. My ass was covered with dozens of tiny little red dots, broken capillaries from the serious lashing Blake had dished out. A deep blush colored my cheeks.

Bound and at his mercy in the darkness of the night, I'd survived Blake's unexpected return, overcoming my panic and fears. More than that, somehow I'd needed it, to break through all the craziness in my mind. My fears had seemed so small and insignificant in the face of impending tragedy.

I showered and dressed. I glanced out the window. Blake's Tesla sat out front. A few cars down, a black Lincoln was parked on the street and I swore I caught a glimpse of red hair moving in the driver's seat. A clatter in the kitchen tore my attention away.

I stepped into the living room tentatively, my nerves on edge. Sid was making his breakfast at the toaster. I relaxed slightly, relieved that Blake hadn't come back. At least he hadn't been there this morning. I didn't have the energy last night to anticipate how I'd deal with waking up to him. I hadn't planned for any of that. None of it.

"You're up early," I said.

"Yeah, trying to get on a better schedule. Our hacker friends must be on vacation so I haven't had to pull any all-nighters, which helps."

"Really? They just stopped?"

"Seems that way."

"Wow." I thought back to the meeting with Trevor. He didn't seem to have an ounce of forgiveness in his heart, and our conversation had hardly convinced him to stop the attacks. Maybe tracking him down at his house had shaken him enough to make him stop. I wondered if he'd done the same for Blake's other ventures or if he'd just decided to spare me.

"Hopefully they stay away so we can finally get back to work."

"Do you think they will?"

"I have no idea. The code is so solid now I have a hard time imagining how they could breach us again, but we can't defend what we can't see. I guess we have to wait and see if they resurface."

"Right," I agreed. "Listen, Sid. I'm sure it won't make much difference to you, but I'm going to be staying with a friend for a little while, so if you don't see me around here much, that's why."

"You still coming to the office?"

"Of course."

His face was passive as he sat behind the counter. He broke up his Pop-Tart, but I caught a flash of concern in his eyes when he looked up at me.

"Is everything all right?"

Unaffected as he tried to be, knowing that he cared meant a lot to me. We had a strange friendship that had deepened in its own way over time. I didn't quite know how to answer him.

"I think it will be. Time will tell."

Sid simply nodded, even though I was being cryptic and only half believed it myself. Thankfully he wasn't one to pry.

★ ★ ★

I knocked quietly at Blake's door, even though I had my finger on his key in my pocket. He greeted me with a smile that nearly took my breath away. He was gorgeous in his tired worn-out blue jeans and a simple white T-shirt. His hair was wayward and messy. Despite the long night, he looked rested and happy.

"Hey, beautiful." He lifted me off my feet and kissed me.

I returned it, slave to the habit of melting into his touch and craving his skin on mine. What the hell was I thinking? Nothing about this was going to be remotely easy.

"What do you want for breakfast?"

He lowered me back down but stayed close, twisting a strand of my hair around his finger. I shook my head and looked away, physically incapable of looking at his eyes straight on.

"You okay?"

"Yeah." I stood there awkwardly, paralyzed. "Can we…

talk?"

"Okay." His eyes narrowed slightly and he stepped back into the apartment, closing the door behind us. He walked farther in, but I lingered by the door, not wanting to get too comfortable. I couldn't get pulled into the usual routine between us.

I shifted my weight back and forth a few times. He raised his eyebrows a fraction. Shit, I should have just emailed him. I couldn't do this face to face.

You can do this. You have to do this.

"I think we need some space." My teeth clenched against the tremble that threatened to take over. I fisted my hands, determined not to lose it.

All signs of warmth and humor had left his face. "What does that mean?" His voice was low, eerily so.

Shit, this was happening. This was really happening.

"I'm going to stay at Marie's for a while. I need some time, and I think it would be easier if I wasn't here."

"Time? How much time?"

"I don't know."

I had no idea how long. I hadn't nearly given up on the idea that I could get us out of this mess, but I needed time with Daniel to figure out how to get us there. I couldn't risk Blake's life in the meantime. His life… I couldn't gamble with it. The thought of Daniel making good on his threat hit me again—a terrible, sobering thought that gave me the resolve I latched onto now.

If I did nothing else, I would protect him. He'd chosen me, tried to protect me, and now here we were.

"Where the hell is this coming from? Did I do something wrong?"

I shook my head, not wanting him to blame himself but knowing he'd probably find a way to anyway.

"Everything is just too much right now. I'm falling behind at work. I can't focus. And then this news about Mark came as such a shock. I haven't really had time to process everything." Sadly, most of that was true, which was probably the only reason I could get the words out. "And I can't do that with you around right now."

He shook his head, his eyes wide. I was leaving the safe world of Blake, slipping further out of his reach.

"No. I—fucking *no*. We can figure this out, whatever it is. We haven't even had a chance to talk since I got back, Erica, and now you're dropping this on me?"

I cut him off quickly, afraid to let him take over the conversation. "I thought about things a lot when you were gone too." *About how much I love you, can't breathe without you.* "And I think this is the best thing right now. I care about you, Bl—"

"You *care* about me?" His brows knitted tightly together. I'd struck a chord.

He took a step closer and I stepped back against the door, as if the volume of his voice could knock me down. His anger felt like a physical blow. The venom in his words rapidly worked its way through my system. The tears threatened and I squeezed my eyes closed, fighting them.

"Please, Blake. Just give me time. That's all I'm asking for." My voice was a whisper.

"Is this about James?"

I let the thought roll over in my mind a moment. He'd handed me a reason, one that would hurt him deeply. I could admit to the lie and he'd believe me. Surely the thought of an infidelity would be devastating enough to sever the love he felt for me, with no question whether I was actually telling him the truth.

I shook my head. I couldn't stomach the backlash that might come from that false admission.

"No. This has nothing to do with James."

"You're not telling me something, Erica. How do we go from you drunk wanting phone sex to last night, which was amazing by the way, and now this?"

He'd need answers. He wouldn't let me go without them. Maybe after we'd had some time to come to terms with the separation, I could give him some reason that made sense. But not now. Everything was too raw. He'd see right through me.

Too much was unsaid, but I couldn't tell him the truth. He'd go after Daniel, and we'd be in an even bigger mess. Jesus, maybe none of us would survive it. Like a Quentin Tarantino movie where you can't begin to count the bloody bodies on the floor. We'd be among them, no one winning. Just one big bloody fucking mess.

"I will always love you," I whispered, afraid of saying the words with the passion I really felt. Once I'd said them, I relaxed a little. The truth felt right, and he needed to know that, if nothing else. "I know you're angry. You have every right to be, but please don't doubt that."

He came close, bringing his arm up to rest on the door. I flinched back. Like an abused animal, I'd been hit, and in that split second I expected it. He lowered his hand and stared hard at me. He shoved his hands through his hair. I took a deep breath, wishing I could tell him who'd planted that fear in me, to take that pain away from him.

This is going to hurt. I was here to deliver the blow, not soften it.

I fumbled with the clasps on my bracelets and lifted the two sparkling bangles to give to him. I hoped for a second that he might take them, accept them, but he stood motionless before me, boring into me with those beautiful hazel eyes. I looked away, hating how they pleaded with me, fearful he'd see right into me. When he wouldn't take them, I stepped past him and set them on the counter with his key.

I turned back to leave.

"Stop."

I faced the door, my hand on the knob, ready to bolt.

He was close. His ragged breath caressed my skin.

"You're doing it again. You're running."

"I'm not running. I'm leaving."

"What if I don't let you come back this time? How many times am I going to let you do this to us, for fuck's sake?"

I clenched my jaw, hating the thought that this might be the last chance he'd give me.

"Look at me, goddamnit." He slammed his palm on the door.

I jumped at the sound and the edge in his voice. I took a deep breath and turned slowly to face him.

"Tell me why you're really doing this, and I'll tell you why it's wrong."

"I told you, I need time."

"Bullshit."

"I should go."

"No, you should stay here, with me. This is where you belong."

I closed my eyes and shook my head. I couldn't believe I'd found the strength to come this far, but inside I was unraveling. My love for Blake fought for control over the very real threat that I needed to protect him from.

I needed to leave before I lost my resolve. Before I could, I turned and left him without another word.

I tried to move quickly, but the albatross of emotion slowed my movements, numbing me. I went through the motions of packing in this dazed and detached state as tears blurred my vision. How I managed it I'll never know, but I'd stuffed most everything I might need for a few weeks away from the apartment into my large suitcase.

Sid was hidden away in his room, so thankfully I didn't have to face him again. I stepped outside, and out of pure habit I scanned the street for the black Escalade and Clay. The threat of Mark was gone, and Blake was back in town. We weren't together anymore, so there was no need for a babysitter. Despite the fact that I disagreed with the whole concept of a security detail, Clay had grown on me a bit.

My gaze shot down the street, and I noticed a less welcome presence. Connor leaned against the town car. He tipped his hat toward me. A mere gesture I assumed, since he was likely tasked with reporting my every move back to Daniel. He'd keep it up until Daniel believed that things were done between Blake and me.

I walked toward him, my suitcase rolling loudly behind me. "You can tell him it's done. Now leave me the fuck alone."

His face was as stark and emotionless as it had been the last time I'd seen him. "I'll give him the message."

I walked past him and hailed a cab, starting the journey

to Marie's on the outskirts of the city. As we turned off Comm Ave, I checked behind me to make sure Connor wasn't following. Thankfully, he wasn't. Marie was the last person I wanted Daniel checking in on. He had no idea we were still in contact, and she was one of the only people who knew what he really was to me.

The cab navigated through light traffic. Throngs of people went about their days. Happy, normal people with easy problems. I was leaving the only home I'd ever really known, and Blake was right. I was running away. This was an aimless and desperate escape from a world I'd created, one I truly loved.

CHAPTER TWELVE

Marie didn't question me when I arrived. She just held me so tight it almost hurt. I sobbed into her, letting all the misery pour from me.

"Whatever it is, we'll get through it, baby girl," she promised.

I needed that, for someone who loved me and didn't know a damn thing about anything to promise me that everything was going to be all right. I wanted so badly to believe it.

I spent the day watching mindless television while she went out to run some errands. I wanted to fill my brain with nonsense, anything to drown out the misery.

After I enjoyed an amazing home-cooked dinner and a few glasses of wine, my tension had started to ease slightly. I didn't feel so numb, and I'd finally stopped crying, which seemed like progress.

Marie and I had settled in her den, jazz playing quietly in the background as we curled up on her two large couches. I covered up with a blanket and held a big wine glass between my palms. A comfortable silence had settled between us.

"I'm sorry for just dropping in on you like this."

"Don't be ridiculous. You can always come here. Day or night. This is your home too."

"Thank you. That means a lot." I didn't have many other places to run to, sadly.

"Do you want to talk about it?" She canted her head to the side.

The past couple days' events flashed through my mind. First Mark, and now this. As soon as one burden had been lifted, another replaced it. Despite my complete and utter breakdown since arriving, I'd avoided telling her anything. She assumed something had gone terribly wrong with Blake, and for now, that was enough.

"Not really," I finally said.

"Maybe you should. I've never seen you like this, honey."

I was a mess, true. I looked like hell but I was grateful that I didn't have to put on a happy face, or makeup for that matter, when I was with Marie. I could just be, even if I wasn't planning to tell her the whole truth.

"We're taking a break. That's all. I don't expect it to be easy, but trust me when I say it's for the best."

"What did he do?"

"It's not him, it's me. I...I really don't want to talk about it, Marie. Not right now, anyway."

She didn't look entirely satisfied with my unwillingness to share, but she wouldn't push me. She never had. She was always good about giving me space, not smothering me with concern and questions. Because she was, I typically ended up telling her more than I probably should. But this was different.

"I do want to talk about Daniel, though."

She rolled her eyes and sighed. "Please, not this again. At this point you could probably tell me more than I could tell you about the man."

"Have you seen the news?"

She nodded. "Yes, I saw that his son died. Tragic. Have you spoken to him about it?"

"Yes, he's taking it pretty well."

That sounded more sarcastic than I'd wanted it to. The wine was making me too loose. I set down my glass. I couldn't afford truth serum slip-ups. I had too much at stake to risk getting sloppy.

"I want you to tell me everything you know about him, Marie. Don't worry about sugar coating the past. Trust me when I say I have no illusions about him."

She sat quietly, tracing the rim of her glass. Our eyes met, and I could see there was more that she hadn't told me. No doubt for my own sake.

"Why do you want to know so badly? Don't you ever think that Patty didn't tell you for a reason?"

"I think about that every day."

What if I hadn't been so damn curious? I'd never have found Mark. I'd still have my anonymity and he'd still be alive. Blake wouldn't be half responsible for his death and at risk of losing his own life. Jesus, everything would look so different right now. So very different.

"I want to know because I don't entirely trust him. He wants me in his life. Not publicly as his daughter, of course, but I need to know what I'm getting into. He's not extremely forthcoming, and his wife wants me at a distance. It's complicated. I figured if you could tell me something about his past, that would be a start. At the very least, I'd like to know who he *was*."

She stared into her glass, her mouth in a grim line. "I had no idea you'd find him, but the minute you did, I had this terrible feeling that it would come to this."

"To what?"

"To me having to tell you all this. Patty made me promise to never tell you. Until recently I kept that promise easily because you never really asked. Now you're asking me to go against her wishes after all these years?"

Nothing mattered more now than getting to the bottom of who Daniel really was. What made him tick, who mattered most. I had to figure out how to reason with such a ruthless and uncompromising man. I pushed on, unwilling to let guilt mix into what I was feeling right now.

"You're not going against her wishes. I already know who he is. I did that all by myself. Now all I need is for you to help me fill in the blanks."

"That damn picture." She mumbled a curse under her breath. She rarely cursed. She sighed again. "They were in love. Any stranger could see that. I told you once that everyone loved Patty. That's true. She was pretty, of course, but warm and charismatic too. She had a beautiful energy that drew people to her, and Daniel saw that. Like a moth to a flame, he had to have her. He pursued her, pulled out all the stops. Romantic as hell really, and it didn't take long before she was head over heels for him too. After a matter of months, they were inseparable."

"So what went wrong?"

"The school year was coming to a close. Obviously she wanted to know where the relationship was going and if they had a future. Every time she asked him about it, he'd dodge the question. He'd put her off, saying they'd didn't need to worry about it right now. They'd talk about it when the time came. Of course the time came when she realized she was pregnant. She needed answers. Now or never, she had to know if they were going to be together."

"Did he end it?"

"No, he sent her back to her family in Chicago after graduation. Told her he had to try to work it out with his family. A high-powered staunchly political family like his was bound to have strong opinions about the situation. It didn't matter that she came from a good family. He could play around all he wanted, but they expected him to marry someone strategic, someone who could bring value to the family and the Fitzgerald name."

"Sounds like an old-fashioned notion."

"Hardly. Not when money and power are at stake, trust me."

"So what happened?"

"She came back home and waited. Weeks went by. Finally, he called her and told her that it wasn't going to work out between them. He'd be starting law school in the fall, and having a wife and a baby simply didn't play into those plans. His family wouldn't have any part of it."

"He ended it, just like that?"

"He said he loved her, truly did. She said he seemed sorry, for what it's worth, but he was like a puppet in that family. So dependent on the wealth, slave to the expectations. He had a future all planned out for him that he had to live up to. She, and you, didn't fit into that plan."

I knew the story well, but to imagine Daniel— intimidating, powerful Daniel—like that seemed strange. He'd been like half the people I'd gone to school with at Harvard, independent and cocky as hell until parents' weekend, and then how quickly they fell in line. They couldn't risk losing Mommy and Daddy's financial support.

"Wow."

Who knew how he really felt, but Marie had completely discredited what he'd told me.

"Did he know she was going to keep me?"

"No. He told her she should end the pregnancy, but Patty never told him what she planned to do. They never spoke again, so he might have assumed that she did."

I thought back to our brief time at his house on the Cape, when I'd asked him why my mother had never told me about him. *After she went back to Chicago, I assumed she was going to take care of it. I didn't hear from her, and I didn't want to reach out and raise suspicions with her family.*

Dirty fucking liar.

I sat in stunned silence, trying to wrap my head around why he would possibly want anything to do with me now after cutting us off so coldly before. His life was following the grand plan that had been laid out for him years ago. What was so different that I now fit into it?

Marie came over to sit next to me and took my hands in hers. "This is why she never told you, baby. Do you hate me for telling you?"

"Of course not. I should know this. Really. It just doesn't make a lot of sense that he wants to know me now." I shook my head.

"Erica, I don't know what's happened to change his mind about having you in his life, other than the circumstance of you finding him. But I truly hope he deserves you now, after what he did."

I leaned in to hug Marie. She held me tight, stroking my hair like my mother used to. I sagged into her thin frame, wishing I could cry. I held back, knowing that if I started up again, I'd probably never stop. My brief control on my emotions was slipping. I gave her a kiss good night and excused myself for the night, promising her that I was fine. I was just fine.

I made myself comfortable in Marie's guest bedroom. I'd taken the half empty wine glass with me and decided to empty it all at once. To hell with Daniel. To hell with this terrible fucking day.

I set the glass on the bed stand and unpacked my suitcase. I never minded staying with Marie, but these circumstances weren't exactly what they'd used to be. Summer breaks, holiday weekends. Now I was running away from my life with no ideas about where I'd land next.

I glanced at my phone, and against my better judgment, I picked it up and read a text from Blake.

Call me. Let me fix this. I love you.

★ ★ ★

I barely made it to work on time. I had loosely considered taking the day off, but I had a whole team of people at the office while I wasn't. I'd cried myself to sleep after seeing Blake's text. If texts could kill, his words would have sliced right through me. I turned my phone off after that, determined not to turn it back on until I could get a handle on myself. This crying shit had to stop.

I waved to the crew upon my arrival and disappeared into my office. Risa was immediately there giving me an update, which involved me prepping more contracts for her and coordinating the new account assets with the guys. For once I was grateful for her boundless energy and relentless work ethic. Even though I was exhausted, she threw me right into work, which is really where my focus should have been for the past couple weeks.

My mind had too often been someplace else. Thinking of Blake, worried about Mark, but today I dove into the day's work with a kind of fervor that made everything else blur into the background. If I couldn't make it go away, I'd settle for blurry.

James had mapped out a few campaign options for us over the weekend. The three of us spent most of the afternoon trying to agree on a direction. I wanted to give Risa's opinion more weight, but despite her gusto when it came to landing new accounts, she seemed to go a little soft around James. Whenever he spoke, she emphatically agreed. When he leaned in to point something out, so did she, taking every possible opportunity to touch him casually.

When I finally gave her another task that took her out of my office, James seemed to visibly relax. We talked through the rest of the notes and the conversation was easier. But I caught him giving me questioning looks.

"You okay?"

I tried to avoid his eyes. They bore into me with an intensity I was growing used to. "I'm fine." I plastered on a fake smile.

"You seem tired."

"I am," I admitted, feeling the exhaustion a little more acutely.

"How were things with you and Landon after the other night?"

I closed my eyes for a moment, pushing down the surge of emotion that came with the mention of his name.

"I think we're all set with these graphics, James. Just take care of the few little tweaks we discussed and we should be ready to roll these out."

Anything else was none of his damn business. I didn't want to talk about Friday's weird showdown between him and Heath, or my relationship ending with Blake, or the way he touched me the other night as if we'd known each other far longer and better than we did. I was going to stuff all that right down with the rest of the feelings I didn't feel like facing right now.

"That's not really an answer."

I sighed and leaned back in my chair. "We broke up this weekend, if you must know."

"Does that affect the business with him being an investor?"

"No, he's a silent investor and he can't call the loan, not that he would anyway. Regardless, I'd like to pay him back as soon as we're able to so we can be independent again."

"How are you holding up?"

"I'm fine," I lied. I was grateful that he cared, but I worried that wasn't all he felt.

"I hope you know that you can talk to me. I'm right here."

"Thanks, James."

"Excuse me."

My gaze darted to where Blake now stood at the edge of my office space. He glanced to me briefly before fixing his gaze on James. James met the look with a steely one of his own that I'd never seen before. Holy shit, this wasn't good.

No one moved.

Blake looked back to me, barely able to mask the irritation in his voice. "Can I speak with you, privately?"

I opened my mouth to speak but James spoke first.

"We're in a meeting." He leaned back into his chair and crossed his arms, as if he meant to stay.

"I wasn't talking to you." Blake wasn't masking his irritation anymore. He took a threatening step, prompting James to rise too. They were a few feet apart staring each other down. Blake had some height on James, but James was thicker, stockier by nature. They could be evenly matched, but I'd seen Blake in action before. The way he'd lashed out when protecting me was a wild card that James couldn't begin to fathom.

I rose quickly and grabbed Blake's arm, urging him away from this standoff with James. "Blake, let's go talk outside." He stood still, his muscles taut and unmoving. Finally he relaxed enough to turn and leave the office with me. I led him down the hallway, thankful that we were far enough from the office to have some privacy, even if our words became heated.

"What did you want to talk about?" I asked him tensely.

"Why don't we start with him? What went down this weekend? Did you fuck him?"

I gasped at the accusation, my anger now matching his own. "No! I told you he's a friend. He's just being protective."

"What makes him think that you need protecting?"

"You seem to think I do pretty regularly, so maybe it's an epidemic. Maybe I'm the kind of girl that screams damsel in distress. I don't fucking know, but right now I don't need you coming in here and causing problems. This is where I work. If you want to talk, we can do that, but not here. You can't come here like this."

"I'm not allowed to come here now?"

I hesitated, briefly considering whether that was an appropriate concession to make. Seeing him under any circumstances was risky though. "I don't think it's a good idea, Blake."

"Let me get this straight. You're breaking up with me, for no reason other than you need space to figure out your life. And now you're cutting me out of the business that I've invested four million dollars into, and you're expecting me to just back off? No questions asked?"

I leaned back into the wall, the exhaustion taking its hold on me again. "You're not here on business. If you were, we'd be having a very different conversation."

"You're right. I'm not."

"Then you should go."

I turned my head, avoiding his eyes. He lifted his hand slowly and turned me back, forcing me to meet his gaze, intense and full of determination.

"You're running away from something. Maybe me, but guess what? I'm not letting you this time. You need time to figure things out? Fine, but we're figuring them out together. Let's go back home and talk this out."

Panic welled up. I'd never survive one-on-one with him like that, telling half-truths until he was somehow convinced. He'd keep on this way, stopping in on me, tracking me down until I gave him an answer that made sense. The more we hashed this out, the weaker my arguments would feel and sound. He needed to believe me, once and for all because if Daniel saw us together… I couldn't go there.

"I don't need time to figure out what I already know."

I brushed his hand away. "There's nothing you can say to change how I feel. I'm going to pay you back as soon as I can, but I can't have you involved with the business right now. I'll talk to Sid about taking over the lease as soon as possible, but you'll get your rent either way." I made myself believe it and met his gaze. I couldn't let him doubt it, risking everything because I couldn't end this right.

He bridged the distance between us, catching my face in his palm with renewed determination. My breath caught, and I fought every instinct not to kiss him. His lips were so close. His ragged breathing matched my own.

"You love me." He clenched his teeth as he uttered the words, as if they burned him.

I went to war with the magnetic force between us even as I felt myself slipping, losing control. *You have to protect him*, I reminded myself. His life depended on it.

"If you love me, you'll let me go." My heart broke at Daniel's words used against the man I loved.

Tracing the hard line of his jaw, I felt it soften under my touch. I pressed up on to my toes to kiss him gently. One last kiss. He angled to deepen the kiss, but I pushed him back before he could.

"Goodbye, Blake."

I was all the way down the hall when he finally spoke.

"Don't come back, Erica."

His words leveled me. My insides twisted at the possibility of losing any chance for our future. I turned to face him, scared of what I'd see in his eyes. His hands fisted at his sides and his jaw clenched tight, the muscles bulging.

"If you end this now, don't bother coming back."

With trembling hands, I opened the door to the office

and disappeared inside, closing the door on everything that was most precious to me.

CHAPTER THIRTEEN

The rest of the week passed in a blur. I barely left the office. My once welcomed focus on work had degraded into a compulsion to keep moving forward despite my lack of sleep. Even when I was sleeping, the visions that haunted me weren't conducive to real rest.

Somehow, the fatigue and the pressure I put on myself to keep working masked a lot of the pain. The giant gaping hole in my chest where my heart used to be didn't seem so devastating when all I pretended to care about were numbers and lists and driving the business forward with breakneck speed. Everyone at work was keeping up. At this rate, maybe I wouldn't need Daniel's money after all. I'd wanted to pay Blake back as quickly as possible in any case.

I was in the middle of a meeting with Risa when Daniel called. I let her know I needed to take this and waited to pick up until she had gone.

"Hello."

"Erica, I'm downstairs. I'd like to speak with you." His voice was cold and commanding. "Come out the back."

I hung up and let Risa know I was leaving for an early lunch. I pushed the back door open and found Connor at the wheel of the Lincoln idling in the alleyway. Daniel was leaning against the hood smoking a cigarette, wearing his usual dark suit and white collared shirt. The picture of the politician, I thought, as my mind raced through the reasons for his being here. Marie, Blake... I couldn't speak for the fear that had gripped me then.

"You hungry?"

I shook my head, more out of confusion than to really answer him. "What's wrong?"

"Nothing. Let's get some lunch." He pushed off the car and flicked the cigarette away. He opened the car door and motioned for me to get in, his expression unreadable.

I forced myself to move. Once upon a time, I had warmed upon seeing him, even as intimidating as he had come across at times. I once welcomed our time together, and now I had to force my limbs into action to join him in the car.

"Connor, take us to O'Neill's."

I took a few deep breaths, trying to calm my nerves. O'Neill's sounded innocent enough. Maybe he did just want to have lunch. All those sleepless nights had ratcheted up my anxiety enormously.

"What did you want to see me about?"

"I meant to come see you earlier, but I thought you could use some time. How are things with Landon?"

A wave of relief came over me that Blake was safe, quickly replaced by a reminder of the pain of our separation.

"I wouldn't know. I haven't seen him in days." I stared out the window, hoping he wasn't going to make me regurgitate the details of our breakup.

"Good. He seems to have accepted that, I gather."

I shrugged, trying to ignore the ache in my chest at the thought that Blake might have given up on us finally. That's what I wanted, right? I hadn't heard from him all week, a fact that gave me solace and tormented me all at the same time. I swallowed against the tears that burned my eyes. Now was not the time for that.

"Did he mean that much to you?"

His voice was softer than I expected, and I turned to face him, blinking away the wetness. I swore I saw a flicker of pain there, though I reasoned I was only projecting my own.

I weighed his question. Blake meant everything to me, but what good would it do telling Daniel?

"I asked you a question."

"He's the only man I've ever loved."

He tensed slightly and looked away.

The truth and his strange reaction made me feel a little bold. "I don't really have time for these little meetings. Can we get to the point of why I'm here?"

"Watch yourself."

He narrowed his eyes a fraction that reminded me how frightening he could become in an instant. I silently wondered who I got my temper from, though I'd never hold a candle to Daniel in that department.

"I told you I'm taking you to lunch."

I crossed my arms, making sure I was pressed tightly on the farthest side of the seat. Connor had driven us south of the city, and we passed blocks of row houses until we were driving down the main drag of a small downtown.

"Where are we?"

"The old neighborhood. This is where your grandfather and his father grew up, before being a Fitzgerald meant anything."

I sat back and took it in. I'd never been to this part of the city. A far cry from the clean tourist-flooded streets of downtown. We weren't exactly in the safest part of town either. Connor pulled up in front of a tavern on the corner. A worn sign read *O'Neill's*.

I followed Daniel out and stood awkwardly beside him as he shook hands with the man who sat on a stool just outside the entrance. He was as broad and muscle bound as Connor, but with jet-black curly hair and dark eyes mostly hidden by the hair and the shade of a tweed cap. He greeted Daniel by name and let us pass.

We entered the dark room of the tavern and took a seat in the far corner. Daniel ordered us beers and a couple burgers. O'Neill's no doubt had a limited menu so I didn't argue. That, and I decided to pick my battles with Daniel unless I wanted to get into the habit of covering up bruises. God, was I grateful my mother couldn't see me now.

"I'd like to talk business," he began.

I didn't want to get into that yet. I needed to learn more about him if I was going to find my way out of this mess. "How's Margo?" I asked, hoping to divert the conversation away from his master plan for my life.

"As well as can be expected." He downed a good part of his beer. I let mine sit.

"She wants me to stay away from you, you know? At the gala she told me as much. She won't be happy to see me anywhere close to your campaign or your personal life."

"She means well, but these decisions aren't up to her."

"Won't it cause tension if I'm blatantly disregarding her wishes?"

"Margo is the least of our concerns."

"Perhaps you could enlighten me of your concerns. Are threatening to kill Blake and liquidating my business still high on your list of priorities?"

He grinned slowly. "If you think that mouth won't get you into trouble because we're in public, you've got another thing coming."

I glanced around quickly. The bar was sparse, and its patrons didn't seem to be the type of people who would care much about a little lunchtime quarrel. Not to mention Daniel appeared to be a preferred customer here. Maybe these were the people who took care of his wet work, when people like Mark needed to be taken care of.

Daniel was right. Sassing him would probably get me nowhere fast. I sulked back into the seat.

He dropped a thick stack of paper onto the table and pushed it over to me. "Here's our marketing plan. I don't have time to read it, and if I did, I'm not sure I'd be able to make much sense of it. I'm told its very general since we're responding to new political and local developments daily, and all of that varies. We'll start the hiring process soon to replace the person heading things up now. It's all for show of course, since you're the one I'll be bringing on."

"What about my business?"

"Landon is out of the picture, and you'll get your money from me soon enough. Figure out a way for it to run without you, or sell it. I don't care which."

"If you gave me more time, I could get in the black on my own, without your help."

"How much time?"

"A couple months maybe. I'm not sure," I lied. Realistically, I'd probably need six months or more.

"No, there's no time for that."

I leaned in, hoping to persuade him. "Daniel, I could

help you find someone for this position. Someone with the same background who can bring the same qualities to the table that I can. I don't know why—"

"Erica, this isn't a negotiation." His voice sharpened enough to attract a couple looks from the bar. "You'll be working for the campaign. Working for me. I can see now that you're trying to figure a creative way out of this. As you do, be sure to keep one thing in mind. I don't care what Landon means to you. He could be the father of your children, and I wouldn't hesitate to remove him from the equation. Not for a second would I hesitate on that choice. Do you understand? Because I thought I'd made myself pretty clear last time."

The bartender dropped off our burgers and vanished again without a word. I stared at the plate with no appetite, sickened by the threat.

"Erica."

I closed my eyes and delivered my next words as calmly as I could. "I understand you perfectly. If you're hiring me to use my brain, however, you might want to tell me at what point I should lie down and let people walk all over me. Or are you the only person who'll be doing that?"

"This isn't about you, you little bitch."

He slammed his hand down on the table, attracting a few bored stares from the bar again. Frightened, I sat back in the seat to gain a few more inches of distance from his anger.

"This is about something far more important and far more successful than you'll ever be. My family. *Our* family. We've spent generations crawling out of places like this so that we could do something bigger. You're going to be a part of that now. A small, albeit important, part, and the sooner you realize that, the better off you'll be. Now eat your burger."

"I'm not hungry," I murmured.

His eyes became so cold that I immediately picked up a fry and started eating it. We ate in silence and occasionally our eyes met, cool blue mirrors of each other's. I'd be lucky to escape his wrath on the drive back. This wasn't like bickering with Blake or keeping people on the right track at work. I was poking the giant, and he wasn't sleeping. Daniel might have been proud of my accomplishments, but I didn't have the luxury of being Daddy's little girl who could get away with mouthing off to him like that. Not when Blake's life was at stake. I'd have to somehow learn to shut the hell up or play the game differently, because meeting him head-on wasn't taking me very far.

★ ★ ★

Connor dropped me at the office after a mostly silent ride back, save Daniel's promise to let me know about what time to come into the campaign headquarters so I could meet with the staff there. I made a mental note of it and spent the rest of the drive staring out the window, feeling my life slipping away.

I walked in to find Risa pulled up next to James's desk, smiling and chatting away while he shifted his focus uncomfortably between his computer screen and her. Something about it set me off.

"Risa, can I speak with you?"

She sat up straight, as if I'd broken the spell between them that existed only in her mind. She followed me back to the office.

"This needs to stop," I said bluntly, unable to soften my delivery.

"What?"

"This thing you have for James. We can't have these kinds of distractions. I need you focused on work, not spending half the day at his desk flirting."

"I don't know what you mean." She frowned and tucked her hair behind her ear nervously.

"I know we don't have an official policy on relationships in the office, because frankly I didn't foresee that being an issue, but now that it is, I see why companies put these things in place. Set your sights on someone else. I need him working and I need you focused."

Her jaw snapped shut and her face turned beet red. I couldn't tell if she was more embarrassed or angry, but calling her out had taken her completely off guard. I'd brushed her off before, but never reprimanded her directly like this. I simply didn't have the patience to dance around it anymore. Not today.

"What about you and Blake?"

I'd been pent up with wanting to tell Daniel what I really thought about him for the better part of two hours. I really should have picked a better time to speak with her, but here we were. I spoke slowly, trying to maintain my composure.

"He's an investor, not an employee, and my relationship with him isn't any of your business."

She pursed her lips and tapped her toe on the floor.

"Okay, let's move on. Any updates?" I said, hoping to neutralize the tension and get back to work.

She stared at me for a second before taking in a deep breath.

"I'm attending a fundraiser on Saturday. It's for a foundation that supports tech education for inner-city kids. Max thought it might be good for us to have a presence there."

"Sure, that sounds like something we could get behind."

"I thought so too, but I wasn't sure if donations were in the budget or not."

"I'm sure we can pull something together."

"Great, just let me know and I'll make the arrangements."

"That might be the type of event that I would attend, you know."

I tried not to be offended at her surprised look.

"I didn't realize that. You seem really distracted lately. I didn't want to bother you with it. I know you have other things you could be doing, and the networking thing is my job. Sorry, I guess I should have asked you about it."

"It's fine. I've had a lot going on."

"Did you want to come? I can call Max and try to get an extra ticket."

I considered the offer for a moment. I hadn't been beyond Marie's or the office in a while. The idea of mingling with people when I was still feeling so fucked up was a little petrifying, but I could use the distraction. If nothing else, networking was better than being alone with my thoughts.

"I think I would, actually. Might be a nice change of pace."

"All right. I'll see what I can do." She gave me a tight smile and left briskly.

I sighed inwardly, thankful that we'd talked a little. She

was pissed, but I didn't want tension between us to affect work. And heaven knew I'd been a walking disaster for the past couple weeks. I only knew what it felt like on the inside. I couldn't imagine how I was being perceived on the outside, and most of the time I didn't really care. So much was up in the air right now. Tiptoeing around people's feelings at work wasn't something I had energy for.

The rest of the day went along quickly. I ignored the marketing plan that Daniel had given me. I cared enough about my work to know I'd take a genuine interest in the contents of the document. That was exactly what he wanted, and I couldn't handle the idea of catering to his wants right now. He'd ruined my relationship with Blake, and I was determined to delay becoming part of the Fitzgerald political machine as long as possible.

CHAPTER FOURTEEN

I stopped in at the apartment to find something suitable to wear for the event. I hadn't packed formalwear in my mad dash to leave, and Marie and I couldn't really share clothes with our body types.

Being in the apartment again seemed strange. I hadn't made any effort to find a new place, though. Not as if I'd had much time, but deep down I also couldn't imagine being anywhere else yet. Marie's spare room was fine. A place to try to sleep, and at least I wasn't alone there. I couldn't bring myself to think about starting over someplace new though.

I put my rent check on the counter for Sid. Out of habit, I started to clean up the small messes that had accumulated.

"You don't need to do that."

Cady walked out of Sid's room in a long T-shirt that seemed to swallow her up. She looked tired and content as she padded into the kitchen to help me. Her spiky frosted blond hair was pushed every which way.

I turned to put some dishes in the sink, hiding a grin. Sid was making a girl tired and content. Go him.

"I don't mind," I said.

"I'm not sure how Sid would survive without someone taking care of him." She laughed.

"No kidding. Guys…"

We made quick work of it and she picked up the rent check, glancing up at me.

"You plan on coming back sometime?"

I hesitated. Sure, she was Sid's girlfriend, but she was also Blake's assistant. I could almost guarantee that anything I said to her would make its way back to him.

"No plans to, but I haven't found a new place yet."

She gave me a sympathetic smile. "That's too bad. I'm sure Sid will miss having you around."

"Maybe. He has you now though."

"Yeah, well, I don't think he's the only one who misses you."

I grabbed a bottle of water from the fridge and drank some of it down, not acknowledging those last words.

"I know it's not my place to say anything. Whatever happens with you and Blake is between you two, but for what it's worth, I thought you two were great together. He seemed really happy. And I've known him a long time."

"How's he doing?"

I'm not sure why I asked. As if knowing more about Blake's state of mind would make me feel any better about things.

She gave me a sympathetic look. "You should talk to him, Erica."

★ ★ ★

I settled on a simple black strapless cocktail dress that hugged my curves and fell just below my knees. I pulled my hair into a loose twist and slipped on some black strappy heels and a light shawl in case the venue was cool.

When I arrived at the event, I found Risa and Max talking among a small group. Max flashed me his award-winning smile. The couple they were speaking to waved their goodbyes and walked off, leaving us alone.

"You look beautiful, Erica. Thanks for coming tonight."

"Thanks, I'm glad I did. Risa told me a little bit, but how are you involved with the charity?"

"Angelcom has been a supporter for several years. We sponsor this event once a year to attract new donors and bring visibility to the cause."

"That's wonderful."

I still hadn't quite forgiven Max for pushing me into that last dance with Mark, but I couldn't argue that he'd been incredibly helpful to the business since then. I wasn't giving him the benefit of the doubt, but with Blake out of the picture now, I wasn't going to write him off completely either. Times like these, I had a hard time believing the terrible things Blake assured me were true of him.

"We should probably find our table. They'll be serving dinner shortly," he said, interrupting my thoughts.

I followed Risa and Max to the table and quickly recognized the faces of the others who joined us. Heath rose when he saw me, but my gaze went immediately to Blake and the woman by his side.

Sophia.

I stopped short, frozen with the prospect of facing any of them right now. The man I loved next to a woman I despised. The pain of our separation became exponentially potent. The regret of every moment we'd spent apart hit me with full force, seizing my lungs. My breath left me in a rush.

As much as I'd hated Sophia and what she meant to his past, I wasn't remotely prepared to see them together tonight, or ever for that matter. She looked impeccable in a silky red dress that contrasted beautifully with her sleek black hair falling over her shoulders. With Blake in his suit, the dark gray one that I loved, the two made a beautiful couple. The billionaire and the model. What a match.

"It's good to see you, Erica." Heath broke the silence and gave me a quick hug.

Blake held my gaze, as if he were waiting for me to react. But I couldn't move. I literally couldn't take a single step toward the table.

Risa found her seat next to Max, leaving one unoccupied place between her and Heath. I eyed it warily, uncertain how I could possibly survive this dinner with Blake and Sophia across from us. Maybe I could leave before the event really got underway—feign illness or something.

As if reading my thoughts, Sophia gave me a knowing smile that had me grinding with rage. "So glad you could come, Erica. Join us."

Her words somehow broke the trance, and I needed to move. In the opposite direction.

"Risa, I'm going to grab a drink. Do you want anything?"

She shook her head. "I'm fine, thanks."

Blake rose as I started to leave. I ignored him and carried on toward the bar, reminding myself that I couldn't really sprint in my heels.

"Jack on the rocks," I said to the bartender.

Blake came up next to me. "Same."

We weren't touching but we were close, inches apart. I remembered our first few weeks together when I tried in vain to ignore the palpable energy that pulsed between us, an undeniable attraction that had quickly turned into an addiction, an obsession.

"I didn't know you'd be here." His voice was quiet, laced with regret.

Or what? You wouldn't have brought her?

I took in a slow breath, trying to get a handle on my emotions. He was being nice, and I should at least make an attempt at normal post-break up communications. But the silence that hung in the air between us seemed to be answer enough. I was miserable, work-obsessed, and had no idea how to reason with my power-crazed murdering father so that I could end all this.

Maybe it was too late for that anyway. Sophia had probably picked up right where I'd left off as soon as she realized I was out of the picture. She'd have been a fool not to, and I couldn't blame Blake. I'd told him in no uncertain terms that I didn't want to see him anymore. To let me go.

"How is Risa working out?" he finally asked in another attempt to get me talking.

"She's very motivated. Closing a ton of accounts for us."

"Seems like she's warmed right up to Max."

I glanced back at the table. Risa appeared to be her usual animated self, and Max's attention was fixed on whatever she was saying. I hadn't paid too much attention to how their connection had been evolving over the past few weeks. As she'd aptly noted, I had too many other things on my mind to care as long as she was doing her job and moving us forward.

"He's been helping her connect with advertisers. Seems to be working out well. Revenues are up." My focus shifted to Sophia, who caught me staring. I turned back, catching my reflection in the mirror behind the bar. "Sophia looks beautiful, as usual."

Blake took a sip of his drink. "She's in town for business."

"You don't need to make excuses to me, Blake. I'm... happy for you." My jaw tightened at the complete lie that I'd just uttered in the name of being polite and allowing us to both move on. Then I let half the drink slide down my throat.

"You're a terrible liar."

★ ★ ★

I made my way back to the table and Blake followed without a word. I was grateful to be sitting next to Heath. Somehow at this table of colleagues and ex-lovers, he felt like an ally. We made small talk about the event and how work was going.

"Have you talked to Alli about moving yet?" I asked.

He shook his head.

"Any particular reason why?"

"I guess I'm a little scared of what she'll say. I'm almost done with the program though, so I need to figure it out soon."

"You should talk to her, Heath."

"So should you."

I nodded and made the mistake of looking at Sophia, who was taking every opportunity to touch Blake. Small touches, tracing the angles of his suit over his shoulder. Leaning into him as she spoke, her perky little tits brushing against him. I gritted my teeth.

"She's really worried about you."

I looked back to Heath, unable to relax. "I'll call her soon. I've been really busy with work, you know. Haven't had much time for anything else."

"She's not the only one who's worried."

My gaze darted back to Blake, who was leaning back in his chair, looking bored as he scanned the room. Sophia was murmuring in his ear and laughing quietly, as if they were sharing some private joke. When her hand disappeared under the table, I couldn't take it anymore.

I pushed away from the table and made a beeline to the ladies' room. I regretted eating anything when a wave of nausea hit me. Pushing Blake away had been less devastating when he still wanted me. I could entertain the fantasy that he'd wait for me until I figured things out with Daniel. But that moment had passed. Sophia had moved right in, picked up where I'd left off, and was very likely giving him everything he'd been craving during the time we'd been together.

If my heart hadn't already been broken, seeing him with her had mashed it into an unrecognizable pulp.

I found the ladies' room mercifully abandoned. I looked at myself in the mirror. Despite being an epic emotional wreck, I looked okay. Makeup hid the dark circles under my eyes, at least. I was no runway model, but I'd been good enough for Blake. Once upon a time, I had been the one he wanted. I scolded myself for caring. I could get through this, somehow. I'd been through worse, right?

Before I could answer myself, the door swung open and I caught Sophia's reflection walking toward me. Her lithe runway-ready body sauntered up to the vanity counter where I was trying to pull myself together.

"Everything okay? You seem upset, Erica."

Her voice was the usual sultry laced with bitch that I'd remembered from our first meeting in New York.

I turned to face her. "What do you want?"

She leaned back against the wall casually, crossing her arms in front of her. "I thought we could catch up. I was sorry to hear things didn't work out with you and Blake."

My lips pulled into a tight line. I wouldn't take her bait. "I bet."

"Wasn't a good fit, I guess."

"How would you know?"

"I'm a friend, Erica. He talks to me. I'm sure it was all pretty overwhelming for you, being with him."

"What are you talking about?"

"The sex, of course. Let's not pretend we don't know that he likes it rough." She gave me a full smile and leaned her hip on the counter, cocking her head as if she were sizing me up. "You never struck me as the kind of girl who could get whipped."

I struggled for a breath, unable to hide my reaction. "You don't know a fucking thing about me, Sophia."

She laughed. The sound stung, as if she'd slapped me in the face.

"Oh, I think I know plenty."

I fisted my hands by my sides. What I wouldn't do to smack that look off her face. And Blake. A sickness spread through me. He'd told her personal things about us. Jealousy and betrayal was a lethal cocktail of emotions, and I'd had about all I could take.

"Laugh all you want, Sophia, but I'm not the one pining after a man who wrote me off years ago. Then again, maybe you'll get lucky and he'll take you back. Either way, I couldn't care less."

I pushed through the doors and returned to the table to grab my shawl. Feigning illness wasn't too difficult, because I literally felt sick. I said some quick goodbyes to Risa and Heath, ignoring Blake, even though I could feel the heat of his gaze on me. I couldn't face him now. That our memories meant so little to him that he'd share them with Sophia cut me far deeper than I'd ever thought possible.

The city lights flew by as the cab headed back to Marie's. The sparsely lit towers disappeared behind me, along with any hope I'd held for being with Blake again. Something felt devastatingly final about all this. The urge to cry and the gut-wrenching despair was replaced by a cold, emotionless finality. Blake was gone. I'd finally lost him.

I'd lost people before. I knew how to say goodbye, forever. But I couldn't remember anything hurting like this before. My reason for living, for waking up in the morning, anything that had kept me hoping before had been stripped from me. But I knew I'd survived this kind of devastation before.

Somewhere in the depths of my soul, I stopped bleeding. The relentless pulsing pain slowed, and the memory of who we'd been together became another scar.

I knew how to live with scars.

I wiped away the last tear, swallowing down the urge to cry until I went numb, my body's natural reaction when faced with unrelenting emotional pain. My love for Blake had changed, becoming a dark and bittersweet memory forever imprinted on my past. My greatest love had become my greatest loss.

CHAPTER FIFTEEN

"You staying late again?"

James took a seat across from my desk. It was the end of the day and we were the only ones left. More and more days were ending this way. I couldn't stop myself.

"Thinking about it," I said.

"I don't know what the numbers are, but I'm pretty sure you don't need to be pushing yourself this hard."

"I don't mind long hours. Keeps me out of trouble." I was only half-joking. I wasn't exactly resigned to the new life Daniel wanted for me yet. Not that he'd given me a choice, but I had agreed to meet with his team in a few days. I'd been dissecting their marketing plan in the meantime and trying to game plan strategies that would allow me to contribute in a capacity that would satisfy Daniel without writing off my own business.

"You're going to burn out. Do you realize that?" James leaned forward, resting his elbows on his knees and bringing his hands to his chin.

"Why do you care, James? Honestly. I'm not putting it off on you guys."

"I wouldn't mind it if you did. Sometimes you just don't seem very happy."

I sighed. "Does it really matter? Happy or not, I'm here and we're getting things done." Who cares if I wanted to work myself into the ground? That was my prerogative.

"Actually I don't think it's good for you or the business. If you break down, who do we have? The team's not big enough to sustain without you. If you keep going like this, you're going to be worthless in another week or two. Then what? What if something goes down and we really need you?"

"You're making a big deal out of nothing," I muttered, wondering what I could say for him to ease up.

As closely as I was working with Risa, I definitely had a better connection with James. When it came to work, he seemed to understand what I was looking for without really asking. A silent rapport that builds between two people who work closely for a long time already seemed to exist between us, and somehow that made this line of questioning more tolerable. But he couldn't possibly begin to understand my life right now.

"All right, will you at least take a break? Let me take you out for something to eat."

"I'm not hungry." I wasn't. I rarely was these days. I'd probably be waif thin like Sophia in no time, but not by choice. I simply had no appetite for food, or much else, for that matter.

"Okay, how about a walk. Just give me an hour and then I'll leave you alone, I promise."

I rolled my eyes.

"Please?"

He gave me an innocent but determined look that was hard to resist. I couldn't fathom why he cared so much, but I couldn't deny that it pulled at my heartstrings a bit.

I pushed away from my desk. "Fine. One hour. I have to finish edits on these contracts tonight." I didn't, but if pretending like I was fine for an hour meant getting out from under his relentless interrogation into my mental health, I would do it.

We walked down the block and James stopped in front of his motorcycle. He unhooked a helmet and handed a second one to me from a different compartment.

"Uh, no. I don't do motorcycles."

"I've been riding since I was a teenager. I promise you'll be safe. I'll go slow."

"This wasn't part of our deal."

"There were no clauses about motorcycles. Jesus, Erica, you've been writing too many contracts." He gave me a little smirk that melted my anger. "You gave me an hour. Relax, okay? It'll be fun."

I reluctantly put on the helmet, feeling a little ridiculous. He helped me buckle it and gave me a little pat on the top of the head that only added to my self-consciousness. I carefully took the seat behind him and we started moving.

The engine roared to life. He grabbed my hand and wrapped my arm around his waist.

"Hold on!"

I did, not caring how unprofessionally close it meant we'd be. I was suddenly and perhaps irrationally petrified of flying off as he eased out onto the street and propelled us ahead. I held on tight, trying not to totally freak out. He covered my hand with his own and gave it a squeeze.

I had no idea where we were going and didn't bother asking. I finally relaxed a little, not enough to loosen my hold on him but enough to feel the thrill of the speed. We zipped through the busy city streets and past the cars that were still stuck in the rush hour traffic heading home after work.

We drove until we were riding along the ocean. The beach was mostly empty, dotted with a few runners and people kite surfing farther away from the shore. James parked and helped me off. We walked down to the beach together, slipping off our shoes at the end of the path.

The air was perfectly warm with the ocean breeze blowing over us. The waves crashed gently onto the shore. I didn't come to the ocean much, but whenever I did, I had a really hard time worrying about anything. Something about the hypnotic and soothing motion of the waves and the endless horizon of the sea washed away the noise and the stress that had taken up residence in my mind. Even now, with everything I was dealing with, I felt a rare sense of peace.

I wanted to hold onto that for as long as I could. I made a silent mental note to get out here more. The long train ride would be worth it.

"Let's go in."

I laughed. "Are you kidding? Do you have any idea how cold it is in there?"

"I know exactly how cold it is. I've been swimming in the ocean up here all my life. Come on, don't wimp out on me." His lips curled up into a mischievous smile.

"No, thanks. I'll stick with heated pools and warmer seas."

He stripped off his shirt. The dark ink that peeked out under his sleeves was on full display now, the flames of an ornate design licking across his skin. He was undeniably gorgeous. He wasn't as lean as Blake, but he was definitely toned. He'd spent a few hours in the gym, I guessed.

"You know what they say about salt water."

I shot my gaze back up to his, embarrassed that I'd been gawking. People could look at tattoos, right? That was normal.

"What do they say about it?" My eyes wandered again.

"Ocean and tears are the cure for all ills. One dip in that ocean, and you'll be as good as new." He stood there before me half naked in his board shorts.

I tore my gaze away and drew a line in the sand with my bare toe. Ocean and tears, huh? If that were true, I'd be cured for all the tears I'd cried over these past couple weeks.

Before I could get lost in my own thoughts again, James hoisted me up and over his shoulder. The sand traveled below us too quickly as he carried me to the water.

"No, James. Let me go!" I screamed, trying to be legitimately angry, but I laughed as he waded in. I rotated my shrieks with uncontrollable laughter, kicking and trying to wriggle free from his grasp. He was past his waist now and I was really starting to worry. He wouldn't really throw me in, would he?

"James, stop, don't you dare! Put me down!"

"Whatever you say boss." With that, he tossed me in, giving me just enough air so that I crashed loudly into the water. I sucked in a quick breath. The cold ocean water rushed around me, shocking my senses. I let myself sink until I nearly touched the sandy bottom. The buoyancy of my body and the undulation of the ocean brought me back to the surface a moment later.

I filled my lungs with another breath as James swam away. I smiled and swam after him as fast as my arms and legs would take me. He was going to get it now. He turned just in time for me to catch him. I leveraged myself on his shoulders and tried to push him down into the water with all my strength. The effort was pointless. Humoring me, he feigned the dunk. He disappeared under the water.

I stood there and waited. I tried to follow his path but lost him, feeling anxious and oddly giddy. The moment lasted long enough that I started to worry a little. I scanned the waters around me. Then his arms banded around my thighs and lifted me out of the water. I screamed again and giggled. He loosened his hold, and I slid down his body, slowly and, damn it, suggestively. There was nothing between us but the thin cotton of my clothes—leaving little to the imagination.

My smile slipped at the sensation. My heart ratcheted up, my body coming alive in a familiar way. The water didn't seem so cold anymore. The waves lapped against our skin as he held me firmly. The bright blue of his eyes darkened slightly as his gaze dropped to my mouth. I was panting softly. Definitely from the swimming and the shock of being thrown in the water, I assured myself. Except I couldn't catch my breath now, and the hand that wasn't holding me close to him slid down my thigh, catching me at the knee to hook me around his waist. My hands were frozen on his shoulders. I was afraid to move. He positioned my other leg so I was completely wrapped around him, my lips inches from his.

"God, you're beautiful," he whispered.

He brushed his fingertips along my cheekbone and down my jaw, the way he had at the office after I'd met with Daniel. Except his eyes weren't filled with concern. They were filled with something far more serious, a hunger that was slowly working its way through me. My fingers itched to move, but I resisted.

My eyes closed, and a vision of Blake passed behind them. The familiar pain shot through me, like an ice pick through my heart. I winced and untangled myself from James's body. Without waiting for a reaction, I ducked under the water as he had, swimming as fast as I could toward the shore. *Fuck, fuck, fuck.* This was the absolute last thing I needed right now.

I stepped clumsily out of the water, the pull of the tide nearly knocking me over as I tried moving in the opposite direction. Stepping into the air chilled me further, but the sun was still high in the sky. I wrung out my shirt, shorts, and my hair as best I could. Lying down on the warm sand, I welcomed the healing heat of the sun. I closed my eyes against the brightness and tried to concentrate on the sound of the waves.

My breathing slowed, and I idly wondered if my hour was up yet. What the hell was I doing? This was wrong. Way wrong.

James lay down beside me with a quiet rustle of his shorts and a shaky exhale. I opened one eye to see him lying on his side. He was propped up on his elbow looking at me, a pensive frown marking his beautiful face.

"There it is again." His voice was quiet.

"What?"

"That look. I was really hoping that somehow I could make that go away, but there it is again."

I sighed and draped my arm over my eyes. I wanted to melt away, wash away like the sand in the tide. "I'm sorry."

"Why would you be sorry?"

I should just get this over with. Lay it out for him so we

could stop dancing around it. I couldn't handle hurting two people. Somehow I had to make him understand that we could only be friends. What if he didn't want my friendship though?

I looked at him.

"You were right. I've been a mess, and right now work is the only thing keeping me from losing it completely. I'm trying to figure some things out, and focusing on work is the only way I know how to do that right now."

"You know, it's okay to feel messed up sometimes. Doesn't mean you have to push everyone away though—especially the people who care about you."

I sighed. "I know."

James wasn't the only one trying to get through to me. Marie had given me space, but I knew she was concerned. I still hadn't talked to Alli, and the growing distance between us weighed on me. Still, I couldn't bring myself to reach out to her beyond my vague texts. She was too close to Blake, and right now I needed as much distance as possible from him to keep him safe.

"This wasn't so bad, right?"

I gave him a small smile. "This was fun. I do feel better."

I wanted to say more, but against the advice he'd just given me, I decided that keeping him at a safe emotional distance was probably just as well. A part of me wanted to tell him that I felt more, to acknowledge the intense albeit brief moment we'd shared in the water, but to explain that it was a major breach in my non-existent company policies and procedures. But if I told him all that, I'd have to tell him how I was still hopelessly in love with my ex, who was probably tethering Sophia to a bedpost and fucking her senseless right now. Then I'd have to admit to myself that I'd probably never be over Blake, no matter how hard I tried.

★ ★ ★

Since we were in the neighborhood, I asked James to take a short detour on our way back into town. He drove us down the quiet street that I recognized by way of its new homes and meticulously manicured lawns. When he pulled up in front of Trevor's house, I was shocked to find a real estate sign stuck into the overgrown lawn that marked the property as sold. Somehow the place looked even more abandoned than it had before.

The cautious relief I'd felt before disappeared. This was a bad sign, literally. The only line I had to Trevor was this place. Blake probably hadn't dug anything valid up with the investment company in Texas since he'd never mentioned it. Then again, I hadn't given him a chance. I was too busy breaking up with him, and now, avoiding him.

"I'm guessing this place wasn't for sale when you came by before."

I shook my head. "No. This isn't good."

"Maybe he gave up hacking and started a new life somewhere else. Took up a new career or something."

"And put himself on the map for the first time ever? I seriously doubt it, but you get points for positive thinking."

"Seriously, there's no point in worrying about it. Be happy that he's giving us a break, and let's hope he's lost interest."

I sighed. "Let's hope."

He revved the engine, and we were off again.

We drove down Comm Ave and pulled up in front of the apartment. I slid off and returned the helmet to James. I was mostly dry, but I still felt awkward standing there. Especially after what had happened, I wasn't sure what to say.

"Thanks for the break."

"Sure thing. We should take breaks more often." He gave me a shy grin.

I didn't want to discredit his effort to cheer me up, but the attraction between us was real, as much as I wanted to downplay it. I wasn't sure if this was all a side effect of the breakup or something more. All I knew was I didn't need any more complications.

"I'll see you tomorrow, okay?" I gave him a little wave and headed up to my apartment.

I made my way to the bedroom and stripped off my clothes and my bra, still damp from the ocean. I rummaged through my drawers looking for a suitable replacement.

"Erica."

I screamed and spun around to find Blake in the doorway, his hands on either side of the doorframe.

"What are you doing here?" In the space of a few seconds my heart was racing. I was on display, clad only in my underwear now, as he stalked closer.

"Who was that?" His voice was calm and low.

"James."

His hand went to my shoulder, gently brushing the sand off of my skin. My body warmed at the contact. I secretly wished his hands would roam, but they slid away. He crossed his arms and stared.

"Frolicking on the beach with James. That doesn't

sound so innocent."

It wasn't, but I'd never tell him that.

"Are you fucking him yet?"

I rolled my eyes. I was growing tired of his insistence that I was sleeping with James. "Don't you think if I were fucking him, I'd be doing it right now?"

"Not unless you want me to bludgeon him to death. If so, by all means invite him up next time."

He came closer. The air crackled between us. The heat of his body rolled off in waves with the sexual tension that was about to drive me straight out of my mind. All the progress I'd made trying to work him out of my system had just disintegrated. I ached to fist my hands in his hair, crush my body to his.

"What about Sophia?" My voice was low. I almost hoped he hadn't heard me so I wouldn't have to hear his answer.

"What about her?"

My jaw clenched. "Are you fucking *her*?" I wasn't supposed to care, but I had to know.

"Would it matter?" His expression was impassive, cold even.

A wicked jealousy blazed through me. I narrowed my eyes. I had no right to be angry, but I was. She was a vile bitch, and I wanted nothing more than to scratch her fucking eyes out every time I saw her.

That she could give Blake what he needed in bed only added fuel to the fire. I turned around and tried to ignore the pull of Blake's body behind me. I fished out some jeans and a V-neck T-shirt that was tight and always gave him a good view of the girls. He couldn't keep his hands off me when I wore it. My brain was short-circuiting like crazy. I should make this quick and leave before I did something stupid.

I opened my underwear drawer and grabbed a dry pair. Before I closed the drawer I paused. I spun back around. "Have you been in here?"

"Missing something?" He grinned.

"You stole my vibrator. Who does that?"

"I told you before I was the only one who was going to make you come. By the sound of it, that hasn't changed."

I was speechless.

He closed the distance between us, nudging my legs apart with his thigh. He placed his hand over my throat and drew a broad path of fire over my breast and down my hip.

"I have a feeling you're due though."

My breath hitched at the sudden contact of his hands on my skin. With painstaking patience, he traced the band of my underwear, then over my ass and back down the front where he teased the flesh of my inner thigh. His touch was electric, jolting through me almost painfully. I mustered the strength to push his hand away, praying he'd leave me be, but he only came at me again, cupping me more aggressively through the thin cotton of my panties.

"Don't, Blake. I can't." But God, did I want to. His mouth and hands on me, to end this terrible torture.

His fingers pressed deliciously against me, stroking me through the separation of the fabric.

"This is mine, Erica. I own your pleasure. You and I both know it," he whispered in my ear, kissing my neck and trailing his tongue along the curve of my ear. *Sweet Jesus.*

"I can't... I can't do this."

"Yes, you can. You even want to."

He pushed my panties to the side and thumbed my clit.

"Fuck, you're already wet for me." His voice was rough, almost pained.

I sucked in a sharp breath, stifling a moan. The direct contact of his expert strokes sent me into orbit. My head fell back and I wanted to cry out for the feelings that rushed over me.

"Do you miss this? My hands on you, fucking you?"

I bit my lip, not wanting to answer. Seconds later, I was coming. I gripped his shoulders for balance as the force of the orgasm consumed me. My nails dug in as wave after wave pulsed through me. Heat prickled my skin, and my mind filled with the singular pleasure that only Blake could give me. Fuck, it had been too long. *Need this. Need you.* I wanted so badly to tell him.

He pressed soft kisses along my neck and shoulder as the aftershocks tapered off.

"More?"

The vibration of his voice almost launched me into a frenzy all over again. His fingers slid lower into my folds until he was right at the entrance of my pussy, exerting the slightest pressure as if he meant to push into me. He could be there so easily, and then his cock. The bed was right there. We could steal a moment and no one would know.

But one indiscretion would only lead to more. I had to get back in control. I had to. I shook my head and took a deep breath to calm my frayed nerves.

"No." My voice was breathy, almost pleading. I pushed his hand away and sidestepped him. I moved unsteadily to the bed with my clothes, my legs weak. My head buzzed as

I quickly dressed. He watched, his face seemingly calm, but a storm brewed in his eyes.

I knew that look. It usually came seconds before he had me pressed up against some hard surface, fucking me or making me wish he were. He leaned back onto the dresser, crossing his legs at the ankle, and sucked the moisture from his fingers. His jeans strained over an erection that he made no effort to conceal.

Fucking hell. I tore my gaze away and struggled with the button of my fly. My hands were trembling too hard. I finally managed it and paused briefly in front of the mirror to assess the tangled sandy mess that was my hair. I couldn't risk a shower right now. Tangled and sandy would have to do.

I met his gaze again. "I have to go."

"With him?"

"No, I'm going home."

"This is your home."

CHAPTER SIXTEEN

I spent most of the next day vacillating between fantasizing about Blake's hands on me again and scolding myself for letting him put them there to begin with.

His words had hit me hard. Homeless and rootless, I'd been floating through my life since leaving him. A satellite in orbit with no destination, no purpose. The most solid ground for me was with Blake, a place I'd abandoned. Even when our lives hung in the balance, I couldn't deny that.

The moment at the apartment had been brief, but I was walking a dangerous line. What if he started pursuing me again? I'd finally gotten Daniel and Connor off his scent, and here I was dancing with disaster again.

My phone dinged with a text from Alli.

A: Can you talk?

I waited a few minutes before responding, not wanting to seem like I really had time.

E: Tied up at work. Will call later.
A: I've heard that before. You're a broken record.

I set the phone down, noting the time. She was on her lunch break with limited time. If I could get through the next half hour, I'd be in the clear until she got off work, which was always late. I jumped when the phone rang. She was calling me. I turned off the volume and let it go to voicemail. I couldn't talk to her right now. I had no idea what Heath had told her or what I would say. I'd rather say nothing than lie to my best friend.

A: If you don't call me soon, I'm going to hunt you down. You realize that, right?

I smiled. Alli and her empty threats. I opened my photo app and flipped through the last photos I'd taken. I'd snapped a series of selfies with Blake in the limo on the way to the gala. He looked dashing in his tux and was making funny faces in half of them, pretending to be attacking me in the background.

I laughed and my heart twisted. I rubbed at the ache in my chest. My heart, that empty place, had started pulsing back to life again. Since I left the apartment yesterday, I'd remembered what being happy with him felt like, as happy as I'd been in the photos. The last time I felt anything close to that was at the beach with James, but the moment had been short-lived. By some miracle, he'd had me laughing and forgetting my reality. I had to give him credit for that.

I put the phone down. I needed to stop torturing myself. I'd come a long way to keep Blake safely out of my life. Further than I ever thought I'd come. Now I was on a high-speed train moving backwards, letting the addictive, potent moments I'd shared with Blake take hold again.

I checked the clock. Time to make my daily attempt at a meal. What I really wanted was an adult beverage, but that would have to wait. I moseyed down to Mocha and looked over a menu at a table in the corner.

"Hey, woman."

Simone slid into the chair opposite me.

"Hey," I said.

"What's new?"

"Oh, you know. Same old stuff. Work is busy."

"Yeah? How's investor guy?" She pursed her lips and propped her chin up on her hand. She looked like she was in the mood to gossip. This worried me, because I wasn't.

"He's fine."

"And how's James? Still in love with you, I imagine."

"I'm not sure that's what I'd call it."

"In lust?" Her eyebrows shot up, as if that wasn't entirely a bad thing either.

"No, it's not like that. He's a good guy. I don't know. There's definitely an attraction there."

"Are you thinking about ditching investor guy for him?"

I shook my head. "I'm not with Blake anymore, but no, I'm not ready to be with anyone else. I like being friends with James, but I also feel like I'm not being fair to him because I know he wants more. Does that make me a bitch?"

She shrugged. "He's a big boy. If you consider him a friend, I'm pretty sure he picked up on the fact that you're probably not ready for another relationship. If he wants to push the issue and risk being rejected, that's on him."

I sighed. "Maybe you're right. I just don't want this to blow up in my face one day."

"There's always that chance when you let relationships blossom at work."

"I know. I get it, but I feel like it's too late for that

now, you know? I can't just tell him that we can't be friends anymore without causing a lot of tension."

"Sounds like you've already got enough tension."

I groaned. "I know. Jesus, what a mess."

"Well don't break his heart too badly because when you drop him, I'm coming in with a vengeance."

I laughed. "Why wait? Do me a favor and deflect some of this off of me."

"Believe it or not, Erica, I consider you a friend, and I'm not about to voluntarily engage in a love triangle with you."

"That should be easy because I'm not in love with James. I don't expect I ever will be."

"What if he loves you though?"

I shook my head. "That's impossible." We'd only known each other a few weeks. Plus, he worked for me. Then again, Blake and I had known each other only a few weeks before I was already head over heels for him. But James and I weren't sleeping together. Nothing was nearly as intense as my relationship with Blake in the beginning. I'd fought so hard to stay away, only to find myself back in his arms, happier than I'd ever been. Our happiness had been too brief.

"What are you thinking about?"

I frowned. "Why?"

"Because you just got all dreamy. I have to know, who were you thinking about just then?"

"I was thinking about Blake actually."

She smiled. "Well, there you go."

I stared back at Simone. She was like a wise Sufi in her own right.

I rubbed out my frown. "I wish it were that simple. I really do."

"Well, don't fret, okay? You'll figure things out. I don't know what to tell you about Blake, but when it comes to James, be honest with him. That's all you can really do."

"I know. You're right."

"Let me get you something to eat before you waste away on me."

"Sure." I grabbed a menu and hoped something would catch my eye.

★ ★ ★

James popped in at the end of the day, his smile a welcome sight.

"Hey, I'm hitting the gym after work tomorrow. Do you want to come with me?"

I laughed a little. "Are you trying to tell me something?"

His eyes got wide for a second. "Definitely not. You have an amazing body. But I thought you might want to blow off some steam. That usually helps me when I'm stressed out."

My face heated at the compliment. He needed to stop saying things like that. I should have told him, but I didn't.

"Are you stressed out?"

"I don't know. Maybe." He shifted his weight a little, as if the question made him uncomfortable.

I tried to ignore the little voice saying that was probably my fault.

"What do you say?" He abruptly interrupted my little voice.

"You're determined to cure me of my malaise, aren't

you?"

He grinned. "Yes. I like happy Erica. I also like drunk Erica. We should go out for drinks again sometime."

My thoughts went back to that night at the bar, when he couldn't keep his hands or his eyes off of me. "Let's stick with the gym."

"Cool."

I hadn't been to the gym in a while. A little part of me wanted to bow out when the time came the next day. The fatigue alone was enough of a deterrent, but James was right. I needed an outlet. Maybe I'd wear myself out enough to get some decent sleep for a change. We decided on a place down the street where he'd just picked up a membership.

James showed me around and went to hit the weights. I found an empty treadmill and set what I thought was an aggressive program. I wanted to sweat and burn, see if I had enough mental strength to physically run myself into the ground. Maybe I could crush out the last of this pain. I put in my ear buds and pushed myself into a rhythm, almost eager for the challenge ahead.

I vaguely noticed someone step onto the machine next to me. I stayed focused on the music and my pace until my headphone was yanked out. I nearly lost my footing. Blake stood next to me. My breath caught at the sight of him. I thought we'd have more time apart before I had to face him again.

"What are you doing here?"

"I work out here. Wanna race?"

He smiled, reminding me of the playful, teasing lover I used to wake up to every morning. He also reminded me of all the orgasms I wasn't having since we'd broken up, except for that one delightful slip up.

"That hardly seems fair."

"Maybe not. I'm a little out of shape though. My endurance isn't what it usually is."

His meaning was obvious. If his endurance had taken a hit, mine had been pulverized. He was always in incredible shape, a well oiled machine, lean and powerful.

I rolled my eyes, wishing he'd leave me alone, but knowing that wasn't his style.

"I thought you liked to be challenged?"

Without waiting for my response, which would have contained some choice words, he leaned over to change my settings to match his. My comfortable incline soon increased until we were both in a full sprint. I wanted to dish out some trash talk but saved my breath for the run that I felt certain would be testing me shortly.

What the hell was I thinking? I hadn't exercised outside of the bedroom or a yoga studio in months. I couldn't remember the last time I'd slept through the night. I was running on fumes. My lungs burned and my muscles ached as I struggled to keep up speed. Only sheer pride kept me from admitting defeat. I couldn't give him the satisfaction, even now, when it hardly mattered.

Several minutes later, I was silently praying for relief, unsure how much farther my legs would take me on the mile sprint Blake had committed our machines to. Drenched and drained beyond recognition, I finally slowed to a walk.

Blake hopped off his machine and leaned casually on the railing behind us. I could barely stand, let alone walk. Somehow I kept my legs under me and disembarked, wondering how I was going to drag my sorry ass home in this condition.

"How are your legs?"

He gave me a smirk that made me want to slap it off his beautiful face.

"Fuck you," I managed between the jagged breaths. I took a long swig of my water. Our little jaunt clearly hadn't had nearly the same effect on him. He barely looked winded.

"Gladly, but you seem a little wiped out. Hope you didn't have any plans for later."

He lifted the bottom of his T-shirt to wipe the light sheen of sweat from his forehead, blatantly showcasing his abs. They looked as good as ever. He wasn't exactly letting himself go.

"Hey." James walked up to us, his chest puffed out at the sight of Blake.

Blake gave him the kind of look he reserved for other unfortunate men who had made the mistake of getting too close to me. Pure disdain, as if James's mere existence offended him. This wasn't good on any level. As much as I insisted that James and I weren't sleeping together, Blake had an uncanny propensity for finding us in the same place at the same time.

"You done?" I said to James, hoping to break the stare down between them.

"Yeah, ready when you are." James's eyes didn't move.

"I'll see you later, Blake."

I gave James a gentle push on his chest, prompting him to turn and follow me out. When I looked back, I caught Blake's tense expression, his hands fisting tightly around the railing.

CHAPTER SEVENTEEN

Friday was the day I was going to meet with Daniel's campaign people. I chose a chocolate brown scoop neck dress that flowed loose at the hemline. I paired it with a thin belt and my nude heels. The look was sophisticated and more in line with who I *was* professionally rather than who I was auditioning to be. I refused to wear a suit at this pretend interview for a job I didn't even want.

The governor's election was still a couple months off, but people buzzed around the headquarters office as if today were the big day. Campaign signs filled every window. Paperwork was everywhere, scattered on people's desks and piled up on every available surface. A dozen or so people were on the phone talking, their voices mingling into one unintelligible audio blur.

Young men and women my age passed by me, moving across the office as if they were coordinating the moon landing or something. The perpetual sense of urgency put me on edge.

I stood there somewhat stupidly, taking it all in, when a tall young man emerged from one of the few enclosed offices and walked toward me.

"Erica?"

"Yes."

"I'm Will, the assistant campaign manager. Come on back and we can talk."

We stepped into his office. The room was windowed on two sides. He shut the door and all the noise of the main room with it. I relaxed, immediately relieved by the separation. Thank goodness I didn't have this reaction to our office. Even Blake's office, which had two or three times more people, didn't feel this hectic.

Will sat down at his desk and shuffled through some papers. He was probably in his mid-thirties. Attractive with dark blond hair that seemed slightly shaggy and overgrown, he looked like a more mature version of the interns and volunteers out on the floor. His eyes were slightly glossy and he radiated a kind of energy that I knew from personal experience came from copious amounts of caffeine and minimal sleep.

"So thanks for coming in. I understand that you know Mr. Fitzgerald already?"

"Yes." The word came out awkwardly. We sure knew each other, but Daniel hadn't prepped me on how we were supposed to know each other officially. "We have some mutual business connections." I hoped that was vague enough to discourage any further prodding on the subject.

"That's always good. I'm assuming you are up to speed with the position's requirements?"

"I am, but I'd love to hear your take on what exactly you're looking for."

We spent the next ten minutes discussing the structure of their marketing efforts, shortcomings, and concerns, and how they were hoping to improve. I listened intently, taking notes to fill in the gaps from the documents Daniel had given me.

"I'm probably not supposed to mention this in an

interview, but we don't have a lot of time to dance around things here. Mr. Fitzgerald seems especially eager to find a way to work with you. I'm guessing you feel the same way?"

Wow, was that ever a loaded question. I clicked my pen. The stubborn part of me wanted to scream out, *No!* Instead, I smiled politely and withdrew a thick document from my bag. The size of it rivaled the marketing plan that Daniel had given me the week prior.

I dropped it on his desk. "Will, I have a proposal for you."

★ ★ ★

The meeting with Will went well, but I wasn't sure how or when Daniel would react to what I'd proposed. I had a feeling he wouldn't be too pleased, even though I'd laid out a plan that made perfect sense for everyone involved. He'd likely see it as another attempt to negotiate the hard line he'd drawn. I'd still try to convince him all the same. I had to.

Mark was dead, but as long as Blake was safe, I was going to fight Daniel on this. Because the kind of life he had planned for me wasn't much of a life at all, as far as I was concerned. At least for now, I was willing to face the repercussions of standing up to him and hope for the best.

Letting someone else run my life went so far against the grain of who I was as a person. I was growing weary of Daniel's attempts to coerce me with violence and fear. In the long run, no one could possibly win. Any talent he expected to extort out of me would be swiftly crushed if I followed him blindly into this new life.

I pushed the apprehension out of my mind. Daniel would let me know his thoughts on the matter sooner or later. I wouldn't worry about it in the meantime.

Back at the office, I was talking with Chris and Sid when something caught my eye out the window. Blake's Tesla had zoomed up to the curb. My heart leaped. Even without seeing him in the flesh, the terrible ache that haunted me resurfaced. The ache was quickly replaced with a fiery rage as I watched him help Risa out of the car. She was smiling and laughing, her hand flat on his chest.

Oh hell no. I found my legs and rushed downstairs, meeting them a few seconds later.

"Erica, hi." Risa froze, a white-knuckle grip on her purse.

I quickly assessed her, desperate to find a hair out of place, some indication of what had gone on during her overlong lunch hour. I continued to stare, imploring her to feed me an excuse.

"Um, Blake wanted to go over some of the new marketing numbers with me. So we decided to grab lunch."

"Did he?"

She nodded anxiously. I stared at her a moment longer. I couldn't stomach even the loose vision my imagination was stringing together right now.

Blake going behind my back to get information about the business was one thing. Coercing Risa into bed, with presumably very little effort, was another matter entirely.

"I should go up and get back to work," she said.

"You should."

I turned my focus to Blake, whose face twitched with the slightest of satisfied smirks. He circled the vehicle and slipped into the driver's side before I could say anything. He zoomed off as quickly as he'd arrived, while I stood there trying to figure out his angle.

Risa had long disappeared into the building by the time I walked back in. I was hoping to buy myself some more time. My mind was spinning with the things I wanted to say to her. Trying to separate professional from unprofessional might have been a lost cause at this point. James met me on the landing, looking concerned.

"What's going on?"

"Blake just dropped Risa off from a 'business lunch.'"

"Okay, so what?"

"First of all, he has no right to meet with my employees behind my back, and secondly, I could tell right away that the meeting was anything but innocent. First I had to tell her to leave you alone and now she appears to have set her sights on Blake. She's fucking relentless. The nerve that he has, showing up like this." I was talking fast, not taking much care with what I was saying. "No part of that is going to fly. There are plenty of other people out there. He can stay out of my office."

Risa sure knew how to get what she wanted. That was all fine and well until now. Blake knew better. I paced back and forth over the landing. He wouldn't get away with this.

"You go on in. I'll be back in a little bit." I turned to go back down.

Before I could make the first step, James caught my elbow and spun me toward him.

"Where are you going?"

"I'm going to give him a piece of my mind."

"Why don't you wait a while and cool down. You're

taking this too personally."

"No, I'm not. This is totally unacceptable."

"Why are you letting him get under your skin?" He frowned, seeming genuinely irritated.

I didn't care. I was furious. "I'm not letting him screw my employees, okay? I don't think that's him getting under my skin."

He took a step forward, bringing our bodies dangerously close. I tore my gaze away from his penetrating eyes. I focused on the wall behind him, trying not to think about how he made me feel when he was this close.

"You have no idea if he's screwing her or even pursuing her." His voice was low and matter-of-fact. "But you can't stay away."

I shut my eyes tight and prayed for strength to get through this moment and the rest of the day without losing my mind.

"Erica."

"What?" I kept my gaze low, unable to face him. I couldn't give him what he needed. I was barely surviving in the aftermath of my break up with Blake. I had no heart left to give to someone else.

"Will you hear me out, first, before you go running to him?"

I bristled slightly at the way he said that. I didn't like how it sounded at all. "What do you have to say?"

His expression softened slightly, as if he sensed my irritation.

"I know this is complicated. You and me. But as much as you want to ignore it, there is something between us. I can feel it, and I know you can too. I care about you, and

I can't stand to see this guy torturing you, ripping your goddamn heart out."

I sighed. "Believe me when I say you truly don't understand what I'm going through."

"The only thing I don't understand is why you can't admit that you have feelings for me. Why do you keep fighting this?"

I couldn't give him an easy answer to that.

"I'm not so blind that I can't see what I do to you." He ran his thumb across my cheek lightly.

"Maybe you're overestimating your effect on women," I lied. He had an effect on me. I had no idea why. Since I'd met Blake, other men didn't come onto my radar, but James was right in front of me, impossible to ignore.

He laughed softly. "You flush whenever we're close like this, like you need to catch your breath around me." His thumb came down along my jaw and brushed over my lower lip. "And the way you part your lips when you do…it's all I can do not to kiss you right now. Because somewhere underneath it all, I know you want me to."

My breath rushed out of me. The second my eyes flashed to his, his mouth was on me, kissing me with soft and tender strokes that stole my breath. I tensed, waiting for the voice in my head to start screaming at me, but she didn't. Maybe she was as tired of fighting as I was. Something inside me let go. Through all the doubts, I gave myself permission to want James in this moment, for as long as this moment lasted. When he tightened his embrace, I arched into him and slipped my arms around his neck.

"James." I whispered his name, letting the sound of it settle over me. I tried not to think about all the ways he felt different from Blake. The way he smelled, the way his body felt against my own.

"I'll make you forget all about him. Just let me in, Erica," he whispered between kisses. His hands were everywhere, soft, tentative touches, but instead of fire, they left a chill across my skin. I shivered as I played his words over in my mind. *Just let me in.*

No. The little voice had just enough energy to speak up. James's lips tried in vain to coax me back, but whatever I'd felt in the heat of the moment had passed. The fire that had swept through me and overtaken my senses so quickly had faded just as fast.

And that's when I knew. Blake was the only one I'd ever let in. Somehow he'd rooted himself in my soul, and no amount of lusty chance encounters with James would change that.

"What's wrong?"

I shook my head. "I can't do this."

"What do I have to do? Please, just tell me."

"You don't want to be with someone like me. God knows, I don't even want to be with myself most days." I straightened and took a step back, trying to gain some distance between us.

"Why don't you let me be the judge of that?"

"There's nothing you can do, James. I can't be what you want me to be. This... This isn't fair to you."

"Will you stop? Don't push me away because you're scared of what you're making me feel. I can watch out for my own feelings."

"Maybe I'm scared for myself then. You're right. I am attracted to you. I can't deny that, but you need to understand that I *can't* love you." The truth of the words struck me as I spoke them. I wasn't capable of loving anyone else right now, or possibly ever, no matter how great of a person he might be.

"I'm not asking you to love me. I'm asking for you to give us a chance. You have no idea what we could be because you won't even let us start."

I squeezed my eyes shut. For weeks I'd been holding myself together with the emotional equivalent of duct tape. All I wanted was someone to help put me back together again, but James wasn't that person.

"You want him. You're going to go running to him." He stared at me a long time, his expression pinched with the frustration that seemed to bubble just below the surface.

"I'm not running to him."

"It's pathetic to watch you doing this," he snapped. "Chasing after him when I'm standing right here. I *want* you. I'm losing my mind wanting you, and all you can think about is getting another chance with him."

Anger surged through me at his assumption. "I'm not chasing him, James. I left him. *I* left *him*. Okay? I broke my own heart. This is all my doing and you don't understand the first thing about it. So stay out of my head and my heart, and keep your fucking judgments to yourself."

I wrung my fingers in an attempt to slow the tremble that hummed through me now.

He seemed to relax, his shoulders sagging slightly. His expression softened. "I can't understand why you'd hold a candle for someone who hit you."

"What?" I frowned. Had I heard him right?

"My dad had a heavy-hand too. I know it when I see it,

trust me. But for the life of me, I can't understand why you'd tolerate it, no matter how much you cared about him."

"I—oh my God. James, that day… Oh, shit."

I let my head fall into my hands. I'd been so wrapped up in dealing with my own feelings that I'd never once thought about what he might think to see me like that. No wonder he hated Blake so much.

I took a step closer and put my hands on his chest. I didn't want to fight with him like this, and he needed to believe me. "Blake has never hit me. I promise you. Please trust me when I say this whole situation is more complicated than you'll ever realize."

My proclamation didn't have its desired effect. He stepped away, and my hands dropped down with his movement.

"Whatever you say, Erica."

The defeated look on his face added an impossible guilt to my already shattered emotional state.

He turned and disappeared down the hallway and back into the office.

★ ★ ★

I had no idea what I would say if Blake happened to be at his office. He'd get an earful of everything I was thinking and feeling, one way or the other.

I marched through the bullpen with enough speed and focus that heads turned, my heels clicking as I went. I stormed through his office door, ignoring Cady's greeting, and slammed it behind me as soon as I found him at his desk. He swiveled in his chair.

"Erica, I wasn't expecting you so soon."

"Fuck you." I walked up to the side of his desk, ready to give him a piece of my mind.

He rose gracefully and faced me. "I thought you took fucking off the table when you broke up with me. If you've changed your mind about that, I'll admit I'm still interested."

"Not making progress quickly enough with Risa?" I lifted my eyebrows and my lips firmed into a tight line.

"Not as quickly as she might like."

I clenched my jaw. His words sliced through me like a thousand little knives. How could he change this way? Had he always been this cold? I took a breath and prepared myself for the fight.

"You can screw whomever you want, but stay away from my employees."

"You seem to be taking a pretty liberal stance on workplace relationships."

"I don't know how many times I need to tell you, James and I are friends."

"Is that so?"

"Yes," I insisted. I didn't know why, but I really wanted him to believe it.

"Looks to me like he's hopelessly in love with you."

I swallowed hard. "So now you're using Risa and Sophia to get back at me, to make me jealous? Is that it?"

"Are you?"

He came closer, trapping me between him and the end of the desk. I backed up against it, feeling unsteady.

"How long was I supposed to wait for you, Erica? Or did you just come here to get off." He slipped a hand up my thigh and reached for my panties.

I slapped his hand away. "I didn't used to hate you." I swallowed against the tightness in my throat.

The cold look in his eyes changed. They darkened with emotion. "Loving me wasn't enough. You've made me desperate."

I shook my head, confused.

"No? Maybe it wasn't love then." He canted his head slightly.

"Blake—" I winced at the insinuation. How could he ever doubt it?

"You could barely say it, Erica."

My mouth opened but the words caught. I wanted to tell him I loved him, hated him, and missed him desperately. Explain how so very tired I was of this painful and draining separation.

"Say it," he bit out. "If there's anything worth waiting for, I need to hear you tell me now."

Unshed tears burned my eyes. "Why would you wait for me?"

"Because I can't fucking help it," he snapped. He raked his hands through his already messy hair. "Jesus Christ, did you really think I'd just stop wanting you? Just like that? Flip a switch and everything would change? That I'd feel nothing?"

I squeezed my eyes closed, though I could feel his gaze burning into me. He cupped his hand behind my nape, bringing our faces so close. My eyes flew open at his rough breath against my lips. My heart pounded against my chest. His expression tightened, painted with all of the anger and frustration I'd spurred.

"Whatever it is that took you away from me, I'll fix it,

I promise."

"You can't fix this, Blake."

"Like hell, I can't. I'll do anything to get you back. Do you understand? *Anything*."

The tears burned and streamed down my cheeks. The asking in his intensely green eyes took hold of me, enveloping everything. The pain behind them penetrated my soul. His expression softened, and he wiped away my tears, kissing the path they'd made down my face.

"You're the only one, Erica. There's never been anyone else."

"But—"

"Not Risa, not Sophia. No one comes close. Believe me, no one ever will. If we can't make this work…" His grip on me tightened slightly. "I can't even think about it. God help me, I'll keep trying until I break you down. Say it. Baby, please."

The softly worded plea shredded me.

"Say it," he whispered, kissing me sweetly.

"I love you." The words came out in a sob. I swallowed down the urge to breakdown completely, strengthened by the pressure that lifted slightly by saying the words. "I love you so much."

He answered by lifting me up to rest on the edge of the desk. "Then don't give up on us. Love me, damn it. Please, baby. Let me love you."

He slid his hands up my thighs, bunching the fabric of my dress as he went. He silenced any thoughts of refusing with another deeper kiss, devouring my mouth with hungry, urgent strokes. I linked my hands behind his neck, meeting his resolve.

"Jesus, I need you," he growled and pulled away. In one swift movement he yanked off his shirt and divested me of my panties, careful to ensure that my heels stayed on.

"Blake, the office," I whispered, vaguely aware that we were breaking an unwritten rule of not fucking in his office.

"Don't give a shit. I need to be inside you more than I need to breathe right now. I don't care who knows it."

With one arm, he swept the contents of the desk behind me to the floor. Everything landed with a loud crash. He pushed me back, crawled over my body, and wrapped my legs snuggly around his waist. He covered me with fevered kisses, sucking my neck until my skin prickled with heated desire. He tugged down the top of my dress, freeing my breasts. He took my nipple in his mouth, circling the tender tip with the pad of his tongue and repeating the motion on the other.

"I thought I'd lose my mind seeing you walk away from me last night."

"I didn't want to leave you, Blake."

"I couldn't sleep from wanting you so badly. Wanted to bury myself so deep in you, hear you scream."

I whimpered, desire thick in my veins. I shifted anxiously beneath him, desperate for more contact. I scrambled for his belt, unfastened it, and pushed down his jeans to free his cock. Frantic for him, I lifted my hips, meeting him as he shafted easily into me. He ground his hips, staking his claim inside me as I stretched around him. He filled me so completely. His ragged breathing matched my own.

No one had ever made me feel this way, and no one ever would.

He took my mouth, his tongue seeking mine with deep

velvet strokes until I could scarcely breathe. I moaned as he pulled back and then plunged deeper.

"Say it again." The command left his lips in a strangled groan.

He gripped my hip and thrust again, so deep.

"I love you, Blake." I sobbed from the pleasure of it. "Oh God, you feel so good. It's so good."

As if something invisible snapped, the thin veneer of control slipped from his features. No longer could I make out the familiar lines of restraint on his face. Only his intense animal need to possess me. He pumped into me rapidly. The friction of his fierce movements made me wild. I grasped at anything—his hair, shoulders, the edge of the desk. Anything to ground me when I slipped perilously into oblivion.

He took my hands in his own and held them tight above my head, firmly enough that I couldn't escape. My breasts jutted out, tantalized by the soft hairs of his chest. I moaned and cried out unintelligible things. I'd lost my mind in the pleasure.

Our bodies collided over each other's, slick and taut with the tension coiled tight within each of us. The slow burn of my desire was raging now, the fire taking over as I clenched helplessly around him. His hips slammed mercilessly against me, my body anchored there and by his mouth where he kissed me. Passionate bruising kisses that I fully met like a person who'd been starved of them.

"Fuck, fuck, fuck. Erica. Come, baby. I can't stop."

His words spurred me right into my orgasm. I let out an intoxicated cry, my fingers threading tightly with his. His eyes never left me as he took his pleasure, the cords of his muscles strung so tight. The taut knots of his abdomen clenched once more before a spasm rocked his powerful frame.

My body hummed. My chest expanded with warmth, and I inhaled his scent, basking in our sudden and fierce closeness. Love—a heady, pulsing, possessing wave of love—held me in its clutches. Everything that I'd been trying to forget and subdue when he was near came rushing in, overtaking my senses. Forehead to forehead, we caught our breath between slow, passionate kisses.

He stilled for a minute and looked up. "Damn it."

"What?"

"I have a conference call in a few minutes, otherwise I'd take you home and finish this." He shook his head. "Never mind, I'll have Cady reschedule it."

He thickened inside of me, impossibly ready for me again. I tightened in response, overwhelmed by how much I wanted him again already. I wanted to gorge myself on everything I'd been missing for so long.

Then reality slowly resurfaced. This had been amazing. Heart-wrenching, toe-curling, amazing sex, but it didn't solve things. I pressed my hands on his chest gently.

"Let me use your bathroom."

He pulled out of me. I bit my lip, suppressing a whimper at the loss. With his help, I slid off the desk and collected myself enough to escape into the adjoining bathroom. I shut the door and cleaned myself up. How would we get through this now?

Before I could begin to think about it, he knocked on the door. I pulled myself together quickly and met him at the doorway.

"Everything okay?"

"Sure." I pushed by nervously. "I'll let you get back to work, I guess."

I'd barely passed him when he tugged me close. "What if I don't want to let you go yet?"

I avoided his eyes, unable to keep from relaxing into the warmth of his body.

"Let me see you tonight." He paused, penetrating me with his gaze.

I contemplated a response. He'd just stripped me down emotionally and called my bluff on this whole breakup. What else could I say to keep him away that he would possibly believe or accept at this point? He was the definition of undeterred.

"I don't think that's a good idea."

His eyes widened slightly. "We're back to this?"

I sighed inwardly. We were so far from being back to normal. I was no closer to being able to tell him everything he didn't know.

"You're killing me with this shit, Erica. After what we just did, you won't let me take you out?"

I tried to weigh my options, the possibilities, and all the things that could possibly go wrong. In the middle of this trying thought process, Blake kissed me. I kissed him back, twisting the fabric of his T-shirt into a fist as I pulled him even closer. Everything melted away as it so blissfully had earlier.

"I'll meet you after work, okay?"

I nodded without thinking, drunk on the taste of him once more. Before I could tear myself away to leave, he spoke again.

"About Risa…"

My gaze shot up to meet his. I sobered momentarily with apprehension about what he might say.

"It's not what you think."

"Oh?" *Then what the hell was it?*

"Her loyalties don't lie with you."

"What do you mean?"

"You said you wanted to make your own mistakes, so I'm letting you. Do your homework. You'll figure it out."

CHAPTER EIGHTEEN

On the walk back, I'd pulled my hair up into a twist so I didn't look like I'd very recently been nailed on a writing desk. I returned to the office and ignored Risa's guilty look in my direction. I couldn't make eye contact with her. As soon as I passed the partition, James was behind me.

"How did it go?"

His tone had an edge, reminiscent of the bitter jealousy that I'd recently unleashed onto Blake. I sighed, wishing I hadn't chosen to come here first.

"Fine. We're on the same page now."

"I can see that," he said quietly, thumbing a tender spot high on my neck. He shook his head and turned to leave as quickly as he'd come.

I sat down and opened my compact. In the tiny mirror I saw a quarter-sized violet bruise where James's hand had grazed.

My face heated. *Goddamn it, Blake.*

He was ruthless in his jealousy, and now James was obviously pissed that I'd gone and done exactly what he'd said I would.

I sulked back into my chair, overwhelmed. And to think I'd once been worried about office culture. I would be lucky if James didn't quit before I had a chance to rip Risa a new one for shamelessly pursuing my ex, or whatever Blake officially was right now. In that moment I was incredibly grateful for Sid and Chris's generally uneventful social lives. I created enough drama for the whole office all by myself.

I waited until everyone left at five. For the first time in a long time, James didn't stay late. I knew he was upset when he didn't bother saying goodbye. I bolted the door and went over to Risa's desk. I looked through her paperwork carefully. Everything seemed to be in order. Contracts, notes, print collateral.

I sat in her chair and moved her mouse. Her computer screen lit up and I started looking through her files. I clicked over to her email and scrolled through dozens of messages between her and clients, myself, and others on the team. Everything looked normal. I hoped Blake wasn't sending me on a wild goose chase to justify their lunch.

I checked her sent mail and scanned down a few pages. I stopped on an email to Max titled "Files."

Max,
Here are the files you asked for.
xo,
Risa

Attached were a handful of spreadsheets with all our user data, along with confidential documents for the business that I'd shared with her when we met with Alli weeks ago.

My jaw dropped. I'd brought Risa on and shared every resource with her, taught her everything I knew, and given her the opportunity to be someone important on the ground floor of our company. Sure, we had a few personality conflicts, but this was too much.

I called Sid immediately. "Hey, can you change Risa's

email password?

"Sure, what's going on?"

"I don't fully know yet, but it looks like she's in cahoots with Max, the guy who was supposed to fund us originally."

"I don't get it."

"She sent him a database dump of the site and all our advertiser contact info, plus a ton of financials for the company that I'd shared with her when she started."

"Whoa. Why?"

"I don't know, but I don't have a good feeling about it."

"Have you spoken with her?"

"Not yet. Send me her new password and I'm going to do some more digging tonight. I want to figure out as much of this as I can before I approach her, but it's safe to say she won't be coming in on Monday."

"All right. I'll do it now."

I hung up and continued to fume. As pissed as I'd been with her this afternoon, she'd crossed a new line that we couldn't come back from.

★ ★ ★

I showered quickly at the apartment and picked out something to wear. I had no idea what we were doing, so I decided on a light sleeveless top and a short floral skirt that Alli had accidentally left during her visit. I didn't have much choice but to wear my hair down since Blake had branded me with a hickey. I brushed on some light makeup and curled a few chunks of my blond strands into beachy waves and called it good.

I checked the street below, indulging the remnants of

my paranoia that Connor might still be lurking, but I saw no sign of the Lincoln. Maybe that would be the end of that. If so, sneaking time with Blake might be feasible. But Blake probably wouldn't be interested in a relationship with me under the radar without some sort of explanation. Things between us were changing again and everything felt out of my control.

I texted Blake that I was at the apartment, and he was downstairs a few minutes later. I opened the door when he knocked, and he scooped me into his arms before I could even say hello. He lifted me off my feet, tilting his head up for a kiss. His smile was contagious. I lowered my head to kiss him sweetly, my hands cradling his face. He held me hostage with his kiss, drawing me into the passionate strokes of his tongue until I was breathless and wanted him all over again.

He lowered me finally, keeping our bodies close. "Perfect."

My face heated at the word. I'd felt anything but perfect for so long. How could he possibly think so?

"Where are we going?" I asked, eager to shift the focus away from my supposed qualities.

"You'll see. We'd better go. It's a little bit of a drive."

After navigating through some weekend traffic, we found the coast and drove north. Gradually the city landscape changed as we passed into the smaller suburban towns. Unlike the palette of cedar-shingled mansions on the Cape, the seaside homes north of the city were more historic and quaint. The farther we went, the more impressive they were. We pulled off the main road onto Marblehead Neck, an exclusive neighborhood reaching out into the sea. Each house was majestic in its own way, grand both in size and architecture. We pulled into a large circular driveway leading up to a sprawling brick home overlooking the ocean and the Boston skyline. A few other cars were parked in the driveway to the side of the house.

We sat in the car a moment. Blake held my hand tightly in his.

"Are you going to tell me where we are?"

"This is my parents' house."

My eyebrows shot up. "Oh."

"They've been wanting to meet you. I figured this was as good a time as ever."

I checked myself in the mirror. This was all so sudden.

He smirked. "You look perfect, baby. Don't worry. They're going to love you."

He opened my door and we walked up the brick pathway to the main entrance. Blake's mother answered the door a moment later.

"Erica!" She smiled and pulled me over the threshold into a warm hug.

"Erica, this is my mother, Catherine."

Catherine was a petite woman with short blond hair, tanned by the sun. She had cool blue eyes that reminded me of my own. She stepped back, smiling.

"Sweetheart, we have been *dying* to meet you! Blake has been keeping you all to himself." She slapped him playfully on the arm before grabbing my hand. "Come on in. I want you to meet Greg."

She led us into a large kitchen where Blake's father was pulling trays out of the oven. He was wearing an apron over blue jeans and a T-shirt. Now I knew where Blake got his fashion sense.

"Greg, come say hello to Erica."

Blake's father pulled off his oven mitts and the apron and joined us at the edge of the room. Tall, with graying dark brown hair, he was handsome and had a kind smile, his eyes glittering when they met mine. I saw so much of Blake in him.

"Wow. Good work, son." He laughed heartily and surprised me next with a big hug. "Wonderful to meet you finally. Blake speaks very highly of you."

I fell speechless at the compliment. In fact, I hadn't been able to speak since I'd stepped into the Landon home. All of this was complete and utter overload.

"I hope you like chicken parm," Greg said, easily filling the silence.

"I love it." I smiled warmly.

"Oh that's right. Blake tells us you're a phenomenal cook. Damn, I hope this measures up."

Blake laughed as he took two beers out of the fridge. "All right, guys. Tone it down. Seriously. Want to get some fresh air? Otherwise these two will literally suffocate you with questions and compliments."

"That doesn't sound so bad," I joked. Blake's parents seemed amazingly sweet. I was definitely feeling overwhelmed, though.

"Go on you two. Everyone's out on the deck," Catherine said, motioning us out of the kitchen.

Blake caught my hand in his, and we passed through a large living room and onto a deck that spanned the length of the house, overlooking the ocean.

Heath and Alli turned toward us from their position at

the railing.

"You!" Alli crossed her arms defensively and gave me a terse look.

Oh shit. She'd been right about hunting me down.

"Hey," I said timidly.

She pushed off the railing and came closer, pointing at me with her manicured finger. "Don't *hey* me, Erica. You are in huge freaking trouble. Do you have any idea how worried I've been about you? Who doesn't call their best friend back for weeks at a time? I mean seriously—"

"Calm down, babe. She just got here." Heath rested his arm over her shoulder and gave her a little squeeze.

I recoiled a bit, leaning back into Blake's body, hoping he could somehow save me from the wrath of Alli. She was completely overreacting, not to mention killing the moment.

"Is there anything else you need to get off your chest? Now's the time," I said, only half-joking.

She twisted her lips into a half smile. "I love that skirt on you. I want it back."

I laughed, and before I could say anything, she crossed over and pulled me into a hug. I hugged her back, realizing how much I'd missed her.

"Don't you ever do that to me again."

"Sorry." My voice muffled quietly into her shoulder. I'd been keeping the truth from so many people for so long, sometimes I didn't even know who I was anymore.

"Apology accepted." She stepped back. "Now, do you want to explain to me what the hell is going on?"

I glanced up at Blake and back to her. "Let's talk later, okay? I'm sure their parents aren't interested in hearing about my drama."

"I wouldn't go that far," Heath chimed in, his eyes wide. "Fair warning. You'll be lucky if we can get through dinner without getting the third degree on why you and Blake aren't together anymore."

My eyes widened anxiously. This was looking more and more like an intervention that might end in tears and rehab for me too. No one could fully appreciate how fragile I'd been these past few weeks. I'd been worn down to the point where I seriously wondered if I was taking years off my life with the stress.

Blake kissed me on the cheek and whispered in my ear. "Don't worry. I'll keep them occupied. Just relax and have fun."

Catherine joined us, with Fiona in tow. Fiona looked perfect in a teal striped top and short white shorts.

"Erica, I'm so glad you could come," she squealed, giving me a tight hug.

My throat tightened with emotion. Too much hugging. I couldn't handle all these people being so happy to have me close. Before I could overthink it, Catherine announced that dinner was ready. We all settled at the table outside on the other side of the deck. I sat between Alli and Blake, which was a relief.

"Erica, tell us about your family," Catherine began as we started digging into the meal.

"Mom," Blake snapped.

"What?" She shook her head, wide-eyed, and looked back to me.

"It's okay. Um, my mother passed away from cancer when I was thirteen. My stepfather remarried while I was away at boarding school, so I don't really have a lot of close family now."

"Oh, sweetheart, I'm so sorry."

I shrugged, not wanting to seem emotional or upset about it. Plus, I'd barely scratched the surface. "Thank you. It's fine, though. I get to make my family wherever I go now."

Alli grinned and leaned into me a little.

Greg finished a bite of salad. "Tell us about your business. Blake tells us that you're part of a rare species of women in technology."

I glanced over to Blake whose lips twisted into an annoyed grimace. Greg opened his mouth, but before he could speak, Heath cleared his throat.

"Sorry to interrupt you there, Dad, but we have an announcement."

The blood drained from Catherine's face. Alli rushed to speak.

"I've decided to move back to Boston."

"Oh, wow." Catherine laughed, putting her hand over her heart like she'd been moments from a heart attack.

My own heart experienced a burst of happiness at the news. I shifted in my seat to face her.

"Oh my God, are you serious?"

She nodded. "It's official. Heath and I talked about it this week. I'll be on the job hunt and moving as soon as I can."

"That's so wonderful," Catherine said with a warm smile. Greg peppered Heath with suggestions about apartments in the city and I nudged Alli.

"I'm interviewing for marketing directors. You wouldn't

happen to be interested?"

She frowned and sat back. "Are you serious?"

"Actually, yeah. Things didn't work out with Risa. I'll fill you in on the details later, but suffice to say, we're severing ties completely and irrevocably."

"Wow. In that case, yes."

"Really? Are you sure that's what you'd want to do?"

"Are you kidding me? I've spent the past two months pulling twelve-hour days for prima donna designers. Coming back to Clozpin would be like being on a tropical vacation by comparison."

"I thought you wanted a career in fashion though?"

She gave me a half-hearted smile. "I thought I did too. I guess sometimes you don't realize what you have 'til it's gone. I definitely got some perspective and learned a ton, but this move feels right in every way. Heath's going to be happier here, his family's here to support him, and you're here. I couldn't think of any better reasons to make the change."

"You won't hear any arguments from me. Obviously I've been dying to have you back since you left. And frankly, with what's going down with Risa now, I feel like I'll never be able to trust anyone in that position again who isn't you."

"Don't worry. We'll figure it out. We built this business. No one's better suited to grow it."

"Cheers to that."

CHAPTER NINETEEN

I breathed a sigh of relief as we left the bustling dinner with Blake's family and escaped to the beach below. I left my sandals on the steps, and Blake and I walked barefoot along the shore as the sun began to set.

"Sorry. They're completely crazy," he mumbled.

"It's okay. They're really sweet actually." A quiet happiness bubbled inside me at the unexpected turn this evening had taken. "This may sound strange, but why didn't you introduce me to your parents before? You know, when things weren't so messed up between us."

"Like Heath said, they're nosy and overwhelming. On one hand, I didn't really want to share my time with you, and on the other hand, I knew that once I let them loose on you, it was all over."

My heart sank a little. "All over?"

"Now that they've met you, they're going to be hounding me nonstop about you. Don't think for one second this is going to be your last Landon family dinner."

I laughed. "Listen to you, Mr. Angst. You make them sound so burdensome. You're incredibly lucky."

Our eyes met and he took my hand as we walked. "I don't mean it like that. They've always been great. I guess I was too caught up in being with you to realize that you'd probably enjoy this a lot more than I typically do."

"I don't have much to compare it to, but I'd give

anything to have a family like yours, you know? Don't ever take them for granted, Blake. Everything can change in an instant."

"Yeah, you're right."

Ahead of us, at the edge of the enormous property, stood a gazebo. We walked up some old wooden steps from the beach. Inside, the structure was ornately built and offered an impressive view of the skyline. Daylight was fading now, and the ocean air cooled around us. I sat close to Blake, and he wrapped an arm around me as we settled back to take in the scenery. I rested my head on his shoulder as he traced circles down my arm.

"You were right about Risa," I said after a while.

"Yeah. Did you find what you were looking for?"

"I think so. My question is, how did you?"

He stayed silent.

"Blake."

He sucked in a slow breath that whistled through his teeth. "You're not going to like it."

"So what? Tell me."

He pushed the errant strands of hair away from his face only to have them fall back. "I hacked your email account."

I stilled. "What?"

"I was worried about you."

"That's a major invasion of privacy, Blake! Why—"

"Trust me, I wasn't the only one worried about you. Marie even reached out to me at one point to grill me about what I did to upset you so much."

My jaw dropped. Marie. Damn it all.

"I just wanted to take a spin through your mail to see if there was anything I should be concerned about. While

I was in there, I checked out Risa's and Sid's, purely out of curiosity since you'd decided to shut me out of the business for the time being."

"And you saw her messages to Max?"

"Don't say I didn't warn you."

"I don't understand why that specific information would be helpful to him though."

"The investment company you told me about…the one who's sending Trevor fat checks? It took me a while to get past all the layers of corporate privacy, but I finally tracked down the people behind it."

"And?"

"Seems like our friend Max is using the company as a front to fund Trevor's efforts. He's basically been paying Trevor to run this group and be a full time pain in my ass."

"But the attacks stopped."

"I'm not totally sure why, but my guess is that once he had an in with Risa, compromising the site was possibly doing more harm than good. Wasted effort maybe."

"Why would he need our data though?"

"I have no idea. Have you spoken to her yet?"

"No, not yet. I'm not sure if she'll tell me when she finds out she's getting fired though." I thought for a moment, trying to piece everything together. "Did she reach out to you for the meeting today?"

"No, I contacted her."

"Oh."

"I wanted to feel her out. With very little effort, I'd convinced her to leave your company and come work for me, and we'd made plans for a more intimate dinner this weekend. She was willing to jump ship, screw your ex, and finagle herself into my business before we'd even gotten the bill."

"You're an asshole." I started to move away but he pulled me back.

"What? I was testing her. Obviously I'm not interested. Relax, baby."

"Why would that be so obvious? A few days before that Sophia was all over you, and I didn't see you protesting."

"You don't need to worry about Sophia."

"Right."

I stood up and walked to the other side of the gazebo. I steadied my hands on the rail, holding on tightly as anger rushed over me anew.

"Sophia was here on business, like I said. Outside of our shared stake in her company, there's nothing there beyond friendship."

I turned to face him. "Maybe for you, but she's borderline obsessed with you. Do you know how happy she must have been to know that I was out of the picture finally? She's probably counting down the days until she can be your little submissive again. And for the record, I don't appreciate you talking about our sex life with her."

His brows drew together. "What do you mean?"

"Sophia told me about your little heart-to-heart." I tried not to sound as bitter about it as I felt, but I couldn't help it. That he'd confided in her hurt me more than I wanted to admit.

"Did she say something to you?"

"Yeah, she seemed really broken up that I was seemingly unable to satisfy your kink factor." The sarcasm was coming out thick now.

He blew out a breath. "I'm sorry."

"I know I might not be the most experienced person with this 'lifestyle' as she calls it, but I never thought you'd be one to kiss and tell, especially to her."

"She asked about you. I told her we'd broken up, and she asked if you were submissive. I didn't go into details, but I was kind of a mess at the time. She was trying to be a friend."

"A friend? Are you kidding me?"

"I get it. You're jealous. She's jealous of you too, but I can't cut her out of my life. You're bound to run into her now and then with our business dealings."

I started to leave.

He bolted up to stop me. "Erica, wait."

"I don't want to talk about it anymore. Let's go back to the house."

He stood at the entrance and blocked me. "I didn't know what to think about why you left, all right? I thought maybe I was too rough with you that last night we were together, and that's not a conversation I can run by too many people. Frankly, I'm still worried that *is* why you left."

The memory of that night invaded my thoughts. The intensity of letting him hurt me, of desperately wanting him to. *What if I take things too far, and it's something we can't come back from?* His words echoed through me. If he'd thought that's why I left, I struggled to imagine how much that would have hurt him to believe it.

I shook my head. "That's not why."

He seemed to relax a little. "I can see now that I shouldn't have talked to her about it, and I'm sorry. From now on, she's completely out of our personal lives. No matter what happens."

"If you're such great friends, was that also why she was all over you at the charity dinner?"

He scowled and half turned away, looking past me. "Christ, Erica. You know, you broke up with me, and I'm the one explaining myself here."

He had a point. I took a breath and tried to adopt a less accusatory tone. "You said you wanted to be with me, no matter what, so if that's something I'm going to consider, I think I should know what's really going on between you two."

He hesitated, his gaze fixed on me as if he were searching. I started to worry. That familiar sickness spread as I imagined what they'd done together. And I'd have no one to blame but myself. Whatever had happened between them had happened because I'd pushed him away.

"When she realized we weren't together, she didn't pass up a chance to try to hook up. I shot her down, of course. No matter what was happening between you and me, I wouldn't ever go back to her, Erica. Our relationship was never exactly fulfilling, and you know how she is to some extent. Try to imagine being in a relationship with that. She's a nightmare."

I couldn't argue. I often wondered how they'd managed to be together as long as they had, but people did change, for better or worse. Maybe she hadn't always been as much of a malicious cunt when they were together, but I didn't want to give her the benefit of the doubt.

"So…" I cocked my head, waiting for him to continue.

"Since she and I broke up, she's always been physical like that with me. Honestly, I never thought much of it until you showed up that night, and by then it was obvious how jealous you were. I took a gamble."

"You wanted to make me jealous."

"Nothing else was working." He brushed my cheek with his fingertips. "Seems like making you insanely jealous does the trick though. I'll have to remember that next time you decide we need 'space.'" He gestured with air quotes.

I caught myself smiling, but it soon faded. Blake was talking about all these things like they were in the past tense. Our problems weren't nearly behind us yet.

I searched for the right words. "Blake…"

He hushed me. "I have a feeling you're about to tell me something I don't want to hear, so how about you let me kiss you instead?"

Angling over my lips, he did, and I let him. I savored the sweetness on his tongue. I breathed him in with the salty air and let the ocean wash away all the things we didn't want to hear or talk about. We stood there for what seemed like forever, simply kissing. We let our hands roam, eagerly but not frantically. For now, I was content to be this close. I could do this for hours.

The night had gone almost completely dark, and voices approached.

"Hey, lovebirds," Heath called. "Mom's going to come looking for you soon. Dessert's ready."

Blake groaned and rolled his eyes. I laughed and nuzzled into his shoulder, bashful and entirely too wound up to be presentable.

"I need a minute," I whispered.

"No kidding. I'm so hard it hurts."

"Mmm, I know the cure for that." I slid up against him,

his erection straining against his jeans at my hip.

"You're seriously not helping. I can't have her catch us out here."

I took a breath and a reluctant step back. The ocean waves crashed closer to the retaining wall as the tide came in. Alli and Heath walked hand in hand back toward the house. I was so happy that she was coming back. We could do this more often, all of us together. Maybe.

"Where did you two wander off to?" Catherine asked when we got back to the house.

"They were making out in the gazebo," Heath blurted.

Blake punched him in the shoulder. Heath retaliated until they were laughing and grappling on the floor of the deck like wild animals.

"Boys! Boys! My lord, seriously. Greg, come control these boys!" Catherine flushed, a mix of laughter and embarrassment flashing across her features.

Alli, Fiona, and I were doubled over with laughter as the two continued their wrestling match a safer distance from where we sat. Greg emerged with a giant pot of water and dumped it on them.

They cursed and finally separated. When Blake returned, he had a silly grin on his face. He leaned in to give me a hug, making his best effort to get me wet too.

"Blake, stop it," I giggled.

"Just trying to share the wealth."

My phone rang. I pushed him away playfully and fished it out of my purse. I froze. It was Daniel. I looked around, half expecting to see Connor, but we were completely secluded. He was probably calling to bitch at me about the interview, but it was the last thing I wanted to think about.

I ignored the call and tried to think about how I was going to handle this shift between Blake and me. We were falling hard and fast into our old ways, the normal rhythm of our relationship. I was at his parents' house, for heaven's sake, having a great night with his amazing family. This was way too far outside the scope of acceptable behavior according to Daniel.

He called again, and I turned my phone off. I didn't care. I had so much love around me right now. Between Blake and me, Heath and Alli, among his warm and caring family, how could I let Daniel's evil penetrate something that felt so right, so good? I pushed him out of my mind, unwilling to let him ruin the best day I'd had since I said goodbye to Blake. I didn't want to think about that part of my life, at least not yet.

We spent the rest of the evening talking and listening to Blake's family tell embarrassing stories about each other. We laughed and drank and enjoyed the beautiful night. Blake never left my side, holding my hand on his lap possessively, as if he were afraid to let me go even for a second. I didn't mind, because I felt the same way.

A little tipsy, I said my goodbyes to everyone. Alli, Fiona, and I proclaimed that we loved each other no less than a dozen times. Heath bore witness, affirming the statement with us each time in his ever-patient sobriety. Catherine held me in a firm hug that seemed to last forever. I hugged her back. Hugs were good. Blake finally coaxed us apart. We stepped outside, and I stumbled a bit toward the car.

We got in and I snuggled up to Blake, kissing his neck and biting his earlobe. "I want you."

"You're drunk, but I will absolutely take advantage of

you. These are extenuating circumstances."

I giggled. "Good. You should pull over somewhere and do me in the car."

"Wow, baby. Keep talking like that and I just might. First, let's put your seat belt on, okay?" Blake pulled out of the drive. "Then take your panties off."

I smirked and slid them down my legs, giddy for whatever plan Blake was cooking up.

I looked up from my seat belt endeavors just in time to notice a black sedan parked across the street. I twisted in my seat. The lights turned on and the car began to follow as we meandered back toward the main roads. My gaze fixed on the side view mirror. I blinked and tried to shake the buzz. I wasn't imagining this. The car kept following us, a safe distance behind.

"You okay? You haven't been this quiet all night."

My heart raced as the cold reality of the situation became clear. My indiscretions with Blake were officially on the radar. Between that and trying to manipulate my way through the interview, Daniel would be furious. I powered on my phone. Daniel had called twice more, never leaving a voice mail.

The complacency I'd felt earlier had expired. All my fears could be realized, all because I couldn't stay away. I panicked, my body shaking uncontrollably. Everything was crashing down now.

"What's wrong? Do you want me to pull over?"

"No!" I shouted. "Drive, let's get out of here." *Heaven help me, what have I done?*

Blake's hand tightened over the steering wheel and he reached over to hold my hand in his other. "Okay, here's the deal. You need to talk to me right now, or I'm heading back to the house." He stopped at a stop sign.

"Just drive. It's not safe. They're following us. Go!" This would be the worst buzz kill ever, especially if we ended up dead.

He frowned and kept going. He checked his mirrors.

"Who exactly is following us?"

I shook my head, hugging my arms tightly around my body, as if I'd fall apart completely if I let go.

"Erica, for fuck's sake! Who?"

"Daniel." My voice was a whisper. "They've been watching us."

Blake stared ahead onto the road, his expression unreadable. His speed picked up as we hit the highway. We were going well over the speed limit, zipping down side streets until we hit ours. He parked and helped me out.

Somehow we'd managed to lose Connor. Either that, or he'd simply decided to stop tailing us. Not that it really mattered now anyway. He knew I'd been with Blake.

We stepped into Blake's apartment, and he planted me on the couch and brought me water. My body had calmed down a little, but I was filled with an empty kind of despair—that dark unknown that I'd envisioned so many times if Daniel changed his mind about sparing us. I said us, because if anything happened to Blake, I wasn't sure I'd be able to go on.

While I drank, Blake made a call from the kitchen. His voice was low and the call was brief. He returned and sat across from me on the table, stroking my thigh.

"Can we talk about this now?" His voice was gentler.

I didn't know what else I had to lose by telling him. He

deserved the right to protect himself now that I'd brought Daniel's focus back to him.

"Daniel killed Mark," I said.

His expression didn't change. "I put that one together myself, Erica."

"You threatened him, and it burns him that you did. He's not going to let it go." I bit my lip, staving off the tears that threatened.

"I'm not worried about Daniel."

"Well you should be. He's going to kill you, Blake! He said I had to end it completely with you or he was going to 'remove you from the equation permanently.' Now he knows, and… This is so bad. You don't understand."

"So this is why." His stare was penetrating, piercing my soul.

I swallowed and nodded silently.

"Why didn't you tell me?"

I shook my head. "You don't know how he is. He's ruthless, violent. You have no idea what he's capable of. He killed his own son, for God's sake. I had to try to protect you from him."

"I have information that exposes not just Mark, but him. I had no idea he was going to kill Mark. Not that I'm not infinitely happy he's gone. If I'd known he was going to go that route, I probably wouldn't have approached him the way I had."

"What information?"

He exhaled. "Doesn't seem like there's any love lost between you now, so I don't suppose there's any harm in telling you."

"What is it?"

"Daniel's been covering up Mark's exploits for years. You never reported it to the police when he raped you, but plenty of other women did. He can grease as many palms as he wants to make the problems go away, cover shit up, but he couldn't make everything disappear around someone as prolific as Mark. When I told him I could make certain information very easily accessible, to the press for example, you can imagine that he wasn't too pleased."

"All the more reason to kill you now. He's taken mercy on you to manipulate his way into my life. He wants me to be part of his fucked up political campaign, unofficially, of course. He was going to help me pay you back the money you lent me so I could ditch the business."

"And you agreed to all this?"

His eyebrows shot up, like I'd lost my mind. Maybe I had.

"I… He didn't give me any choice, Blake. He said he was going to *kill* you. I've been trying to figure out a way around it this whole time, but he doesn't make it easy. He's horrible and…persuasive." I sagged back into the couch, not wanting to even touch the fact that he'd been violent with me.

"Drink."

I took a few more sips, wishing Blake would talk.

"I'll go to him, Blake. I can try to convince him that this wasn't what it looked like. He knows we're bound to run into each other. Somehow I'll make him understand, come up with an excuse. And then we'll just have to lie low, figure out how to… I don't know…"

"No. I'm not sneaking around to be with you."

"Then what do we do?"

"He's banking on you reacting just as you have, because you love me. What he's not banking on is me causing so many problems with this election that he'll be too busy to think about much else."

"I don't understand."

"I'll release the information. It's that simple."

"But…" I swallowed, suddenly at war. I cared about Daniel, enough that the idea of ruining his campaign troubled me. Why? Why would I care when he'd made my life hell? He'd threatened me with murder and more. "There has to be another way."

"Then come out publicly as his daughter."

"How would that be any less damaging for his career?"

"Having an illegitimate daughter you supposedly never knew existed is far less damaging than covering up multiple rapes for your stepson. It could be a nice amicable discovery. Not like you're extorting him or anything. Then we could get married and he'd have to play nice, because I'd be his son-in-law. How's that for payback?"

My eyes widened. "What?"

He smirked. "Is that so crazy?"

"Yes, that's completely crazy. Try again." My heart was suddenly beating out of my chest. Between freaking out about Connor following us and hearing those last words, I was completely sober now.

He laughed a little, but his smile soon faded. "I'm not wild about walking around knowing there's a hit out on me, Erica, but we can outmaneuver him on this one. The information I have must scare him because he wouldn't have killed someone to prevent me from leaking it."

"He said he did it for me." I gave a weak laugh. "I think

he thought I'd be impressed that he did. That's so fucked up, isn't it?"

"He probably did do it for you, but we both know how he is. He wouldn't do something like this without calculating every possible risk and reward."

I looked out the window, into the night sky brightened by the city lights. Would we be held prisoner like this until we knew it was safe again? When would it ever be safe again?

He leaned forward and feathered a finger down my cheek, turning my gaze back to him. "Nothing comes between us anymore, okay, baby?"

His eyes were dark and serious. I nodded. That was what I wanted too.

"I can't lose you like that again. I'll go crazy."

"Me too." An argument could be made that I'd already achieved some level of crazy in his absence.

"After we figure out what we're going to do with Daniel, I want you to move up here with me, okay? Or we can get our own place, I don't care."

I paused. "Can't I just stay at the apartment like before?"

"No. Not close enough. You owe me this much after disappearing and destroying my life these past few weeks."

I wanted to protest, but I couldn't fathom being away from him for a minute right now. "How are we going to get out of this mess? I can't take it. I can't lose you."

"You're not losing me. I'm not going anywhere. I'll hire a SWAT team if I need to, okay? Let's not think about that shit right now. All I want you thinking about is being here with me, right now."

I took a deep breath.

"Come on. Let's go to bed. He's not going to be

coming after us tonight. He'll have to get through Clay and his friends first."

I nodded, willing myself to calm down. I trusted that Clay could handle Connor. I liked Clay and I abhorred Connor, so the idea of them facing off was appealing, actually.

Blake went to stand but I pulled him down on the couch with me. I wrapped my arms around his neck and held him tightly, as if someone might come and rip him from me. He held me back, tightening his arms around my rib cage. I breathed him in, feeling settled at the familiar scent that was Blake.

I fought the surge of emotion, relief at having him with me again twisted up with an ever-present fear of losing him again. I draped my leg over his, tangling our bodies together so he couldn't leave.

"I'm sorry," I choked. "This is all my fault." I squeezed my eyes closed and fought the tears.

"Shh, baby. Don't think like that. It's going to be okay now." He brushed my hair back from my face, fingering the tiny mark he'd made on my neck. "I know that now. You were trying to protect me. I appreciate the effort, but nothing is worth going through what we did. You don't like me running your life, and I don't like you making sweeping decisions like this without me. So maybe we can agree to figure these things out together in the future. What do you think?"

I pulled back and he swept away the tear that fell, kissing me sweetly.

"Love me, Blake."

Heat passed over his features. He tugged off my shirt

and bra and moved me so I was lying down on the couch. Slowly, he slid off my skirt, leaving me bared and open to him.

His lips parted slightly. "I want you like this, every night. Naked and waiting for me."

He stood and pulled his shirt over his head, tossing it away. He pushed his jeans down to the floor, revealing the perfectly sculpted man beneath the clothes. I stared, boldly admiring the body I'd come to love, to crave.

He lowered down, settling between my thighs. He slid up my body, his erection hard against my belly as he kissed me from my shoulder to my neck. His hands worshipped my curves, slowly and reverently, leaving trails of fire in their wake. I shifted against the sharp ache between my legs.

"I want to feel you inside me," I said, breathless.

His perfectly masculine body hovered with measured restraint as he circled my opening. I circled the hot flesh of his erection and positioned him at my entrance. His breath caught as he pushed into me slowly. I dragged my eager fingers over the curves of his pectorals, circling the soft disks of his nipples until they hardened under my touch. He gave me a little more. I slid my hands down to his ass and dug my nails into his flesh.

"Ah, Christ." He jerked forward, firmly planting himself inside me.

I moaned, arching into the fullness.

He lowered down, thrusting again gently. He traced the ridge of my ear with his tongue. "You're a bad girl."

I hummed. "You like me bad."

"I thought you wanted me to make love to you."

"When you're inside me, you're loving me and I'm

loving you. Isn't that how it works?"

He hesitated, and then took me with a deep and passionate kiss, licking and devouring me with his mouth as he shafted into me with steady drives. I tightened helplessly around his cock. The fever rushed over me, and my hips bucked gently beneath him.

Then he lifted me so I was straddling him, his cock buried in my depths.

"Oh shit." I sucked in a sharp breath. He was so deep this way. A fine mist of sweat covered my skin. I circled my hips, finding my bearings. "I thought you didn't like it this way."

"You're not exactly putting me out."

I smiled. "You sure?"

He licked his lower lip, and I leaned in to catch it between my teeth. I sucked him and kissed him feverishly. He groaned and lifted my hips. He was only in me at the tip when he slammed me down hard, filling me. I gasped for air at the sweet ache of his cock penetrating me.

"Oh, God." I clenched around him, steadying myself with my hands on his shoulders. "You're so deep."

He caught me by the nape and drew me in for a kiss, deep strokes, gently fucking my mouth with his tongue. He gripped my hips tightly, grinding me down a fraction more. "I can't live without this, Erica. Without you."

My breath left me, but he swallowed it with another devouring kiss.

"You won't have to. I promise. I swear it." I sifted my fingers through his hair, pressing my breasts against his chest. "I love you, Blake. You're the only one. My only love."

I lifted again, my thighs slapping down against him. He

hit the end of me again, stretching the sensitive tissues at my core. His hands gripped me anxiously, and his face tensed with agonizing strain. He lifted me, powerfully working me over his cock, over and over until my thighs trembled.

"Blake." My voice was a plea. "Are you close? I want to come with you."

His cheeks bloomed with heat and he clenched his jaw as he pumped into me. "Now, baby. Feel me come inside you."

His words did me in, the vision of him losing himself, buried in me. My whole body shook with the power of the orgasm that swept over me. My head fell back as he released with a cry and one final drive, pushing us both over the edge.

CHAPTER TWENTY

I woke up to Blake's warm body curled around me. I stretched, and he pressed slow, lazy kisses along the length of my torso. Having sleep—actual restful, nightmare-free sleep—only to wake to Blake's hands and mouth on me. This could be heaven.

He nuzzled my neck, sucking my skin softly.

"No more hickeys," I warned.

He laughed into my neck. "I wasn't sure I was actually going to see you again. I had to leave my mark."

"Yes, you made yourself known."

He stilled and turned me to face him. "James saw?"

I paused. "He noticed, yeah."

His expression was impassive, but I saw emotion storming behind his eyes. "What exactly does he mean to you?"

I bit my lip, wondering what to say that wouldn't send Blake flying into a jealous rage. "Think of him like my Sophia. He's a friend who wants more, but a friend all the same."

"If he wants you, then I want him gone. You can find someone else to do what he does."

I rolled my eyes. "And I want Sophia gone. So we're probably both going to be disappointed for a while."

"This is completely different. Sophia lives in New York. You work with the man face-to-face nearly every day. If I had someone at my office trying to fuck me every day, you'd lose your mind."

I sighed. "James and I don't have a history, and he's a good person. He's not hatching a plot to get me away from you." I didn't think so anyway, though he certainly wasn't a fan of Blake. "Can we drop it for now?"

"I can't stand that he had his hands on you."

"Then don't think about it, because it doesn't matter."

I lifted my head to kiss him, praying he'd never know that James had had his mouth on me too. I lay back and traced his jaw. His face seemed softer, rested. Maybe he hadn't been sleeping well without me, either.

"Speaking of work, I should meet with Risa at some point and get that mess cleared up."

"Can't it wait until Monday?"

"Maybe. She'll probably wonder why she can't get into her email account though, if she's doing any work after hours."

"Let her wonder. Your time is better spent in bed with me. We have to make up for lost time."

"Oh?"

"I was thinking about kissing you from head to toe until you beg me to stop. And I need to block out at least an hour for licking your pussy." He slid his hand to cover my mound. "Yeah, at least an hour. Let's see, what else…?"

I laughed. "Okay, I get it, but I should go downstairs and get cleaned up."

"Nonsense. You can shower here. No clothes necessary. I want you naked in my bed all day. I'll tie you up if I have to. You know I will." He looked serious but a ghost of a smile passed over his features.

"We'll have to face reality eventually, you know."

"Nah." He lowered his mouth and circled my nipple with his tongue, flicking the tip until a familiar warmth simmered in my belly.

I sucked in a breath and arched into the motion, sliding my fingers through his hair. He slipped a finger into my sex, curling up to the spot that made me crazy.

"I haven't even gotten to use any of my toys on you. And you're in big trouble for all this shit you pulled."

I moaned and lifted my hips to deepen his penetration. I'd wanted dominant Blake. Here he was.

My phone rang, interrupting our moment. Still in Blake's clutches, I reached for it. *Sid. Thank God.*

"Hey."

"Hey, uh, the police are at the apartment."

"What?"

"They have questions about some guy, Mark MacLeod. They said you knew him?"

"Shit. Okay. I'll be right down."

Blake slipped another finger into me and closed his teeth gently around my nipple. My brain skidded, trying to decide which direction to move in. I tried to push him away, but he was firm and unmoving, his eyes twinkling mischievously.

"Oh, you're here?" Sid asked.

My breath hitched. "Yeah, I'm at Blake's. Give me a few minutes."

I hung up and Blake took my other nipple in his mouth, his cheeks hollowing with a long, delicious pull on the tip.

I gave him a gentle shove. "Get up. I have to go."

"Why? Who was that?"

He loosened his hold and I slipped away, throwing on my clothes from the previous night. My mind was racing. Daniel had implied that the investigation would be closed. *What the hell were they doing here?*

"Sid. The police are downstairs. They want to talk to me."

He sat up quickly. "Do you want me to come with you?"

"No."

"Erica, this is one of those things that maybe I should be there for."

"No, Blake. The answer is no. I will deal with this. I do not want you there. Please tell me that you're hearing me on this."

He hesitated. "What do you think they're here for? They're going to ask you about Daniel. What will you tell them?"

"I'll figure it out, okay?"

★ ★ ★

I tried in vain to calm my nerves before I walked into the apartment. I looked a little worse for wear from the previous night, but surely they didn't care about that. I prayed Blake would honor his promise to stay upstairs because I didn't trust him not to say something he shouldn't in front of the police.

I walked in, and two men greeted me. One was tall and thin, his hair a mousy brown, and the other was shorter and thicker around the middle, his hair almost completely gray. They both seemed friendly enough, which I was thankful for because I was petrified by the prospect of speaking with them.

The tall one spoke up first. "Sorry to stop in on you so early here. I'm Detective Carmody and this is Detective Washington. We were hoping to speak with you about your involvement with Mark MacLeod."

My involvement? "What do you mean?"

Washington reached into his jacket and pulled out a handful of large photographs that appeared to have been taken at the gala. In them, Mark and I were dancing, his arm wrapped firmly around me. My back was to the camera. In another, his mouth was an inch from my ear, a smug smile on his face. That was the face I was glad to have missed when he was telling me how he wanted me again. I suppressed a grimace as I remembered his voice, his breath on my skin that night. Instead I looked up calmly, waiting for them to continue.

"These were taken by a journalist shortly before he died. Guests identified you with him here. Did you know him well?"

I shook my head. "No, I didn't know him well at all. I'd met him a couple times through a business deal I was doing that involved his firm."

"He looks like more than an acquaintance here," Washington said.

"I can see that. He was flirting with me a lot. I humored him with a dance, but I didn't see him after this. He seemed nice enough, but I wasn't interested."

"How was he acting that night?"

"He was coming on to me, like I said. He did seem drunk. I don't know. We only talked for a few minutes before the dance, and then I left the gala early. I wasn't feeling well."

The pair glanced at each other. Carmody stuffed the photos back into the envelope and Washington sized me up again. I tried not to fidget or look nervous.

"I guess I'm confused. He killed himself, right? Are you trying to figure out why he did it?" The words left me in a rush, and my heart raced.

Carmody spoke. "When the son of a prominent figure dies suddenly, we have to do our due diligence. We're trying to rule out all other possible causes of death."

"Oh. I didn't realize that. I thought I heard the investigation was closed."

"Not yet, unfortunately." Carmody shrugged.

"Is there anything else you might be able to tell us?"

"I don't think so. I wish I could. Honestly, I was really shocked by the news." That was the truth.

"You're not the first person who's said that, which is why we're talking to anyone who might have known him well."

I nodded. "I feel so bad for his parents. They must be devastated." I tried to appear as sympathetic as I could. I couldn't believe the words that were coming out of my mouth, or how easily I'd slipped into the role of an appropriately ignorant innocent bystander in this situation. Perhaps the weeks of trying to talk myself into being someone I wasn't had done this to me.

"They are. It's too bad. Sometimes there aren't any answers for why people do this though. Anyway, thanks for your time and sorry for the bother."

Washington reached into his pocket and retrieved a business card. "Here's my card. Call us if you think of anything, all right?"

"I definitely will."

They left, and I collapsed into a seat at the counter, grateful I'd survived their interrogation without a breakdown. I honestly didn't think they suspected anything, and why would they? I had no ties to Mark that anyone outside of a few people close to me could ever find.

No sooner had they left, Blake appeared.

"What happened?"

"Nothing. They had photos of Mark and me dancing at the gala. They wanted to know how we knew each other. I explained that we were only acquaintances and he'd been flirting with me. They seemed satisfied and left."

"So they don't believe Mark's death was a suicide?"

"I couldn't say for sure. They didn't seem too concerned that it wasn't. Seemed like they were hitting a bunch of dead ends and about to pack it in. But I have no idea."

"All right, come back up."

"I'm here now. Let me get cleaned up, and I'll come up there when I'm done." As much as I wanted to be in my warm and safe Blake bubble after weeks of separation, I needed a minute with my thoughts.

He paused a second. "Okay, don't be long." He kissed me and left.

I stepped into the shower and washed. I thought about going back upstairs, where we'd be hiding. Sure, hanging out in bed with Blake all day wasn't exactly an inconvenience, but I also knew why we were lying low. So far, the only solutions on the table were coming out as Daniel's daughter, a saga I couldn't begin to anticipate the complications of, or Blake could bring attention to the shady dealings that would undoubtedly ruin Daniel's campaign, possibly his entire career. I had a hard time accepting either as a viable option.

I toweled off and glanced out the window. Connor was parked down the street, almost out of my view. A rush of emotion surged through me, and I knew what I needed to do.

I pulled on my blue jeans and a T-shirt and slipped on my sneakers. I scribbled a quick note and left it on the counter before I rushed downstairs. I stepped outside. Clay was standing guard against the Escalade.

"Ms. Hathaway."

"Clay. Long time no see. Back on the clock, I see."

"Yes, ma'am."

"Well, good luck. I'm walking down to the store. I'll be back in a bit."

He nodded. I started a brisk walk down the street. I only had a few minutes to do what I needed to do. I crossed the street and knocked on Connor's window. He rolled it down, giving me a hard stare.

"Take me to him."

"Get in."

I opened the back door and let him drive us away.

★ ★ ★

I had no idea where we were going until I saw the familiar Boston Sand and Gravel storage tanks come into view. We took several back roads under the tangle of highways until we were in a secluded area, cut off by train cars and warehouses that stood empty on the weekend.

Daniel leaned against his Lexus SUV, dressed in khakis and a white collared shirt. He was smoking again. He should probably stop smoking, I thought idly. He pushed off the car and walked toward me. I scoped out the surroundings. We were so very alone right now. With the bypass above us, no one would hear me if I screamed. I stepped out of the car, fighting the urge to run in the opposite direction. Despite every reason he'd given me not to, I was determined to meet him head-on.

He flicked his cigarette and stood before me with his arms crossed. His lips were set in a firm line.

"Connor tells me you've been all over creation with Landon. I'm pretty sure we covered that."

"Did he tell you that the police stopped by this morning too?"

His eyes widened and shot to Connor. For the first time ever, I saw emotion in Connor's face. He seemed… flustered.

"I didn't see them, sir. I'm sorry."

Daniel looked back to me.

"Must have been on a coffee run. No worries, I had a little chat with them."

"What did you tell them?"

I waited, wanting the anticipation to burn in him.

His lips thinned. "You'd better start talking."

"They had photos of Mark dancing with me at the gala."

"What did you tell them?"

I stared hard into his eyes, keeping my face as steady and emotionless as I could.

"What did you tell them, goddamnit?" He grabbed my

shoulders and shook me.

"Let me go." I wrestled free from his grasp, breathless from the adrenaline that pumped through my veins. "Don't touch me. *Ever.*"

I saw Connor moving from the corner of my eye. He had a wide stance, like he was ready to act on Daniel's command.

"I lied, Daniel. I lied like a pro. You'd have been proud. And do you know why?"

"Indulge me."

"Because as I've much as I've grown to hate you, for some inexplicable reason, I still care about you. I care about your life and your freedom, and I even care about your stupid fucking campaign. My finger's on the trigger, and I can't shoot." I took a breath, trying to keep the tremble at bay. "Because that's not who I am. I'm never going to be like you. I'm never going to play the game for the sick, greedy fun of it."

"I'm sure that's not the only reason."

"It is the only reason. I'm not scared of you anymore."

He shot me a chilling look, his lips curled into a snarl. "Maybe you should be."

"You'd no sooner kill me than I'd send you to jail for murder, Daniel. Oh, and let's not forget obstruction of justice."

His eyes narrowed a fraction.

"Yeah, Blake told me about all that. How does it feel knowing that all those great pains you went to covering Mark's ass paved the way for him to do what he did to me, the same way he did it to so many other girls?"

His jaw clenched.

"Thanks for that, Dad."

He flinched slightly at the word. I was getting under his skin, and that emboldened me.

"The threats, the manipulation, you trying to assimilate me into your world. All this shit is going to stop right now. Today."

He let out a short laugh. "What gives you that idea?"

"When Mom died, I had no one. No one." My voice wavered, but I swallowed to keep the emotion in check. "She gave me all the love she could give, for as long as she could give it. And from that point on, I had to figure out how to make it on my own. I made the rules. I figured it all out. Even when people like Mark came into my life and threatened to destroy everything, I survived. I thrived. And you're not going to take that from me. I've come too goddamn far to live under anyone's thumb. Not yours, not Blake's. No one's."

He motioned to Connor who then walked a few paces away, out of earshot. I relaxed a little.

"You sound very certain of this. I realize you're trying to be strong here, but I think we talked about how I feel about people threatening me."

"I'm not threatening you. I'm reasoning with you because you've been nothing but unreasonable from the start. Don't you think I deserve to have a voice if this relationship means anything at all to you?"

His expression didn't change. He wasn't going to give in easily.

"I realized something today. You've been making my life hell since Mark died, and I would have given anything to make that stop. But I can't watch you go to jail, or even watch your campaign crumble, at my hand. And you can't knock off your own daughter. Somewhere in that cold heart of yours, you care about me. And you can care about me and trust me without owning me. It's not quite like a father-daughter dance, but I suppose in some fucked up version of reality, that's love."

He made no indication that he wanted to speak, so I continued. I'd give him all I had. I had nothing more to lose.

"I know you loved my mom. I see it in your eyes every time we talk about her."

He winced, his jaw tightening. "Don't talk to me about Patty. You don't know anything about it."

My voice quieted. I'd been nearly yelling up to now. "I don't know what went on between the two of you, but I know that if you'd stayed together, my life would have been so different. None of us can change those circumstances now. But trying to take the wheel on my life at this late stage of the game isn't going to work for either of us, trust me. If you still feel a shred of love for her, or regret for what you left behind, I'm begging you to give all this up and be the kind of man she wanted you to be before you wrote her off."

His lips parted slightly, and he looked past me. I caught a flicker of emotion then, the pain I thought I'd mistaken before when I spoke to him about my mother. I was gambling on the chance that somewhere in his heart, he did still love her. Enough to love me.

He let out a slow breath. "It would have never worked. I did her a favor by ending it. She wouldn't have been happy with this life."

"Then why would I?" I threw my hands up, exasperated.

He shoved his hands into his pockets and looked back to me. A long moment passed between us.

Looking into his cool blue eyes filled me with conflicting emotions. We were supposed to be important people in each other's lives. A father, a daughter, and here we were, sparring and threatening. Our hearts were filled with anger and mistrust. Under all of that, there had to be something worth protecting, but it was so faint and buried so far deep under all the muck that I could barely believe it existed.

He broke my gaze and pulled out another cigarette. His hands shook slightly as he lit it. "So you've made your point. Now what?"

I sighed. "No more stalking. I never want to see Connor's fucking face again. And no more threats. You stay away from Blake and me unless, at some point, I feel like I can trust you again."

"He knows everything now, I gather."

"Don't concern yourself with him. I know it's hard for you to trust me, but I'm not really giving you a choice."

"Maybe he's the one I don't trust."

"Hurting you would hurt me. And he loves me too much to do that."

He paused. "What if he stops loving you?"

The words settled over me. I'd spent days in agony, afraid he'd done just that. I'd given him plenty of reasons to stop, but he hadn't given up on us. "I'll never give him a reason to."

"And the campaign work, I suppose you're hoping to bow out of that as well?"

"If I know I can trust you to stop this madness, I will

help you. I spoke with Will and we came up with a good plan that would allow me to consult with your team without giving up the business. He seemed to think it would be a great solution, but he wanted to run it by you. I'm assuming he didn't do that."

He shook his head and a smirk lifted his lips.

I frowned. "What?"

"I honestly can't figure out if you're more like me or her at this point."

I couldn't hold back a small smile.

"Yeah, sometimes I wonder about that too."

I fidgeted a little. This whole conversation had become somewhat surreal. Had I really just won an argument with Daniel Fitzgerald?

"Listen, I need to go before Blake sends out a search party."

"He didn't know you came?"

"God, no. I had to sneak out of the apartment and past a pack of bodyguards. He's probably completely freaking out right now."

His eyes narrowed slightly. "Well, I guess I don't need to worry about him not taking care of you."

I laughed. "Yeah, not a concern, trust me."

He exhaled heavily and flicked his cigarette. "All right. We'll drop this for now, but I'd like to meet again soon to talk about logistics."

I hesitated, sensing an authoritative tone in his voice that threatened to bring us right back to where we'd started.

"I'll call you. Frankly, I need some time to put my relationship and my business back together after all of this."

He nodded. "Fine. Connor will take you back home.

Assuming you can handle that?"

"Yeah, as long as he doesn't plan on killing me and dumping my body in the river."

★ ★ ★

I called Blake on the way back. He'd called dozens of times since I'd left and I knew he was going to be a mess.

"Erica, where the fuck are you?"

"I'm on my way home. Please calm down."

"Where have you been? You leave me a note telling me not to worry, and then you completely disappear?"

"You're not calming down. I will be home in ten minutes. Tell the SWAT team to stand down."

"Where were you?"

"I'm fine. Everything is fine, I promise."

Connor dropped me off down the street. As much as I wanted to see Clay and his friends jump Connor, that wasn't really in the spirit of peace I was trying to cultivate with Daniel. I approached the entrance of the apartment building. Blake was pacing like a mad man, spouting heated words to Clay and another brawny man dressed in black.

As soon as his gaze landed on me, he started toward me. I was expecting him to start yelling and freaking out, but instead he trapped me in a hug that left me breathless it was so tight.

He released me enough to look me in the eyes. His face was tense, his skin tight over the angles of his beautiful features. His hand trembled slightly as he caught my face in his palm. "Don't ever leave like that again. Promise me."

I nodded and swallowed hard, feeling less brave and

more guilty with each passing moment.

"Promise me, Erica."

"I promise. I'm sorry. I had to see him and set things straight."

His eyes widened slightly. "What? Who?"

"Daniel."

He stepped back and shoved his hands through the fine strands of his hair. "You're kidding me. Please tell me you're joking."

"Everything is fine now. I reasoned with him. He was pissed of course, but I think I finally got through to him and made him understand where I'm coming from. He's going to leave us alone."

"How do you know? What if he was just appeasing you? What if he'd... Christ, Erica. I can't even believe you did this."

I thought it over for a second. My meeting with Daniel could have gone all wrong, completely different from how it had. Blake would have never forgiven himself if something had happened to me.

"He's my dad, Blake. He's horrible sometimes, but he's not going to hurt me." I sighed, grateful that I could finally believe that. "We came to an understanding. He promised to back off."

"And you believed him?"

"I believe him."

★ ★ ★

I spent the rest of Saturday regurgitating my conversation with Daniel to Blake, trying to get him to believe that we were going to be okay. He was still skeptical, but I had at least convinced him that he didn't need to release any damaging information to the public for now. I made him swear on our relationship that he wouldn't.

Risa and I agreed to meet at Mocha on Sunday morning. She'd suspect something was wrong, but I had to see her face to face. It was my best chance to get more information on what she and Max were up to behind the scenes.

"Hey." She slid into the seat across from me, looking fresh and sweet, as usual.

I canted my head to the side and stared at her, as if I were seeing her for the first time. In a way, I was. I was seeing the person she'd been the whole time, knowing what I knew now.

"I'm pretty disappointed, Risa. That's what's up."

She paled a bit. "What do you mean?"

"I'm curious. How long did you plan on pretending you were a part of our team before you cut loose? Was it just whenever the opportunity struck, or did you and Max have a long-term plan?"

She hesitated. "I'm not sure what you're talking about."

"I saw that you sent Max the files, so you can start being honest now. What I want to know is how you went from loving your job and caring about my company to sharing confidential information to a third party with a vengeance, because I seriously don't get it."

Her countenance changed, a bitterness washing over her features. "Really? What don't you get, Erica? You've been a nightmare to work with from day one. Everyone thinks you're this great visionary who's built the business, but where would you be without people like me? I've been busting my ass for you, and for what? So you can take all the credit?"

I frowned. "Sorry, isn't that your job?"

"It will be when Max and I start up our own site. It's already in the works, and we're taking all the advertisers with us, so consider yourself warned."

I let out a laugh filled with pure shock. Her betrayal had run far deeper than I'd expected.

"Wow, Risa. You've really outdone yourself. Max too, apparently. Never underestimate the power of jealousy." Max would stop at nothing to best Blake. I regretted that I'd ever doubted Blake's warnings.

"Call it what you want. Good luck picking yourself up after this. You're going to regret it."

"What you fail to realize is the company's success isn't about you. It's not even about me. Any one of us could leave, and the company could survive now. You were part of a team, but I guess you completely missed the point of what that means. Good luck running your business with a founding philosophy based on jealousy and underhanded deceitfulness."

"Go to hell," she snapped.

I stood to leave. I'd heard all I needed to hear. I paused before I walked away.

"Oh, Risa. One more thing."

"What?"

I let a slow smile cross my face. "Blake wanted me to let you know he's not interested."

BLAKE AND ERICA'S STORY CONTINUES
IN THE HACKER SERIES SEQUEL

HARDLINE

HERE'S A SNEAK PEEK...

CHAPTER ONE

My phone dinged.

B: *I'm leaving work in twenty minutes.*

I silenced my phone, ignored Blake's message, and turned my focus back to Alli. She tucked a lock of long brown hair behind her ear and continued to update the team on the weekly stats for our Internet startup, Clozpin. I listened attentively, as grateful as ever to have her back on the team.

Alli had been back in Boston only a few weeks, but she was finally sharing a city and an apartment with Heath again. Heath was happy, she was happy, and I was thrilled to have her reclaim her position as the marketing director after the debacle with Risa. I'd invited Alli back even before letting Risa go for sharing confidential information about the company.

I winced at the thought. Alli was a fountain of optimism, but Risa's betrayal still stung me. I hadn't heard from her since our last meeting, and somehow the silence between us filled me with more dread than anything else. I wanted to doubt her ability to start a competing site with Max, our almost-investor and Blake's sworn enemy, but the unknown worried me. What if they successfully lured our advertisers away? What if they were able to build something that was legitimately better and filled a need that Clozpin didn't?

With the kind of money Max was bringing to the table plus Risa's inside information gleaned directly from everything I'd learned in my short tenure as CEO of the company, anything was possible. And something about the way she left, filled with so much venom and resentment, spoke to every insecurity I had about running a business. I was still fledgling, without a doubt. I wanted to think I could hold my own, and in many ways I had, but I had a lot to learn.

Another text message arrived on my phone, no less distracting as it vibrated against the glass top of the conference table.

B: *Erica?*

I rolled my eyes and quickly tapped out a reply. I knew he'd pester me until I acknowledged him.

E: *I'm in a meeting. I'll call you after.*

B: *I want you naked in my bed by the time I get home. You should leave soon.*

E: *I need more time.*

B: *I'll be inside you within the hour. Your office, our bed, your choice. Wrap it up.*

The air in the room was suddenly too cool against my skin. I shivered and my nipples beaded, grazing uncomfortably against my shirt. How did he do that? A few well-placed words, delivered via text no less, had me checking my watch.

"Erica, do you have anything else you want to cover?"

My eyes locked with Alli's. She cocked an eyebrow like maybe she knew I wasn't paying attention. All I could think about were the consequences of keeping Blake waiting, and the physical response to that anticipation was already becoming difficult to ignore. I corralled my thoughts away from Blake's promises and back to the present.

"No, I think we're good. Thanks, everyone." I collected my things quickly, eager to get moving. I waved off the rest of the group, and they dispersed to their workstations. Alli followed me back into my partitioned office.

"What's up with Perry? I didn't want to bring it up at the meeting since it's kind of an odd situation."

"Not much. He emailed me again, but I haven't replied yet." I didn't have time to get into the complexities of that situation right now and meet Blake's deadline.

"Are you thinking about taking him on as an advertiser?"

"I'm not sure," I admitted. I was still conflicted on the matter.

Her big brown eyes were wide, questioning me. "Does Blake know he reached out to you?"

"No." I gave her a pointed stare, making it clear without words that I didn't want him to either. The last time I'd seen Isaac Perry, Blake had him pinned to the wall by his throat threatening to de-limb him if he dared touch me ever again. I didn't want to make excuses for Isaac's bad behavior that night, and I didn't want to forgive him any more than Blake did. But this was business.

"He's not going to be happy if you end up working with him."

I stuffed my laptop into my bag. "You think I don't know that?"

Blake's associations colored more strategic business decisions than I cared to admit.

Alli leaned against my desk. "So what are you going to do? Perry must be offering something impressive if you haven't completely shot him down yet."

"Perry Media Group represents a dozen multimedia publications that span the globe. I'm not saying I trust him, but I can at least hear him out."

She shrugged. "Whatever you think is best for the company I'll support. I don't mind dealing with him directly either, if you're more comfortable with that."

"Thanks, Alli. I'd rather get the bottom of this myself though. We can talk about it more later. I need to head out. Blake is waiting for me."

MORE BOOKS BY

MEREDITH WILD

On My Knees
(BRIDGE SERIES #1)

★ ★ ★

Hardwired
(HACKER SERIES #1)

★ ★ ★

Hardline
(HACKER SERIES #3)

★ ★ ★

Hard Limit
(HACKER SERIES #4)

★ ★ ★

DISCUSSION QUESTIONS

1. Erica chooses to end her relationship with Blake in order to protect him from Daniel. Do you think she did the right thing, or should she have confided in Blake from the beginning? What do you think would have happened had she not pulled away from Blake after talking to Daniel?

2. Daniel takes Mark out the equation as a way to protect Erica and himself. Despite his actions, does Daniel's character have any redeemable qualities?

3. Erica's strength continues to grow throughout the book as she faces more challenges both professionally and personally? If Erica's past wasn't what it was, do you think she would have become as strong as she is in the present?

4. As Erica begins to settle into building her company, her relationship with James becomes something more than just a working one. Why do you think James affects Erica in the way that he does? Does Erica's friendship and attraction to James force her to see what she truly wants and needs?

5. Erica has an intense moment of vulnerability when she is with Blake after speaking to Daniel. Why do you think she

chooses that moment to break down the walls of control around them? How does this emotional moment alter the way Erica feels about Blake and their relationship? How do you think Blake feels while Erica is having this moment?

6. What do you think is going on in Blake's mind when Erica ends things between them? Should he have done more to stop her? Do you think he realized there was more at play and purposefully let her walk away rather than force her to stay?

7. In this book, Blake's vulnerability is shown in many instances to Erica. He finally opens up about his past, and some of the choices that he has made. In which moments do you think Blake was the most vulnerable? Why do you think Blake is so hesitant to reveal his past and open up to Erica after all they've been through? Do you think there is still more that he has yet to reveal to her?

8. There are many moments in story in which either Blake or Erica decide to fight back in their relationship with one another, subsequently enraging each other. What do these moments of reveal about Blake and Erica individually and as a couple?

9. Erica and Blake continue to challenge one another during their breakup. Do you think they do this out of hurt or anger, or are they pushing the buttons to see what it'll finally take to bring them back together?

10. Erica wants to stake her claim over Blake just as much as he does over her. What do these moments of possessiveness reveal about Erica and her relationship with Blake? Do her moments of possessiveness differ from his, or do they come from the same place?

11. Do you think Erica and Blake are stronger individually and as a couple after the events of *Hardpressed*? Were the events of the story worthwhile in that they brought Blake and Erica together more so than they might have been without those events?

ACKNOWLEDGEMENTS

This book belongs to my husband. Thank you for bringing me snacks and making me protein shakes when I refused to stop writing. Thank you for being the good parent, the chef, and the soccer dad so I could pursue another dream. Thank you for being my best friend, my biggest fan, and for letting me talk endlessly about everything.

I can't imagine being who I am today, having done all that I have, without you by my side every step of the way, helping me believe that anything is possible. Who we've become and the life we've built together are better than any life I could have imagined. For this, I will be eternally thankful.

Whew. Okay, drying my eyes… Who's next?

While writing is a fairly solitary effort for me, when I do come out of my cave, there are people whose support and enthusiasm give me the boost I need to keep going!

Thanks to my momma for your unconditional love.

Thank you, Susan, for your friendship, support, and for loving spicy fiction as much as I do.

Special thanks to my editor, Helen Hardt, for not letting me get away with *anything*, and for inspiring me to make chapter ten far kinkier than I had originally planned. I'm still blushing.

Lauren Dawes, thank you for your eagle eyes!

Thanks to my Twitter peeps for the writing sprints

that pushed me through the tough spots and to all my social media pals who make me feel popular and loved!

Big, big thanks to the many fans who have kept me motivated through this journey. Your enthusiasm gives me purpose and warm fuzzies when I need them the most! You ladies are rock stars, pure and simple.

ABOUT THE AUTHOR

Meredith Wild is a #1 *New York Times*, *USA Today*, and international bestselling author of romance. Living in the White Mountains of New Hampshire with her husband and three children, she refers to herself as a techie, whiskey-appreciator, and hopeless romantic. When she isn't living in the fantasy world of her characters, she can usually be found at:
www.facebook.com/meredithwild

You can find out more about her writing projects at www.meredithwild.com

,